OTTO PENZLER PRESENTS
AMERICAN MYSTERY CLASSICS

S. S. MURDER

Q. Patrick was one of the pen names under which Hugh Callingham Wheeler (1912–1987), Richard Wilson Webb (1901–1966), Martha Mott Kelley (1906–2005), and Mary Louise White Aswell (1902–1984) wrote detective fiction. Most of the stories were written together by Webb and Wheeler, or by Wheeler alone. Their best-known creation is amateur sleuth Peter Duluth. In 1963, the story collection *The Ordeal of Mrs. Snow* was given a Special Edgar Award by the Mystery Writers of America.

Curtis Evans is the author of several studies of classic crime fiction, including *Masters of the "Humdrum" Mystery*, *The Spectrum of English Murder*, and *Clues and Corpses: The Detective Fiction and Mystery Criticism of Todd Downing*. He edited the Edgar-nominated *Murder in the Closet: Queer Clues in Crime Fiction Before Stonewall* and blogs at The Passing Tramp.

S. S. MURDER

Q. PATRICK

Introduction by
CURTIS EVANS

AMERICAN MYSTERY CLASSICS

Penzler Publishers
New York

This is a work of fiction. Names, characters, places, and incidents either are the product of the author's imagination or are used fictitiously. Any resemblance to actual persons, living or dead, businesses, companies, events, or locales is entirely coincidental.

Published in 2024 by Penzler Publishers
58 Warren Street, New York, NY 10007
penzlerpublishers.com

Distributed by W. W. Norton

Cover image: Andy Ross
Cover design: Mauricio Diaz

Paperback ISBN 978-1-61316-537-9
Hardcover ISBN 978-1-61316-536-2

Library of Congress Control Number: 2023922347

Printed in the United States of America

9 8 7 6 5 4 3 2 1

INTRODUCTION

Peripatetic Anglo-American mystery writers from the Golden Age of detective fiction did their share of sailing over deep waters, not merely metaphorically but in fact, so it is no surprise that in the years between the first and second World Wars that shipboard mysteries, like those set in locked rooms, quaint villages and country houses, became a notable subgenre of their own. (They might be considered a subset of transportation mysteries, which included not only ships but planes, trains, buses and automobiles.)

Intriguing examples of Golden Age shipboard crime novels—fine reads all—include Rufus King's *Murder by Latitude* (1930), C. Daly King's *Obelists At Sea* (1932), Q. Patrick's *S. S. Murder* (1933), Elizabeth Gill's *Crime De Luxe* (1933), John Dickson Carr's *The Blind Barber* (1934), Agatha Christie's *Death on the Nile* (1937), Freeman Wills Crofts' *Found Floating* (1937) and Carter Dickson's *Nine—and Death Makes Ten* (1940).

S. S. Murder, the tale of murderous charm and verve which concerns us here, was produced by a pseudonymous author who is one of the most enigmatic crime writers ever to have put typewriter key to typing paper during the Golden Age of detective fiction. Or in this case I should say not one, not two, not three, but *four* authors, for "Q. Patrick" was in fact nothing less than a quartet of distinct—and distinctly talented—individuals.

The author was launched in 1931 by thirty-year-old Philadelphia pharmaceutical executive Richard "Rickie" Wilson Webb, a restlessly energetic native Englishman who had a yen for mystery writing but preferred working in collaboration with others. Rickie's first writing partner, who joined him in the composition of *Cottage Sinister* (1931) and *Murder at the Women's City Club* (1932), was Martha Mott Kelley, an Amazonian twenty-four-year-old graduate of Radcliffe College of genteel Philadelphia heritage who rather resembled American aviator Amelia Earhart. Her family and friends nicknamed her "Patsy."

Together Patsy and Rickie devised the mystery writing pseudonym of Q. Patrick by combining "Pat" and "Rick" to make "Patrick" and then adding the letter "Q" because, the pair later explained, they considered "Q" the most intriguing letter of the alphabet. With the publication of *S. S. Murder* in 1933, readers were informed that the "Q" stood for "Quentin"—though this name was never otherwise acknowledged. Three years later Rickie would reverse the names Quentin and Patrick to derive what would become the most famous of all his pseudonyms: Patrick Quentin.

After the publication of the second Q. Patrick novel, Patsy abandoned Rickie for another man, as it were, wedding another native son of England and leaving the United States with him to reside in his home country for the remainder of her life.

Having been left high and dry by his erstwhile partner, Rickie wrote the next Q. Patrick opus, *Murder at Cambridge* (*Murder at the 'Varsity* in the UK), solo, drawing heavily on his own experiences in England as a student at Cambridge in the early Twenties.

Apparently he found the experience unduly onerous, for when it came to producing the fourth Q. Patrick crime tale, *S. S. Murder*, later that year, he turned to another female collaborator, thirty-one-year-old Mary Louise White, a reader at *The Atlantic Monthly*. Descended, like Patsy Kelley, from an old genteel Philadelphia Quaker family, Mary Lou, as she was nicknamed, had graduated from Bryn Mawr, done additional studies at Harvard and Yale, and, like Rickie, spent heady youthful days in Paris during the Jazz Age.

Taking advantage of their wide experience of Transatlantic travel in the Roaring Twenties, Rickie and Mary Lou in September 1933 published *S. S. Murder*, an ingenious and zestfully written tale which draws on the then hugely popular card game of bridge, anticipating by three years Agatha Christie's detective novel *Cards on the Table*. As in Christie's classic mystery, a tabulation of bridge scores is included in the volume as a clue. There is as well a footnoted sort of Challenge to the Reader in the teasing style of Ellery Queen.

Probably much of the writing of *S. S. Murder* was done by Mary Lou and the bulk of the plotting by Rickie. Like *Murder at Cambridge* before it, the novel was published, in contrast with the first pair of Patricks, by a major book company, Farrar & Rinehart, who included in its stable that bestselling author of mysteries (and mother of partners in the firm) Mary Roberts Rinehart. Additionally the next year Farrar & Rinehart would pick up Rex Stout, whose Nero Wolfe detective series would quickly become one of the most popular in crime fiction.

Befitting its prestigious publisher, *S. S. Murder* produced Q. Patrick's best reviews to date.

In the *Saturday Review* "Judge Lynch" (aka William C. Weber) proclaimed that the tale stood "high among popular aquatic mysteries," with "[l]ively dialogue, spooky atmosphere, and [a] puzzling problem," while in the *New York Times Book Review* Isaac Anderson opined that a "more cleverly constructed murder yarn than this one would be difficult to find anywhere." In England, the *New Statesman and Nation* approvingly declared: "The plot is sound, the style lively and dramatic with plenty of surprises."

S. S. Murder was also admiringly referenced by miracle problem maestro John Dickson Carr in "The Grandest Game in the World," his landmark essay on Golden Age detective fiction. It is fair, I think, to suggest that it influenced Carr's shipboard radio mystery play *Cabin B-13* (1943), filmed a decade later as *Dangerous Crossing.*

Two notices from lesser known sources are especially striking in their praise of *S. S. Murder*. "Here is a dandy item for the mystery fans," wrote a delighted reviewer in the *Salt Lake Tribune*, adding: "Q. Patrick, who is a mystery himself, or herself—the latter would be our guess—shows admirable inventiveness and constructive skill, and the story's shocks and thrills are counterbalanced by a lively humor reminiscent of Mary Roberts Rinehart. 'S. S. Murder' . . . is no penny thriller; its characters are flesh-and-blood people, and the story has literary competence." Going several steps further in her laudations, Dorothy Williams of the *Camden (New Jersey) Courier Post* proclaimed the novel

> guaranteed to give you an evening of breathless entertainment, whether or not you like detective stories. . . . There are several suspicious people on board and I selected the murderer before I was halfway through the book. I was wrong, to my great chagrin, but I had a perfectly swell case against the original one.

> You can't possibly appreciate the suspense in this book till you read it. This reviewer can truthfully say that she can't remember the day when a book of this type kept her biting her nails so furiously.

Like Wilkie Collins' landmark detective novel *The Moonstone* as well as Margaret Cole's *Burglars in Bucks* and Dorothy L. Sayers's *The Documents in the Case*, both published a few years earlier in 1930, *S. S. Murder* is also an epistolary mystery novel. It is told in the form of letters written to her journalist fiancé by the appealingly presented Mary Llewellyn, a prominent lady newspaper columnist, while she is traveling from New York City to Rio de Janeiro aboard the luxury ocean liner *S. S. Moderna.*

In an amusing bit of meta-fiction in the foreword—the kind of thing mystery writers often indulged in during the Golden Age, when death was so frequently treated as a game—we learn that the letters were turned over for publication to none other than that clever mystery writer Q. Patrick.

From reading Mary's letters we learn that on the second day of the voyage of the *Moderna*, wealthy elderly businessman Alfred Lennox suddenly dropped dead from strychnine poisoning during a pleasant game of bridge in the ship's smoking room (floor plan included). The finger of suspicion is soon pointed at a nondescript passenger named Mr. Robinson, who had been one of the bridge players at the table on that fatal night, but since has unaccountably vanished. Other significant passengers on the ship are:

- The late Lennox's younger second wife (now widow) Mabel, formerly in show business
- His seemingly sweet-natured "flapper niece" Betty

- His handsome young secretary Jimmie Earnshaw, who has dark hair and a "black mustache like [film actor] John Gilbert's" and "seems practically plastered to [Betty]"

- Widowed Mrs. Clap—formerly Marcia Manners, the famed monologist—and her mannish companion, Daphne Demarest, "who looks like an Olympic discus hurler"

- Mr. Wolcott, "white-haired, goateed and very much a gentleman"

- Senor Silvera, "so dark and Spanish and sinister looking that you know he must be henpecked or kind to animals or that he practices the flute in his cabin"

- Mr. Daniels, "a funny little Cockney"

- Adam—not Aaron—Burr, a "nice and restful" individual (though possibly an aspiring "sugar daddy"), who quickly befriends Mary Llewellyn

Two days after Mr. Lennox's demise, another passenger is thrown overboard to his/her certain death—could this be the fatal hands of the mysteriously missing Mr. Robinson at their murderous work yet again? Is there a clue in Mary Llewellyn's letters to her fiancé? Certainly the murderer seems to think so, for he starts sending threatening missives to Mary! Despite the presence of a callous double slayer aboard the ship, however, the spirited journalist's account of events, while exciting, never loses its savoir faire and firm focus on the question of whodunit, in keeping with the carefree canons of classic detective fiction.

After examining Mary's letters the captain of the *Moderna* pronounces, in another amusing meta moment, that they constitute as good a crime saga as anything ever written by "[Arthur] Conan Doyle or Mrs. Rinehart"—a reference not only to the late Grand Old Man of mystery but to the mother of Q. Patrick's publishers. Elsewhere, Patrick goes himself one better by having Mary backhandedly compliment his own immediately previous detective novel, *Murder at Cambridge*:

> I got undressed after I'd finished writing to you and settled down in bed with a novel—a detective story you gave me by that friend of yours, Quentin Patrick. I found it very nice and restful after the thrills and horrors of this voyage—pleasant milk and water after a steady diet of highballs. And, as I read it, I couldn't help thinking if your ingenious buddy can make so much out of a synthetic situation in a dull old English university, what could he not do with a real, red-hot, full-blooded sort of mystery as we've been having on board the *S. S. Murder*?

The answer to Mary's question is that Quentin Patrick did quite well with it indeed. Something in the American air seemed to invigorate Rickie Webb. Certainly his writing partner helped him as well. Unfortunately the talented team of Rickie and Mary Lou was fated to be one of mystery's one-hit wonders. On New Year's Day, 1934, Rickie's collaborator wed Edward Campbell Aswell, her former boss at *The Atlantic Monthly* and an editor at Harper & Brothers who would become closely associated in the thirties with the works of novelist Thomas Wolfe.

In contrast with Martha Mott Kelley, who withdrew from literary endeavors after her marriage, Mary Lou Aswell, as she was now known, herself became the hugely influential fiction editor at *Harper's Bazaar*, in which position she fostered the careers of such literary luminaries as Eudora Welty, Truman Capote, Carson McCullers, and Patricia Highsmith, all of whom remained her lifelong friends.

After divorcing Edward Aswell (with whom she had a son and daughter) and her second husband, novelist Fritz Peters, author of the classic 1951 queer novel *Finistere* (both Aswell and Peters were gay), Mary Lou relocated to Santa Fe, New Mexico, where she maintained a long-term same-sex partnership with the artist Agnes Sims and in 1957 authored a single solo domestic suspense novel, *Far to Go*.

In Santa Fe she and Agnes were occasionally visited by Patricia Highsmith, who during a 1970 sojourn to the city recorded in her journal: "Here lives Mary Louise Aswell, who bought 'The Heroine' for *Harper's Bazaar* when I was twenty-three. She lives with Agnes Sims in a very pretty house with some Ibizan dogs." ("The Heroine," a nasty psychological murder tale, was Highsmith's first published piece of fiction, written when she was a student at Barnard College.)

Rickie Webb likewise took up with a same-sex partner in the 1930s, a prodigiously talented and devastatingly handsome young English university graduate named Hugh Wheeler. Rickie and Hugh would live together, some martial months during World War Two excepted, for the next eighteen years, from 1933 until an acrimonious parting in 1951. Together under three pseudonyms, Q. Patrick, Patrick Quentin, and Jonathan Stagge, the two men would produce some of mystery fiction's finest crime novels.

Hugh would continue writing Patrick Quentin tales solo—not to mention write the Tony award-winning books to the seventies musicals *A Little Night Music*, *Candide,* and *Sweeney Todd*—after he evicted Rickie from the "firm" and their home in the Berkshire Hills of Massachusetts. Rickie returned to Paris, where he died obscurely in 1966.

Plagued with a variety of physical and mental maladies and heartbroken after the loss of his adored Hugh, the love of his life, Rickie died something of a broken man; yet he always took pride in having originated not one but a full trio of the most notable names in crime fiction. Along with Q. Patrick's devilishly perverse *The Grindle Nightmare*, the delightful *S. S. Murder* is the finest detective novel which Rickie wrote without apparent help from Hugh. (*Grindle* sometimes is mistakenly co-credited to Mary Lou Aswell.)

Readers are urged to enjoy this classic Golden Age shipboard mystery in remembrance of Richard Wilson Webb, one of the most sadly underappreciated men of classic mystery.

—Curtis Evans

FOREWORD

I had this record from my friend, David Donnelly, of the New York *Herald.* He had it, so he claims, from the cellar furnace which, fortunately, was not burning when the manuscript was thrust there (more in sorrow than in anger) by his wife, Mary Llewellyn, the well-known columnist. I believe both Mrs. Lincoln and Mrs. Kipling made literary rescues of a somewhat similar sort—hence the Gettysburg Address and the "Recessional." At any rate, the document was repudiated by its original owner for reasons clearly set forth on page 216. I have done little besides adding a few commas and the introductory letter, which I persuaded David to relinquish. I have also changed all names, and expurgated certain indiscretions not germane to the story. But above all I have tried not to destroy the quality of *breathlessness* which seems to make this record stand out from the synthetic mystery of fiction. Here, I thought, was a novelty—murder, written up, one might say, on the field of action. Here was emotion, not recollected in cold tranquillity, but poured on to paper while it was still molten, and before the final shape could even be guessed at. Here were living impressions of exciting incidents—informal without being formless and seen through the eyes of a trained writer who thinks with her fountain pen and knows how to manage her climaxes. For commas and footnotes I take credit. For the rest—my name is appended like a label on unclaimed baggage.

Q. PATRICK.

S. S. Moderna,
Friday, November 13th.

To David Hall Donnelly, Esq.,
56½ W. 12th Street,
New York City.

My Darling,

I must get a note off to you by the pilot, but it's been such a little time, counted by minutes, since you kissed me goodbye, that I naturally haven't much news for you. Did I remember to tell you, in the dust and heat of my departure, that I love you? Is that news, Davy? Well, it'll be front page stuff in a little while—three months, three weeks and three days from today to be exact (see how I've reckoned it all out!) when you slip the ring on my finger and call me Mrs. David Donnelly for the first time. A real newspaper romance with torn up fragments of my *Star* and your *Herald* for confetti and yards of ticker tape for streamers.

We had so much better things to do than talk just before you left that I never told you, as I meant to, what I've resolved to do on this trip. Dr. Klein said I must sit quiet as much as possible, at least for the first week, so I'm going to keep a journal for you describing all the details of the voyage—all those intimate day-by-day happenings which may give you an idea of what really goes on in the head of the sweet young girl reporter whom you hope so soon to make your very own!

I know the doctor's orders were NO WORK. But even the hardest-boiled doctor living couldn't call it work for a girl to write a daily line to her one and only. (And while I'm on the subject, did I tell you that I conscientiously turned down fifty bucks for a series of five special articles from South America signed "Miss Rio de Janeiro"? Wasn't I the obedient patient?)

There'll be no nonsense on this trip, Davy. I can promise you that much. I'm going to be such a good girl you'll be glad you're not along with me. I shall keep my legs up and my hands down to recover from that ghastly "appendectomy" which almost made you a widower before you had tasted the doubtful sweets of married life, and which has left me so light and airy that I'm scared to go out on deck lest a puff of this riotous November wind should blow me overboard to the whales and sharks.

I promise to take my convalescence very seriously, doing only just enough writing to keep in practice. I shall bore you with my journalese descriptions of shuffleboard contests, deck sports, bridge battles at a twentieth of a cent and catty chit-chat about my fellow passengers. It won't be a thrilling affair like the diary I kept for you when I was off on the Laubenthal case. Remember? It will be a modern imitation of your beloved Jane Austen, "in the inimitable style of Mary Llewellyn, whose daily paragraph in the *Star* has brought cheer and entertainment, etc., etc." Perhaps we'll read it over together when we play Darby and Joan in the twilight of our declining years.

Now, dearest, we are getting into deep water and I must catch the pilot before we drop him for good and all. The pilot—my last link with you and New York and civilization for a whole month. I don't quite like it, Davy; my illness has left me a timid, stupid creature and I can almost find it in my heart to wish that I were safe back in my hospital bed with that lovely night nurse bending over me and handing me a soporific glass of hot milk. Or, better still, I wish that we were safely installed together in that brand new apartment of ours and that you could hold me in your arms and never let me go. But I suppose it's all for the best that I should go off by myself and get well and strong again. It's not for so very long—after all!

So good-bye, darling, and thank you once again for the flowers, the fruit, the books and the beautiful letter, and, above all, thank you for being just you and for wanting to marry a plain scarecrow who hasn't even got a decent appendix to recommend her. I am wrapping Aunt Caroline's fur coat around me and wishing it were you! I'll post my first installment from Georgetown. God bless you, Davy; as I used to say when I was a baby—Mayangelskeepyou.

Your own,
MARY

P.S. I love you.

S. S. Moderna,
Friday, November 13th.
9:30 P. M.

Well, Davy darling, we're really out to sea at last and rolling down to Rio in the approved style. It's one terrible roll too, so you must excuse this wobbly writing. We've dropped the pilot, who brings a note from me to you with all my love; we've opened our letters, bon voyage telegrams and parcels; and we've all looked one another over with the usual first-day-out suspicion, hatred and distrust. And then, of course, some of us are very sick—oh, so green and gruesome! No, dear, not this one. I may be a poor weak woman, but seasick—never! Those trips up and down New York harbor to interview Peggy Hopkins Joyce have inoculated me against seasickness once and for all. But only thirty rather wilted-looking individuals turned up for dinner and there are sixty-seven first class passengers on this tub.

And for all its modern name, it *is* a funny little tub, Davy. We knew when we picked it, of course, that it would be small and slow (as well as cheap), but there's an atmosphere about it which reminds me irresistibly of a third rate summer resort on the Jersey coast. Four weeks of that, Davy. Just imagine! I can even smell the dried seaweed and antimacassars—not to mention more subtle dining room odors which are enough to cause even stouter hearts than mine to quail.

Of course, I could change my booking when I get to Rio, but the round trip rate is so good that I hate the idea of paying extra for my prescription. "Rest and sea air" is possible on any boat and I daresay I'll feel better about this one tomorrow. You mustn't blame me for being a bit blue just now, because it's only natural I should feel that all the most attractive people (and one in particular) got off when the "All Ashore" sounded. However, I suppose I'll soon settle down and reconcile myself to being without you, and life will be as simple as slipping on a negligée or a piece of orange peel.

What are you doing at this moment, I wonder? Writing to me, I hope, or playing bridge at the City Room with your "Front Page" cronies—anything but slaving away at that vile Brooklyn report which kept me so isolated, even in the hospital, that I almost began to believe it was not a report at all but a peroxide blonde with red polish on her finger nails. Your favorite combination before you met me, as you once admitted yourself!

But I must return to my muttons and tell you about my jolly little shipmates before they lose that first fine careless rapture of novelty. Most of the lady passengers look as though they were designed to fit the Writing Room in which this journal is now being precariously penned. You know the idea, Davy; thin little tables with old, wobbly legs—a dove-grey carpet and pink plush curtains. Is there need for me to say that I shall not be lacking adequate chaperonage after that? The odd thing is that most of them are married too; the tired wives of tired husbands, either accompanying their better halves on rest cures or business trips. But they are not missing a trick, Davy, on a boat where everything is included, and while they are mostly too sick to eat or drink, they make up for it by staring disapprovingly at my open work stockings and the blue velvet tea-gown which was the outcome of my interview with Helen Mencken.

You see I'm beginning to be catty already!

So much for what you are pleased to call the "Women in Bulk." Now for the men—and one in particular. (No, dear heart, there's nothing to worry about; he's over fifty and bald as a cantaloupe.)

Well, Davy, all my life to date, like that of the eminent Boston spinster, has been distressingly free from insult. But this afternoon I really thought that it had come at last. I was actually picked up by a man—and all without the slightest provocation. It did more to make me feel good than any of Dr. Klein's tonics or Aunt Caroline's pick-me-ups.

I had gone to the upper deck in order to find a nice quiet place for my sun cure, when he came up to me and said:

"I'll arrange to have your chair put next to mine, if you don't mind. I'm by way of being an invalid too and we really might have quite a lot of fun comparing symptoms. Mine was a gastric resection with adhesions—what was yours?"

In spite of the fact that I rather liked his voice, I flashed my eyes and my engagement ring at him in a manner which I'm sure you would have approved. Even on board ship a nice girl can't be too careful.

"Oh, I saw the ring," he said smiling. "In fact, I wouldn't have spoken to you if I hadn't. Unattached young ladies on board ship are a positive menace—especially to an old widower like me. Even the fact that I resemble nothing so much as an albino plum is no protection. I simply am not answerable for my actions at sea—the sunsets, moonrises, long halcyon days, foreign countries, all the glamour—"

"Glamour," I snapped, misquoting from some trashy novel, "is a state of mind, not of geography."

My retort seemed to please him mightily, for he immediately summoned the deck steward and said:

"Bring a chair over here, steward, and label it Miss—Miss—?"

"Llewellyn," I replied grudgingly.

"Good; and my name is Burr."

"Aaron?"

"No, but the next best, or rather the first best thing—Adam. A. B., Adam Burr, at your service—for just as long as you can keep me—from making a fool of myself, that is," he added hurriedly and apologetically.

I found him very diverting and we chatted away until it was time to go and dress for dinner. I think I am going to like him. At least he's nice and restful.

At dinner he turned up again at the captain's table—where, thanks to the dear old Fox, I have one of the seats of honor. To my left is a safe old party named Lambert (of Lambertville, I expect), who sports a rather pretty wife, a flapper niece and a nice-looking young secretary who has dark hair, a black moustache like John Gilbert's and who seems practically plastered to the flapper niece aforesaid. She is an uneventfully wholesome girl who answers to the name of Betty.

Then there is (or at least there was at lunch time) a widow, Mrs. Clapp, and her supposedly female companion who rejoices in the soft, clinging name of Miss Daphne Demarest, but who looks like an Olympic discus hurler. Daphne is English and clips her g's. Mrs. Clapp obviously adores her and is quite touchingly dependent on her Amazon. There's also a Mr. Wolcott, white-haired, goateed and very much the courtly gentleman, and a Señor Silvera, so dark and Spanish and so sinister looking that you know he must be henpecked or kind to animals or that he practises the flute in his cabin. But whatever he does in private, he presumably does it in Spanish, for his English can only be described as splendidly null.

The twelfth chair is occupied by a funny little Cockney of about thirty-eight, who does nothing but blink his funny little eyes and attend to his food with a kind of fussy concentration which makes one wonder if he's used to dealing with more than one fork.

Captain Fortescue is a peach. Nice, hearty, rather ponderously jovial, and always British—oh, so very British. He has a wife and five daughters in a place called Squaling or Ealing, or something like that, all of which rather dims the romance that might otherwise be inspired by his magnificent uniform and gold braid. Alas! his eyes are not for me. They are glued on the Lambert party, who are obviously the most consequential people on the boat and apparently our gallant skipper knows on which side his ship's biscuit is buttered. And, incidentally, the Lamberts have invited the whole table to drinks in the smoking room tonight at ten. I know I shouldn't—but! Well, it's the first night out and a girl's only young once, you know, and not so very young at that!

In the meantime, you ought to feel perfectly comfortable, my pet. Your Mary is safely launched on the deep blue sea with not a playmate under forty in sight, unless one happens to show himself when the sea gives up its sick; not a familiar name on the passenger list and the one eligible male obviously hanging on the smiles of a rich young flapper.

And so, as I said before—and as Kipling said several times before me—we go rolling down to Rio!

Here comes my Adam to fetch his Eve—or, as he calls me, not very flatteringly, his safety valve! Would you believe it, the sun on the upper deck must have caught his bald pate because it has actually turned a delicate pink? In November too! What fun I am going to have watching the "plum" ripen into glorious crimson maturity. And keeping the flies off it according to our contract! That's a new rôle for a promising young girl reporter.

And so to the bar, but not, I hope, to cross it.

No more now.

Stateroom,
Saturday, November 14th.
2:10 A. M.

Did I say "no more," Davy? Did I say that? Did I also say—oh, my God, what didn't I say? And what haven't I to tell you now?

I tried to send off a radio to the paper, but it was promptly suppressed. If only you and I had arranged a private code, Davy, we'd have the greatest scoop in our careers tonight.

You'll certainly have had the news long before this frantic scrawl reaches you, but I'm going to try and collect my scattered wits sufficiently to keep as full a record as I did for the Laubenthal case. You remember what a help that turned out to be in solving the mystery—and here on board this very ship, Davy, is a mystery that makes the "L" case look as simple as a jigsaw puzzle of only three pieces!

And won't Aunt Caroline crow! She'll say it all came from taking a boat that sailed on Friday the thirteenth. And she won't be so far wrong either. Since sleep is now impossible, I'll begin at the beginning, or rather where I left off earlier this evening. (Was it really this evening—just about four hours ago? Seems like a million aeons since I had a moment of peace or tranquillity!)

Probably the first half of my story, at least, is irrelevant and immaterial, if not incompetent, but it just might supply a clue, so here goes.

You remember how I said that the Lamberts had invited our whole table to the smoking room for drinks at ten? Well, I drifted in with Adam Burr a few minutes after I'd finished writing to you and found Mrs. Lambert sitting in state with old Wolcott. Mr. Lambert was playing bridge with the funny little man I described earlier whose name turned out to be Daniels,—Mr. Burr (who had gone out to fetch me while he was dummy), and another man whom I hadn't seen before. In addition there was a steward behind the bar, but I am quite positive that there was no one else in the room.

Mrs. Lambert greeted me as I came in, so I sat down with her and the courtly Wolcott and our positions were like this:

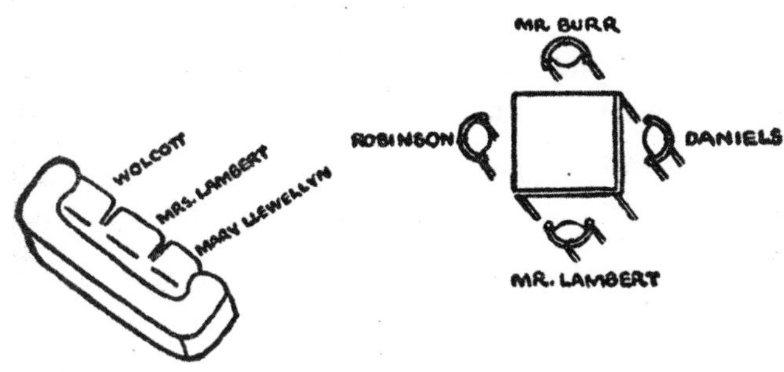

My hostess was most affable and we became quite girl-to-girl on the subject of my special articles, which she always reads over her Sunday breakfast. She is one of those women who are actually about thirty-eight, don't look a day over twenty-eight, and act all of eighteen. Still, she was pleasant enough and old Wolcott took his cue from her and together they flattered me so that

I really began to believe that there is something in the power of the press—after all.

Mrs. Lambert asked me if I'd like to order a drink now or wait until the bridge players joined us. They looked as if they were just about to finish a rubber so I naturally said I'd just as soon wait a while. From time to time I managed to escape from her dithyrambs and strolled over towards the bridge table in order to watch the play. Although the stakes were not high, everyone seemed to be very intent on the game. So much so that I was introduced only in the most casual manner to the member of the party whom I hadn't met before, a Mr. Robinson, I believe his name was. As I remember him, he was an uneventful person, of any age between thirty and fifty; cleanshaven; wore glasses, and had thick sort of brownish hair and a wonderful coat of tan. This, he explained in rather a squeaky, high pitched voice by saying it was the result of a prolonged vacation in Florida. I can't for the life of me remember his saying anything else.

It was not long before I realized that something was rotten in the game of contract—or at least, that Mr. Daniels was not very well satisfied with his partner's play. They had, apparently, won two rubbers more by good luck than good judgment, but now things were beginning to go against them.

"Well," snapped Daniels in pure Londonese which I will not attempt to reproduce, "since I'm incapable of getting my partner to give me the correct lead, I propose a drink, if you've no objection, sir,"—this to Mr. Lambert. "Now, I have the recipe for a gin rickey—may I order one all around?"

"No, no," cried Mr. Lambert hospitably. "The party is on me, but I'll buy anything an Englishman suggests in the shape of a new concoction."

He smiled genially and summoned the steward. Mrs. Lambert and I said we'd take a glass of sherry. Mr. Burr and Mr. Robinson both had highballs, while Mr. Daniels laboriously wrote out the requirements for his rickey, which was finally ordered for himself and Mr. Lambert.

They then resumed their bridge, with the same partners, and much as I love to watch the game, I remembered my manners and rejoined Mrs. Lambert on the couch.

I proffered some banality about her charming niece, asking why she was not with us.

"Oh, Betty's out on deck," she said, with an arch little smile. "Youth must have its fling, you know—"

I flippantly inquired with whom youth was flinging.

"Why, Jimmy Earnshaw, *of course.* He's such a *nice* boy."

Here she lowered her voice as if to impart some fearful indiscretion,

"They've been seeing a great deal of each other lately and—well, we are hoping this cruise may turn out to be something more than a business trip after all."

Her eyes had assumed the avid expression of the confirmed middle-aged matchmaker, who eats too much candy, reads too many novelettes and tries to get a vicarious thrill out of other people's emotional experiences.

"Well," I remarked, "I'm not surprised. She's an awfully pretty girl and would look nice under any circumstances—even in the dentist's chair."

"Oh, but she doesn't have any trouble with her teeth," cried my hostess, who was nothing if not literal. She then proceeded to explain that, even if distressing dental contingencies were to arise, Betty's parents had plenty of money to give her the best of everything.

You can imagine that I soon got bored with this kind of stuff and finally strolled over to the bridge table again, leaving my hostess a somewhat more sympathetic audience in the person of old man Wolcott.

Now, Davy, at the risk of boring you and dwelling too much on trivial details, I am going to write out a description of one or two of the hands. You know my habit of always noting down interesting looking hands in the hopes of being able to use them when I have to pinch-hit for the "Contractor" on the bridge page. And then, I'm putting down every single detail that I can remember.

So here are the hands as I jotted them down on the back of my dinner menu.

NORTH (Burr)
Spades . . . . K x x x
Hearts . . . . 10 x x
Diamonds . . . . x x x
Clubs . . . . A K x

WEST (Robinson)	*EAST (Daniels)*
Spades . . . . Q	Spades . . . . x x x
Hearts . . . . K Q	Hearts . . . . . . J x x x x x
Diamonds . A Q J 10 x x	Diamonds . . . . K x
Clubs . . . . J x x x	Clubs . . . . Q x

SOUTH (Lambert)
Spades . . . . . . A J 10 x x
Hearts . . . . A x
Diamonds . . . . .x x
Clubs . . . . .10 9 x x

Lambert and Burr, 80 on game. Lambert, Dealer
Bidding:

Lambert (bidding to score) . . . . . . 1 Spade	*Robinson*. . . . .2 Diamonds
Burr . . . . 2 Spades	*Daniels*. . . . . Pass
Lambert . . . . Pass	*Robinson*. . . . .3 Diamonds
Burr . . . . 3 Spades	*Daniels*. . . . . Pass
Lambert . . . . Pass	*Robinson*. . . . .4 Diamonds
Burr . . . . Pass	*Daniels*. . . . . Pass
Lambert (over-optimistic) . . 4 Spades	*Robinson*. . . . . Double

Pass. Pass. Content.

The dear Lord knows why I didn't lose the paper considering what happened later, but they seemed so exciting at the time that even Mr. Wolcott left Mrs. Lambert and came over to watch them being played.

Even a lesser bridge player than you, darling, will see at a glance that East and West can easily get their opponents down. The double is perfectly good but what does the ineffable West do? He leads the one and only card in his hand which will enable Mr. Lambert to make his contract, viz., namely and to wit—the *lack of clubs.* South takes with dummy ace—plays out trumps, leads clubs and finds (to his great surprise, as you may imagine) that after the queen has fallen on the king, all those in his hand are good. So he makes his contract—doubled—and Mr. Daniels makes cutting remarks about leads.

Here's another hand which struck me as interesting enough to note down, and which illustrates, even better than the last, how a poor lead can completely gum the works.

NORTH (Burr)
Spades . . . . x x x
Hearts . . . . x x x
Diamonds . . . . J x
Clubs . . . . A Q J x x

WEST (Robinson)	*EAST (Daniels)*
Spades . . . . J 10 x	Spades . . . . Q x x x x
Hearts . . . . Q J 10	Hearts . . . . x x
Diamonds . . . . K 10 x x	Diamonds . . . . Q x x
Clubs . . . . x x x	Clubs . . . . x x x

SOUTH (Lambert)
Spades . . . . A K
Hearts . . . . . . A K x x x
Diamonds . . . . . A x x x
Clubs . . . . K 10

No Score on game. Both sides vulnerable.

Bidding:

Lambert . . . . 2 Hearts	*Robinson*. . . . . Pass
Burr . . . . 3 Clubs	*Daniels*. . . . . Pass
Lambert (optimistically) Little Slam in No Trumps	*Robinson*. . . . . Double

Pass. Pass. Content.

Now it's perfectly plain that if West (Robinson) had made the correct lead—a diamond—South (Lambert) was bound to go down one on his contract. But West foolishly led the jack of spades. (The man has a positive mania for jacks.)

Lambert, after losing one heart, was able to throw his diamonds on dummy's clubs and easily made the contract.

When Daniels asked afterwards, "Why on earth didn't you lead a diamond?" Robinson made some foolish remark about not liking to lead from a king.

• • • •

While one or the other of these hands was being played, I distinctly remember the steward coming in and passing around the drinks. After Mrs. Lambert had taken a sip of her sherry, she called the steward back and started to complain (she's the whiney sort, you know) that it wasn't as good as some she'd had before dinner. Mr. Lambert looked over his shoulder and said good naturedly:

"It's probably exactly the same, my dear, only before dinner is the more correct time to drink sherry and it possibly tasted better then! It looks all right. At least I'm sure it would if I could see it, but I've mislaid my spectacles. In fact, I can hardly count the pips on my cards. Do you happen to have seen them? The spectacles, I mean. I searched everywhere in the cabin before I came up."

Mrs. Lambert said rather tartly, "Oh, Alfred, you're always losing them, and you're always telling me what I ought and ought not to drink. It's a woman's privilege to change her mind and her drinks. Anyhow, I think I prefer port after all."

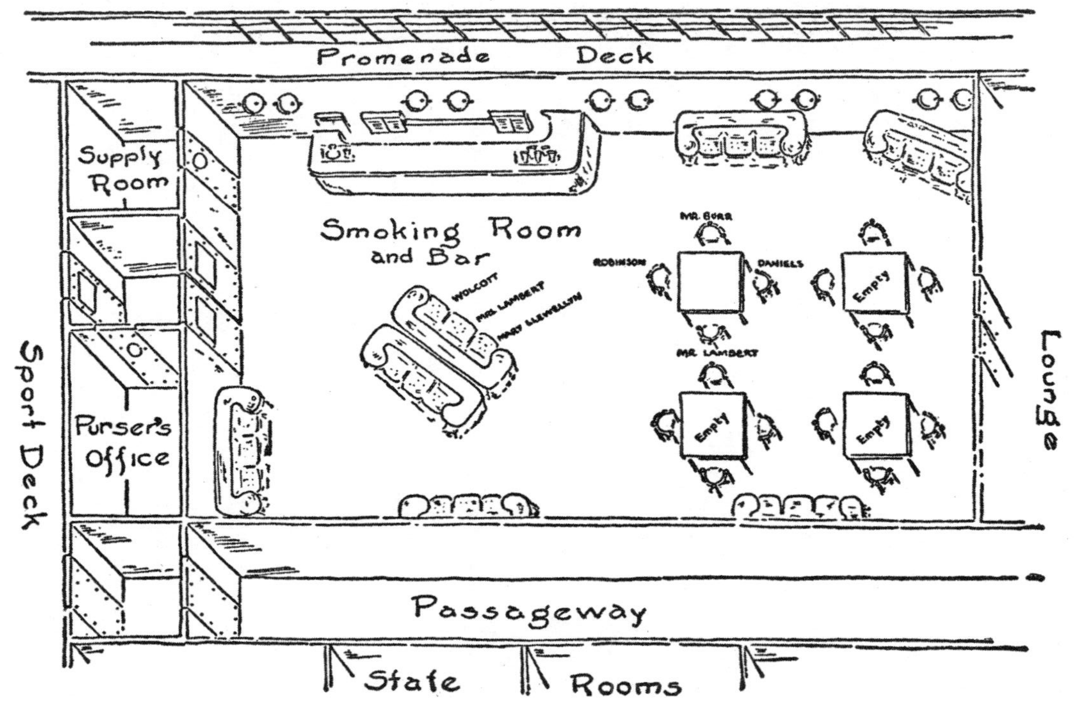
Promenade Deck
Supply Room
Smoking Room and Bar
Mr. Burr
Robinson
Daniels
Empty
Wolcott
Mrs. Lambert
Mary Llewellyn
Mr. Lambert
Empty
Empty
Purser's Office
Sport Deck
Lounge
Passageway
State Rooms

Mr. Daniels made the old bromide about any port in a storm and Adam Burr patted himself and said that port was fattening.

Then Mrs. Lambert started to enumerate (not unkindly) in a stage whisper a few of her husband's physical failings; his near-sightedness, his weak heart, his rheumatic twinges. When he caught the drift of the conversation he looked at us and smiled saying, "Yes, Miss Llewellyn, the old man is falling to pieces fast."

I tell you all of these footling remarks, Davy, because I have a feeling that some time or another they may have some hideous significance. And it looks as if we are going to need all of our ammunition before we are through.

Shortly afterwards they finished the rubber. Messrs. Robinson and Daniels, although they had been handsomely up at one time, were finally losers to the tune of three or four dollars. Mr. Lambert pocketed his winnings with the gleeful chuckle of a rich man who has had an unexpected windfall, and immediately suggested another rubber. Mr. Daniels and Mr. Robinson, who were still suffering from mutual dissatisfaction, finished up their drinks and excused themselves, saying that it was time for bed.

"I'm sure Mr. Wolcott would like to take my hand," remarked the little Cockney as he moved towards the door.

"No, no, I'm afraid my bridge is too rusty. I'll leave that to the younger folks." The nasty old man gave me a bow that was quite unnecessarily courtly. "It's the psychology of the game that appeals to me," he continued, "just the psychology."

Daniels left the room with a grunt. Mr. Lambert suggested rather tardily that the ladies join them for a final rubber. Mrs. Lambert said that she was feeling too sleepy. She'd go and get Jimmy Earnshaw and Betty, she said, and see if either of them would like to make a fourth, adding that she'd ask the steward to bring up her husband's spectacles if he found them anywhere in their suite. Then she said good night all around and in a few minutes the two young people came in from the deck, both looking rather cold and pale (love, I suppose!). Betty was bearing the most beautiful orange shawl I have ever seen in my life. Normally it would have suited her rather well, but its bright color now seemed to throw into relief the abnormal pallor of her face.

While Earnshaw stood by the couch talking to me, Betty went over and kissed her uncle good night.

"No dear," I heard her say, "I'm far too sleepy to play bridge; just one more turn on the deck with Jimmie, then I'm going back to my stateroom."

"Well, just pull the curtain over that open window before you go," said Mr. Lambert. "I believe I'm developing a stiff neck. And ask the steward for a plain gin and ginger ale, will you, Betty? *Mr. Daniels' rickey was positively poisonous.* I want something to take the taste away." I noticed, incidentally, that he had drunk only a little of it.

Betty did as she was asked and then Earnshaw excused himself to me and they both went out together.

We were now in that unenviable position of being three keen bridge players (Lambert, Burr and myself) in search of a fourth. We talked aimlessly for about ten minutes and I was just about to abandon the idea of a game and go to bed when Daphne Demarest entered the room looking even taller and more hoydenish than she had at dinner.

She smiled weakly, saying, "I can hardly stagger, but, if I must stagger somewhere, let it be to a bridge table. Bridge and drinkin' are about the only two things to do in weather like this."

After that I thought it would be mean to refuse to play. I wish to God now I'd never succumbed, but I did and that's that. Finally I partnered Mr. Burr against Daphne and Mr. Lambert, and we started to play at a tenth of a cent a point. Mr. Wolcott stood behind my chair in ceremonious silence, but although stray passengers sauntered into the room now and again, I am perfectly positive that no one stayed there any length of time.

And thus, while we dealt and bid, the curtain went down on Scene I of tonight's hideous drama, and, as I still feel as though sleep is utterly out of the question, I may as well begin on Scene II which contains the climax.

. . . .

Well, first of all, I should mention that our positions were like this:

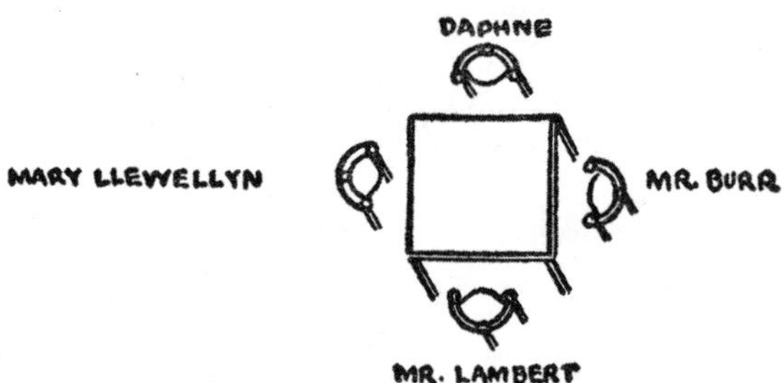

Then, I remembered, the steward came in with Mr. Lambert's gin and ginger ale and put it down by him. Just as he was going away our host called him back and ordered a highball for Daphne ("double whiskey with a splash," as she called it!) and one for Mr. Burr. I said I didn't want any more to drink as I had an operation to consider. Then Mr. Lambert finished the remains of his rickey and the steward took the glass away.

Daphne was not a very good player, but she and Mr. Lambert had the cards and they won the first two hands without any opposition. On the third hand our opponents went up to little slam in spades, and it just happened that, although my hand was pretty worthless in the other three suits, I did hold five spades to the jack over Mr. Lambert's declaration. I doubled and he promptly re-doubled.

I shall never know what the outcome of the play would have been, but I am positive that only a miracle could prevent my setting him at least one.

You know, Davy, there is always a moment of tension after a re-double. Partners look anxiously at each other, give nervous little laughs, and then assume smug expressions in an endeavor to hide their apprehension. We did all these things, I suppose, and then Mr. Lambert remarked, "I'll need a drink if I'm to get home on this one!"

He took a long pull at his gin and ginger ale, put the glass down on the table, and started to play. At this juncture Mr. Wolcott gave a look at my hand, smiled inscrutably and went out of the room.

After the first few leads I noticed that Mr. Lambert's hands were trembling so that he could hardly control the cards, and then—oh God! Davy, shall I ever forget it?—he staggered to his feet with a noise which can only be described as a strangled gurgle. For one perfectly horrible moment he stood there teetering, a ghastly grin on his face, then he crashed forward, dropping his cards, knocking over the three glasses and utterly ruining Daphne's frock. Before we had time to collect our wits he was lying on the floor writhing in convulsions.

For what seemed to me like an eternity we all stood perfectly still—staring at him with a kind of horrified fascination. I have often read stories in which people were poisoned and have thought of it as a kindly, peaceful sort of a death, but no gunshot wounds, no bloodshed could have been more hideous than this. It was the most cruel, the most bestial thing I have ever seen—and at the same time the most pitiful.

I suppose it was really a matter of about two seconds before we recovered, though it seemed an age. Daphne Demarest, who had been contemplating the proceedings in a thoroughly detached manner, was the first to regain her senses.

"Here, take his feet, Mr. Burr," she snapped, "and we'll get him up on the couch. I'm a trained nurse." Then she stooped down and I swear to you, Davy, she lifted that heavy man as easily as if she were putting a new born baby into its bath.

"The doctor, quick," cried Mr. Burr, and the steward, who had been staring at us goggled-eyed, sprang into life and dashed out of the room, as if glad to escape from the hideous thing which it contained.

Don't ask me what happened next, Davy. Don't ever ask me. It is a nightmare which I hope never to think of again as long as I live. I remember being vaguely conscious of the doctor's presence. I remember hearing him say something about tetanus-like convulsions, cyanosis and I caught a Latin phrase—*risus sardonicus* it sounded like—and then plainly, terribly plainly, and distinctly came the word STRYCHNINE!

"Someone had better go off and get the captain. There's nothing more that I can do for him."

I looked eagerly into the face of the surgeon, as they call the doctor on a British boat. Anything—anything to escape from that horrible smoking room.

He nodded. "You'd better come back," he said gently. "That is if you can stand it."

Without waiting for another word I made for the door and rushed blindly out, almost colliding on the threshold with Earnshaw, who was whistling the tune which the orchestra had been playing all the evening. His cheerful expression altered at once when he saw my face.

"In there—the smoking room—Mr. Lambert," I gasped, "you'd better go in and help."

I did not wait to see what he did but dashed on to find someone—anyone—who would direct me to Captain Fortescue.

To reach the captain of a ship at midnight is as difficult as getting in for an interview with John D. Rockefeller. Every member of the crew whom I approached for help told me that it was out of the question to speak to the commander at that time because he was busy navigating. But at last an officer appeared and, having enough sense to realize that something really serious was wrong, he took me straight up to the bridge, where I found the captain looking very solid and reassuring. There was a terrific gale blowing, but I didn't care what it did to my hair or my frock. It was like a heavenly draught of clear spring water to feel the fresh air on my face again after the atmosphere in that stuffy room.

"Captain Fortescue," I shrieked, trying to make my voice heard against the wind, "You are wanted in the first-class smoking room. A passenger—Mr. Lambert—has been killed. The surgeon is there and—and—"

And then I suppose I fainted, for the next thing I knew was that my face was rubbing against the rough serge of the captain's coat. There was a nice mannish smell that reminded me of you—brandy and cigars, I expect—a strong arm around my shoulder, and a sense of pleasant warmth trickling down my throat.

"There, there, now you'll be all right," said the captain comfortingly. "I'll come with you at once. Mr. Billings, the ship's yours."

When Captain Fortescue and I reached the smoking room,

we found the doors locked. The steward opened them immediately at the voice of authority and we entered the room together. The body was still lying on the couch and had—mercifully—been covered by a rug.

As I entered I heard Earnshaw saying to the doctor:

"He had a pretty groggy heart, doctor, and was rather liable to sudden attacks. Mrs. Lambert always keeps digitalis handy."

"This wasn't a heart attack," said the young surgeon grimly, and then he started to talk to the captain in low tones.

The steward, meanwhile, was wiping up the mess of drinks and playing cards with which the floor was littered. Daphne Demarest was calmly smoking a cigarette by the window and Mr. Burr hovered solicitously around me.

After a few moments the captain turned and faced us. He looked far less self-possessed than he had previously.

"You were all present when this—er—accident occurred?" he asked.

"All except Mr. Earnshaw," replied Burr. "Mr. Earnshaw, by the way, is Mr. Lambert's secretary."

Earnshaw nodded. He looked very shaken and upset.

"I can't understand it," he murmured. "He was perfectly well at dinner time. If it wasn't one of his usual attacks—"

"I'm sorry, Mr. Earnshaw," interrupted the captain, "but Dr. Somers says that it looks very much as though Mr. Lambert had died from strychnine poisoning. We have searched his pockets, and—unless anyone has anything which may throw further light on the matter, or unless evidence is forthcoming that Mr. Lambert took his own life, there is only one conclusion to be reached."

There was a moment of absolute silence in the smoking room, while the captain paused, waiting for one of us to speak. When no one volunteered any remark, he continued: "Of course, I don't want to jump to conclusions, but it seems to me—and I think Dr. Somers will agree—that Mr. Lambert has been deliberately *murdered.* I shall ask you to say as little as possible about the matter, of course; we don't want to upset the other passengers. And while the body is being removed, there are one or two questions which——"

At this point Daphne Demarest strode across the room with three long masculine strides. There was something magnificent about her as she stood there, facing the commander with flashing eyes.

"Captain Fortescue," she cried, "we are all very sorry for your predicament, I'm sure, but if this is awkward for you, just think how—how deuced unpleasant it is for us. If Mr. Lambert was poisoned, then one of us three people—Miss Llewellyn, Mr. Burr or myself—must have poisoned him. Except for the steward we were the only three people present when Mr. Lambert ordered drinks. His glass was standin' on the table and—well, there's no need for me to dot my 'i's' or cross my 't's' I suppose. But what I'm really sayin' is this—when I got on board the ship this morning with Mrs. Clapp, I never heard of Mr. Lambert in my life—nor, I daresay, had Miss Llewellyn or Mr. Burr. We happen to have been eatin' at the same table and we accepted his invitation to play cards tonight. As for wantin' to do away with the poor man—" She finished her sentence with a snap of her fingers and lit another cigarette.

"Miss Demarest is quite right," murmured Mr. Burr hoarsely. "And, since we are all more or less implicated, I demand that we all be searched immediately—at least, not Miss Llewellyn, because even in the unlikely event that she had any damaging evidence about her person, she could have got rid of it when she went up to fetch you, captain."

By this time the ship's surgeon had returned from disposing of the body and with him came the purser (a nice lad called Jennings) and—for no reason at all that I could see—our old friend Mr. Daniels.

We were then searched and thoroughly questioned, but since no one brought out any points that have not been included in my record, there's no need for me to go into it all again. The only thing new was the information volunteered by Earnshaw that Mr. Lambert's financial affairs were in perfectly good shape, that he was sixty-two years old and quite happy (as far as he knew) with his wife, (his second effort, by the way), to whom he had been married about two years. That seemed to rule out the probability of suicide.

The secretary added that he was acquainted with the terms of Mr. Lambert's will, in which, with the exception of a few minor bequests, he had left all of his considerable fortune to his wife.

Mr. Burr and Mr. Daniels then gave the captain a few details about the game of bridge that they had played earlier in the evening; he solemnly wrote down the names of those who had been present and made a few notes about the passing of the drinks.

As soon as the steward came back into the room Dr. Somers called him over and gave him what sounded like urgent instructions on some point or other. I did not hear what he said, but I caught most of the steward's reply.

"No, doctor, glasses are always washed as soon as they are taken away. No, sir, the poor gentleman upset all three of the second lot when he fell over."

"Then I suppose analysis of the contents of the tumbler will be out of the question." The ship's surgeon sighed and a puzzled little frown crinkled the smooth skin of his forehead.

It was at this juncture (I think) that Earnshaw suggested that someone ought to go down and tell Mrs. Lambert. The captain nodded, gave a few parting injunctions, and then asked Dr. Somers and Earnshaw to accompany him to the Lambert suite.

It was then, and not until then (believe it or not, Davy!) that I thought of my scoop. An important business man had been murdered under my very nose—and my paper panting for crime news! I dashed off to the radio room and wrote out a message for "The Fox." But it was destined not to be, for I had barely handed it in to the operator when I heard the captain's voice behind me. Oh, well, I suppose I should have known! He was awfully nice about it and explained very carefully what his position was and how they couldn't be absolutely sure that it was murder until they'd gone into the matter more thoroughly. Of course I had to give in, feeling very cheap as you can imagine, especially when he told me that Mrs. Lambert was having hysterics in her stateroom and that all Earnshaw's energies were being devoted to Betty, who was also frightfully upset. "A woman is needed down there," he said succinctly.

I went down at once and did what I could to comfort the poor widow. Finally Dr. Somers gave her an injection and Betty came in to sleep with her. It was nearly two o'clock when I reached my own stateroom.

And here I've been scribbling to you ever since, Davy dear. What a night! A grey streaky dawn is just beginning to break over the ocean and it's about time I tried to snatch some sleep. Incidentally, I'm about frozen.

And all the while the ship has been going steadily onward—just as though nothing had ever happened. Isn't it amazing!

Good night and good morning, darling.

On Deck.
Saturday, November 14th.
12:30 P. M.

It's a heavenly day and the sea is so beautiful that I want to burst into rhapsodic clichés about sapphire skies, pearly clouds and emerald depths. Everything is so peaceful; the passengers have not yet awakened to the fact that there has been a violent death in our midst—and one solitary seagull, wearily tagging after the stern of the *Moderna,* is a reassuring sign that we can't have left the coast so very far behind.

But it's quite far enough for my liking, Davy! I still feel like a dab of whipped cream wobbling precariously on the top of a frozen pudding. And this is the first day of my rest cure!

Well, I got to sleep at last, but it seemed as if I had barely closed my eyes when the stewardess came in with a cup of tea and told me that Mr. Jennings (the purser) presented his compliments and would I kindly stop in his office at 10:30.

I took my bath and dressed as quickly as possible. (I look a fright, and no wonder!) When I reached the purser's office I found him sitting at his desk with a large sheaf of papers in front of him. He asked me innumerable questions about last night and made very careful notes of my answers. The poor lad is obviously worried to death and quite out of his natural element.

Finally I inquired, "Have you definitely established the fact that it was strychnine poisoning?"

He looked a trifle awkward as he replied, "Dr. Somers is performing an autopsy this morning. We can't be positive about anything before this afternoon. And now, Miss Llewellyn, there's a little favor I'd like you to do for me—"

He broke off, very pink and perplexed. I nodded encouragingly.

"The—the captain—has instructed me to interview Mrs. Lambert as soon as possible. It is not—as you may imagine—a commission that I particularly relish. In the first place the poor woman is probably confined to her berth and—I—a mere man—being a journalist, I thought perhaps you'd be used to that sort of thing." He broke off with a gesture.

"Oh, I see, you'd like me to go down and find out how the land lies?"

"Would you?" he asked gratefully.

I felt sorry for the poor fellow and within a very few minutes I had presented myself at the door of the Lambert suite. Betty let me in and gave me a wan smile in answer to my mute questioning. The girl looked absolutely worn out but she seemed to be forcing herself to bear up with remarkable fortitude.

Mrs. Lambert was propped up in her berth, looking ten years older than she had the previous evening. There were dark lines under her eyes and her appearance was not improved by two blobs of rouge on her cheeks—a pathetic attempt, I suppose, at making herself presentable for callers.

I asked after her health and said all the foolish and useless things one does say on such occasions, but she simply looked at me with dazed, frightened eyes and made no reply to any of my questions.

But, all of a sudden, she gave a sharp jerk as if pulling herself back to sentient life.

"Was he—was he really *murdered?*" she asked in a whisper. "My poor husband *murdered?*"

This was my opportunity to carry out the promise I had made to the purser. I told her as gently as I could that nobody was sure about anything as yet, but that she could be very helpful if only she would be kind enough to answer a few questions when Mr. Jennings came down to her room later on.

"Certainly," she said, "I'll answer any questions at all, though I'm sure there's nothing I know that would be of much help. My husband was a happy man, Miss Llewellyn—a very happy man considering his age. He had his business worries of course, who hasn't these days? But our life together has been all that we could have wished. Of course, my family always thought I was crazy marrying a man old enough to be my father—but he was good to me, a good husband, a kind man—"

She dabbed at her eyes with her handkerchief.

"You mean, that you know of no reason why your husband should have wished to take his own life?" I asked.

"No, no, we were so happy," she insisted tearfully. "But there are a great many people who may have wished him out of the way, for all I know." She looked at me with veiled eyes. "How well do you know your friend, Mr. Burr?" she asked suddenly. "He seems to be very attentive."

I replied that I had never set eyes on him before yesterday.

"Well, he *says* he's recovering from an operation, but my personal belief is that he came on this trip to try to get a South American contract away from my poor husband. He is the vice-president of a rival company, you know. Mr. Lambert didn't say anything definite, but I know he was quite upset to find Adam Burr on the same boat."

"I remember you told me that this was a business trip," I remarked invitingly.

Mrs. Lambert glanced anxiously towards Betty, who had been staring aimlessly out of the porthole. The girl immediately took the hint and left us alone together.

"Yes," whispered Mrs. Lambert, "it was a very important business trip. I know nothing of the details, of course, but the whole thing was to be kept a dead secret. That's the reason we brought Betty along. Perhaps Jimmie—Mr. Earnshaw, that is—can tell you about it. But there *is* one thing I can tell you—"

She shuddered as though she were remembering something particularly unpleasant, and once again I noticed the look of fear in her eyes.

"There was something wrong with that glass of sherry which I had last night. You remember how I sent it back and asked for port? Well, I believe that someone had done something to it. The wine tasted absolutely different from what I had before dinner—you heard the steward say it was exactly the same! Can you wonder, Miss Llewellyn, in view of what happened later to my poor husband, that I am frightened for myself—for Betty—even for Mr. Earnshaw, who was my husband's right hand man and *so* devoted to his interests."

She was obviously working herself up into hysterics so I interposed quickly:

"But your husband had a weak heart," I said. "Isn't it possible that—?"

"Yes, he did," she sobbed, "and of course it may have been that. He always went at things so hard—work and play—at his age it was very unwise. It may have been that, oh God knows what it was—"

Here she broke down again, completely, so I summoned Betty, who gave her some aromatic spirits of ammonia and fussed soothingly about her.

After a while I left and went to my chair on the upper deck to enjoy the lovely warm sunlight and try to think things over coolly, calmly and collectedly.

And before I go any further, Davy, I want to say one or two things about Mrs. Lambert. Not that I intend to pose as an infallible psychologist at this stage of the game. I am, however, prepared to bet fifty to one that she did *not* murder her husband, even if she does inherit his money. After all, it takes a great deal of what you so vulgarly call "intestinal fortitude" to commit a murder, and she hasn't any of that in her make-up. She's no fool, of course, and I don't believe for a moment that she was passionately in love with old Lambert—but, kill him in cold blood, never! She's too soft—too feminine. Murderers—especially when they are murderesses—should be made of sterner stuff. She may have deceived him, told him fibs, kidded him along, but she did not actually take his life. Of that I am certain. Besides, she never had an opportunity. She was sitting on the couch all the evening and not once did she come within three yards of the drinks on the bridge table—not even when she said good night. She's a silly woman and I don't particularly like her, but I'm going to do all I can to help her because she is thoroughly scared—and—well, us girls must cling together in a case like this! So much for that.

Now for the next developments, such as they are.

I hadn't been long on the upper-deck, sunning myself and sipping my bouillon, before I was joined by Adam Burr. Apparently he had spent his whole morning either in cross-questioning or being cross-questioned. He has found out that Mr. Lambert's first wife is dead, leaving one child (male) with whom he had not been on speaking terms for some years.

There has been plenty of activity, it appears, from the authorities this morning. The smoking room has been gone over with a fine comb but nothing has been found. The steward (who has been with the company fourteen years and has a blameless record) swears that he fixed Mr. Lambert's drink exactly the same as usual and that no one approached him or came near his tray while he was carrying the glasses to their respective destinations. Mrs. Lambert's sherry was exactly the same as before and he is positive that he opened a fresh bottle of soda water for each glass that required it.

Earnshaw has been given an opportunity to look over every passenger, officer, and member of the crew to see if he could identify anyone as being an enemy of Mr. Lambert's, but he has declared that everyone was a complete stranger—with one exception.

"And you, I presume, are the exception," I interposed quickly.

"Clever child, how did you guess? Yes, I admit I knew Mr. Lambert slightly—only in a business way, of course." Here Mr. Burr pulled out a large handkerchief and passed it over his shiny bald pate. "As a matter of fact, I was very much astonished to see Alfred Lambert on this boat at all. His presence could mean only one thing—that he was after a contract! And he had told me that he was never going to have any more dealings with those 'damned Dagoes' as he called them. His firm got bitten pretty badly last year when the milreis dropped."

He went on to explain that both he and Mr. Lambert were connected with different firms and that there was a big contract now going begging in Rio de Janeiro. He admitted quite frankly that they were business rivals but assured me that there was no personal animosity—on his side at least. "Old Al Lambert," he continued, "was as sharp as a thumbtack, but outwardly he was always a perfect gentleman."

"Do you think his financial affairs were in such shape that he might have wanted to take his own life?" I asked.

Mr. Burr chuckled, "No, no. Alfred is not the man he was, of course, but nobody really is or was as far as I can make out. Still, I think the old boy could still sign a six-figure check without turning a hair. He feathered his nest all right—wish I could say the same. Besides, as I remarked before, Lambert was always very much the gentleman. And no one would say it would be a gentlemanly thing to do—to take poison in the middle of a game of bridge, to knock the drinks all over the ladies' dresses, and to make such an exhibition of one's self in public. Besides, if he *had* been suicidally inclined, he would at least have waited till the end of the rubber. Al's middle name was Contract—in more senses of the word than one."

We then started to discuss the possibilities and probabilities of the previous evening, but Mr. Burr could think of nothing that was out of the ordinary and had absolutely no contributions to offer in the way of a motive. Suddenly it seemed to dawn on us that, considering we were strangers to each other and both under suspicion, we were being extraordinarily frank and outspoken in talking this way. I hope this is all going to sound funny to me some day, but even as I write, I have a horrid, creepy feeling along my spine—. Suppose something got planted among my belongings? I know I'm innocent, but no one else does. Probably Mr. Burr felt about me just as I felt about him—*not absolutely sure.*

Anyway, after a moment he bent over me and looked at me searchingly.

"Forget those dark thoughts, my dear, and let's work in double harness on this. I've never been in cahoots with the press before and it might really be a help to pool our resources. What do you say?"

He looked so kind and paternal that I broke down and told him all about my visit to Mrs. Lambert, my journal, the Laubenthal case—everything, in short, except the name of my bootlegger.

Oh, well, perhaps I was a fool and perhaps not. Anyhow, there goes the lunch bugle and a cup of bouillon won't sustain me for ever.

I must fly.

On Deck.
Saturday, November 14th.
4:15 P. M.

I had a little nap after lunch, Davy, and woke up to find Adam tenderly wrapping my steamer rug round my legs. The old dear has now gone off to fetch me a cup of good strong English tea, so I have a chance to scribble down the item of news which he has just imparted.

It's awful to write about such things on this gorgeous Moby Dick of a day, but I must get pen to paper before medical terms escape my memory.

Apparently Dr. Somers has completed his autopsy and, although he is not a regular pathologist, he has satisfied himself as to the cause of Mr. Lambert's death. An examination of the stomach contents tends to verify his diagnosis of strychnine poisoning, and the amount swallowed seems to have been enough to cause death even in a healthy young man, let alone an old one with a leaky mitral valve. There's no doubt about his heart having been in bad shape, but Dr. Somers says he might easily have lived twenty more years with reasonable care. It was the strychnine that did the trick.

Our young surgeon is quite frank on the subject of his own

inadequacy, but he has apparently done his best with the rough and ready equipment that he has on board ship. He told Mr. Burr (though why on earth he should have been so confiding beats me!) that he is unable to say when or how the poison was administered or exactly how long it took to act. Certain organs are going to be removed (ugh!) for further analysis when we reach Georgetown.

This afternoon the body will be embalmed and placed in an empty stateroom. Merciful heavens! Just supposing it should be next to mine! Imagine how one would feel if one jumped into the wrong bed and found—oh Davy, it's too frightful! But I must keep my own counsel, as the general public still doesn't know a thing. They've been told that an elderly invalid died the first night out and no one even suspects foul play. At least, that is the story.

These are a few pleasant thoughts to carry me through my tea—here it comes incidentally. And later on Adam Burr and I are going to slip away to a secluded spot (dear, didn't I tell you he's got a head like a plum and a tummy like a pear!) and go over everything we can remember about last night. As a matter of fact, I'm going to read this journal to him, all except certain little asides that are meant for your ears and eyes alone. At present I'm afraid I have nothing more to contribute. In the Laubenthal case I did have a hunch. But now I have nothing—except this record which does at least set down as accurately as possible every single thing I observed consciously last night.

Stateroom,
Saturday, November 14th.
6:30 P. M.

Well, darling, it is just possible that I *may* have contributed something after all, although, as you will see later, I am still doubtful. In any case I must hurry if I'm going to tell you because it's getting late and I've got to dress. I have a particular reason for wanting to go down to dinner tonight—a very particular reason!

Adam and I had a long conference on deck this afternoon and first of all I read him my journal (minus terms of endearment and all twiddleybits) from the very beginning, while he scribbled little notations. Finally he said:

"Would you mind beginning again at the part where you *first* mention drinks being served in the smoking room?"

I started at page 18 and went on until he told me to stop. Then I looked at him and he looked at me, and both in one breath we said:

"If—"

Apparently the same thought had struck us almost simultaneously. So before going any further he hurried off to ask the surgeon whether or not the strychnine might have been administered in the first round of drinks.

He came back in a very few minutes carrying a thick green book entitled, CUSHNY'S PHARMACOLOGY AND THERAPEUTICS.

"Dr. Somers wasn't there," he exclaimed, "so I swiped this book from his cabin. Luckily I had one brief and inglorious year in medical school, so dear old Cushny won't be entirely Greek to me."

He opened the textbook at the section on strychnine, which, judging from various markers and marginal notes, had recently been consulted pretty freely by Dr. Somers.

Then Mr. Burr started to read me a highly technical description of strychnine, its action on the human body, the fatal dose and the horrible symptoms which follow its ingestion. Suddenly a phrase arrested my attention:

"—the first complaint is a feeling of stiffness in the muscles of the neck and face—"

"Wait a minute," I cried out excitedly. "Mr. Burr, don't you remember that Mr. Lambert complained to Betty about a stiff neck when she came in to wish him good night? He asked her to pull the curtain over the window in spite of the fact that the room was as stuffy as a hothouse. And this was before he'd even ordered his second drink."

Mr. Burr's only reply was a long, low whistle.

"And," I continued, turning over the pages of my journal, "you will remember that Mr. Lambert had drunk only a little of his rickey at this point. He didn't finish it until page 28, or after you and Daphne and I had begun to play—about fifteen minutes before he finally collapsed."

"Yes, yes," agreed Mr. Burr, in a tense whisper, "and naturally the alkaloid would have a tendency to stay at the bottom of the tumbler. Oh, boy, I believe we have got something at last. Strychnine, apparently, does not act very quickly and the old man might easily not have gotten the full effect until he drained his glass just before the second round of drinks came on. And then he complained of the bitterness of Daniels' famous rickey, didn't he? Well, strychnine has a very bitter taste—oh, my Lord, this looks bad for Daniels!"

We discussed the matter for a while longer and finally decided that Mr. Burr would take it up with the authorities as soon as possible, but, for the time being, we would not tell the others about the new development. Our discovery had, of course, considerably enlarged the list of suspects. If the poison had been put in Mr. Lambert's *second* drink—the gin and ginger ale—then either Wolcott, Burr, Daphne, the steward or myself *must* be guilty. But if the rickey was responsible, then we had to figure on the possibility of Daniels, Robinson, Betty, Earnshaw, and Mrs. Lambert as well.

"I can easily imagine," Mr. Burr concluded, "that our murderer is now congratulating himself on a tremendous piece of luck. Naturally everyone will have jumped to the conclusion that it was the *last* drink which contained the strychnine, especially since it has been impossible to analyze what remained in the glass. It is even probable that he—or she—had a perfect alibi by the time Lambert actually passed out." "Well," I said, "I think the best thing we can do is to find out as much as we can about our fellow passengers and see if there is any one of them who had a possible motive. I'll start tonight at dinner to cross-question the captain as tactfully as I can. You follow my lead. In the meantime, why don't you tell me about the circumstances which preceded the first game of bridge? There might be something illuminating in that."

Adam hemmed and hawed for a few moments and then began his story of what happened during the earlier part of last evening.

He was, he said, in the smoking room at about 8:30 when the entire Lambert party entered. Mr. Lambert immediately rubbed his hands and suggested a game of bridge, but Betty said she didn't feel very well and Earnshaw that he had a date with the moon. Then the young people made their escape. Mrs. Lambert didn't seem keen on bridge either, so she and her husband strolled over to where Mr. Burr was sitting and started to chat with him and Wolcott. Meanwhile a few people drifted in and after Mr. Lambert had finished his cigar (in about half an hour's time), he started to cast covetous eyes around him once again. Mr. Burr said he'd be delighted to play and then little Daniels popped up quite eagerly and said he'd make a fourth with Mr. Wolcott. But Wolcott refused (quite curtly, it seems) and Mr. Lambert was obliged to go over and ask Robinson, who had just come in and begun to play solitaire at a table near by. They cut for partners, settled stakes (one-fifth of a cent) and started in as I had found them when I came in later.

Nothing else important happened until Mr. Burr went off to fetch me—and the rest, of course, I know for myself.

And now, my dear, if I am to vamp the captain and my fellow passengers into telling me all about themselves, I must slip on something very seductive for dinner and do my damnedest. It's an awful admission to make, Davy, but there's a certain part of me that's really enjoying this case, terrible though it be.

Now for a tub and after that my black lace *Chanel*—

Saturday,
Writing Room,
8:30 P. M.

Oh, my dear, dinner was a riot. Shall I ever forget it? It was just one of those things that one tries not to remember all the rest of one's life, only to think of it now and again with an awful *prickly* sensation of shame and disgrace—I feel as though I had been caught stealing lumps of sugar at a garden party!

And my only excuse is that I had been primed by three cocktails before it all happened. Adam caught me just as I was coming out of my stateroom and rushed me off to the bar.—Never drink quickly, Davy, if you want to keep your wits and your manners about you.

Well, I found our table sadly depleted in numbers, though at first glimpse, while I was still suffering from dual vision, I had the impression of vast multitudes. Daniels, Silvera, Wolcott, Burr, Daphne Demarest, and Mrs. Clapp were the only passengers present. I behaved like a perfect lady all through the *hors d'oeuvre* and soup, and it was not until the *agneau farci* that I started to give an exhibition of what happens to a perfect lady when she tries to be tactful on one cocktail too many.

"Captain Fortescue," I said as cutely and ingenuously as I

could, "I've always wondered what it is that makes the captain of a liner invite certain people to sit at his table. Are they chosen for their looks, wealth, social position or their allure?"

Our gallant skipper looked at me the way Aunt Caroline does when you offer her a cocktail, blushed the color of raw beef and muttered something about "people who had special letters of introduction to him."

"Of course," I went on blithely, "I know that's how it happened in my case. The City Editor of my paper (commonly known as 'The Fox') wrote and told you the worst about me, but I was wondering—take Mr. Burr now—surely nobody would be so rash as to give *him* a letter of recommendation?" I shot an arch smile across my shoulder at Adam.

"Mr. Burr," replied the captain stiffly, "has travelled on this ship a great many times. I might go so far as to say that we are old friends."

"And is Mr. Daniels an old friend too?"

The captain looked anxiously towards the little Cockney, who was wolfing his *petìts pois paysanne* and talking animatedly to Daphne at the same time.

"Mr. Daniels—er—brought a letter from our London office—he—"

"Oh, I'm quite okay," interrupted the subject of our conversation, without taking the time to empty his mouth. "Don't worry about me, Miss Llewellyn. My credentials are all right, but like my photographs, they don't do me justice." His piggy little eyes were twinkling with malicious amusement, as he added, "But Mr. Wolcott now—why not ask him how he got in such distinguished company?"

Now I've already told you, Davy, that I don't like Wolcott and apparently Daniels doesn't either. There's something clammy and insincere about him. But still, he is a grey-headed old man, and even after three cocktails I would never deliberately make him feel uncomfortable at the dinner table. Uncomfortable he certainly was, however, when he caught Daniels' remark. His face went deep pink and he laid down his fork as though he was never going to pick it up again.

"I—I—came to this table because I was invited by the captain," he stammered. "If my—er—presence is objectionable, well, there are other tables—"

It was at this point, Davy, just as I was about to try to pour some oil on the waters I had troubled, that a clear, distinct voice rang out in tones of ineffable disgust.

"This is insufferable!"

At first I thought it must be Silvera speaking, but he was munching away and sipping his wine as though he hadn't heard a word of the previous conversation. Daphne's face was a mask of well-bred disdain.

It was Mrs. Clapp who had spoken!

Now, I had never properly noticed the widow lady until this moment. I had been conscious of her as a dark, mournful-looking creature who had appeared once before at lunch yesterday, but who hadn't a word to say for herself. Now, as I looked into her dark, flashing eyes, I realized immediately that she was a person to be reckoned with. I should judge her to be between fifty and sixty, but there's hardly a wrinkle in her face and her eyes are as clear and handsome as those of a girl of sixteen. It was her voice, however, that was the big surprise. It went through everyone at the table like an electric current.

"It is insufferable," she repeated, and though she had not risen to her feet, she gave that impression, for everyone's eyes were fixed upon her. "Why should we be catechized at the dinner table as to our—credentials—our rights to eat when and where we please? We have paid our passage money, Miss Llewellyn, and if you as a newspaper reporter are too young and too ignorant to know who I am—"

At this point the captain interposed a trifle pompously, "I think we are taking Miss Llewellyn's remarks a little too seriously, and, I'm sure, it's an honor for us all to have a great artist like Mrs. Clapp at our table. To those of us who remember her as Miss Marcia Manners, it is indeed an inestimable privilege."

At the words "Marcia Manners" everyone at the table (except Daphne) stared at Mrs. Clapp as though she had been an apparition from another world—as indeed, in a sense, she was. For this mournful, subfusc woman is none other than the greatest of all comediennes—Marcia Manners, who made me laugh at the age of fourteen, made my mother chuckle at twenty-four, and caused my grandmother to hold up her fan to her mouth at forty. This was the woman who created so much fuss and excitement a few years ago by giving up a brilliant stage career to marry a man young enough to be her son; and he had died suddenly, I now remembered, only a few months ago. At last, Davy, I was beholding in the flesh a woman who had counted the world well lost for love.

No one spoke for a moment, but I noticed that Adam Burr had pulled out a pencil and was scribbling frantically on a menu card.

"Yes, Miss Llewellyn," the beautifully modulated voice came across the table, "and I may as well inform you—since you apparently are so interested—that I am—or was—in a manner of speaking, a sister-in-law of Mr. Lambert's. Unless I am very much mistaken, the gentleman at your side is writing that piece of information down for you at this moment." (He was.) "The first Mrs. Lambert was once a Miss Manners. It was a great many years since I had seen my brother-in-law and I will tell you quite frankly that I did not approve of him—nor of the way he treated my sister. Now, Daphne, dear, unless there is any further personal intelligence that Miss Llewellyn requires, I think we may as well leave the table."

With these words she sailed majestically out of the dining saloon, dutifully followed by her companion. The rest of us completed our meal in silence—and as speedily as we could.

I had just come into this room after dinner and was about to start writing my journal when Daphne came in, carrying under her arm an enormous box of chocolates adorned with all kinds of feminine frills and ribbons. She looked like a guardsman about to go calling on his sweetie.

I immediately went up to her and apologized for my share in the dinner-table fiasco, asking her to express my apologies to Mrs. Clapp for my unpardonable crudeness.

"Oh, that's all right," she said good-naturedly, "the old lady loves a scene now and again. I have 'em all the time, but she soon gets over it. She's chucklin' about it in her cabin now. She hates the press, you see, as is only natural, considerin' how much she's been in the public eye, but she's a rippin' good sort at bottom. We're all in a devil of a jam after last night and I don't blame you a bit for tryin' to find out all you can about our jolly little playmates. Have a chocolate, by the way?"

Her manner was so nice and friendly that I accepted at once. It was the most wonderful thing that I've ever eaten—all squishy inside and full of real French liqueur.

"My dear, what heavenly candy!" I exclaimed involuntarily.

Daphne paused with one on the way to her mouth and a doubtful expression passed over her face. I had the idea that she was trying to make up her mind whether or not she would tell me something. Suddenly it came out:

"Look at me, Miss Llewellyn, look as hard as you can and then tell me if you think I'm the kind of woman that would inspire a man's passion at first sight."

I looked at her but said nothing. Indeed, what could I say?

Then she plunged an enormous hand down the front of her dress and pulled out a piece of ship's stationery with some typewriting on it.

"I found this in my room soon after dinner tonight, on top of this box of chocolates," she said brusquely. "Such a thing has never happened in my life before. Here read it. I haven't the foggiest idea who sent it."

The letter went something like this:

Dear Miss Demarest,

I know about last night's murder and I know of your predicament. Also, I know a lady when I see one. If you find yourself in any difficulties, you have a friend at court who is more than devoted to your interests. Just give the purser a note and he will deliver it to

Your friend and admirer,

Anon.

"And do you really intend to eat the chocolates?" I asked, wishing I hadn't been so rash as to take one.

"Hell, yes; no one has ever wanted to do anything to me. I've often wished they would! Isn't it amazin' though? Well, I must be trottin' along to Mrs. Clapp."

With these words she replaced the billet-doux in her bosom and strode out of the room.

Ain't life queer!

Saturday,
10:30 P. M.
Stateroom.

Well, Davy, I've turned in early enough even to please you, and in a few minutes I am going to bed with an allonal tablet *(faute de mieux)* to make up for the ravages of last night.

But before doing that, I must get down the new points which have come up tonight and I'm going to keep the best for the last, because it's frightfully exciting. In fact it's so exciting that it doesn't bear thinking of, so I shan't dwell on it.

I told Adam this evening that he ought to retire from business and join the rocking-chair brigade—he's the greatest old woman for collecting gossip about people. And how he seems to love it! He has discovered (don't ask me how) that Wolcott went to the purser's office immediately after dinner this evening and made arrangements for a stop-over at Georgetown so that he could continue to Rio on another boat. Apparently he doesn't find the atmosphere of this one to his liking. He claims that he is sleeping badly and feeling generally rotten. I must say that, for an old man, he looks the very picture of health. I wonder if my remarks at dinner precipitated this move! Or, I wonder—could this be the breakdown after a desperate act?

And the next item concerns our dark and dangerous Señor Silvera—the mystery man at the captain's table.

You will remember that I told you he doesn't speak a word of English—or, at least, not a word that is recognizable as our mother tongue. He gasps and sputters occasionally, but avoids opening his mouth as much as possible.

Well, my indefatigable Adam who speaks Spanish like a toreador, approached him tonight and started a conversation in what he claims was ninety-nine and forty-four hundredths per cent pure Castilian. After they had been talking awhile, Adam says he noticed that Silvera spoke Spanish with a distinct accent. In short he is a Brazilian, trying for some reason best known to himself, to pass as a Spaniard, whereas, of course, Portuguese is his native language.

Then Adam got to puzzling it out and it struck him further that Silvera's face was quite familiar: he was sure that he'd seen a picture of it somewhere since coming on board. Finally, he discovered it in the current issue of a magazine, *The Engineering Age,* and Silvera is none other than Gil Da Silviera, President of the Rio de Janiero Construction Company. And the article said that he was in America on business and did not expect to return to Rio until next March!

Now, Davy, all you have to do is to put two and two together and make twenty-two. The Brazilian government is building a new breakwater in the Rio harbor. It will cost at least $90,000,000. Mr. Lambert's company was after the job; Burr admits quite frankly that he is too—and Silvera is returning home four months ahead of his schedule. The race, apparently, is to the swift and the contract to the lowest bidder!

We were taking a walk round and round the upper deck while he was telling me all this. It is becoming increasingly difficult to be alone with anyone, for the number of passengers seems to have doubled since last night, and they are all so distressingly friendly. As soon as we had reached a more or less isolated spot, Adam paused and said:

"You know, partner, we've now pinned a motive on almost everybody concerned and made a thoroughly efficient job of it. But, there's one person who seems to have been remarkably backward in coming forward about this whole business—and that's Robinson. Don't you think we ought to have a bit of a talk with him?"

"Gosh! I'd forgotten all about him," I replied. "I hardly believed I'd know him again if I saw him. I vaguely remember that he had a pleasant coat of tan and wore spectacles. But I think your idea is a good one. He's probably in the smoking room. It's open again now—let's go and see. I'm getting giddy walking round the deck anyhow and my face is stiff from smiling at the same people every time we run into them."

We went down the companion-way to the scene of last night's tragedy, where we were immediately accosted by little Daniels, who callously suggested a game of bridge. We both refused, and I said, smiling:

"Why not try your friend, Mr. Robinson? You seemed to admire his play last night—!"

Daniels snorted scornfully.

"And where is he, by the way?" I continued, "I haven't seen him around at all since—since—Mr. Lambert's death."

"The less he hangs around, as far as I'm concerned, the better," snapped Daniels. "Any man who leads the way he does ought to be locked up permanently. I jolly well hope that I never see his ugly mug across a bridge table again as long as I live."

"Well, I thought he had a nice mug," I said mendaciously, "I wouldn't at all mind seeing it again at a bridge table—just so long as he was my opponent and not my partner."

I was about to continue my attempt to draw Daniels out on the subject of Robinson when an incident occurred which even now gives me the strange creepy feeling up and down my spine that is becoming too, too familiar.

The nice Mr. Jennings came into the smoking room with a piece of paper in his hand and a puzzled frown on his face. As he came over and stood near me, I could not help noticing my own name written on his paper and that of Adam Burr, both with crosses against them. In fact there was only one name on the list which had no cross.

"Excuse me," he said politely, addressing the three of us collectively, "but are you quite sure that the fourth bridge player last night was called Robinson?"

"There's no forgetting either his name or his play," said Daniels.

"Would you be so kind as to tell me once again what he looked like?"

Daniels and Burr stared at each other helplessly. Then they both turned inquiringly towards me.

"Why," I stammered, "I didn't notice him properly. It was the first night out, you know, and—and—"

"And Miss Llewellyn is engaged to another man," said Adam facetiously.

"He was sunburnt," I continued, with a withering glance at Mr. Burr. "He wore a dark lounge suit; he has spectacles and thick brown hair and his age is about—"

"Thirty or forty," added Daniels.

"Or fifty," appended Adam.

Jennings looked down at his paper again and the corrugations on his forehead were deeper than ever.

"There's a Mr. *Robertson* in the third class, but he's over seventy years old—a Methodist minister—wears a beard and is travelling with his wife and daughter."

I shook my head, and Mr. Daniels said with some vehemence:

"Good God, Jennings, the man can't have vanished. He was here large as life last night. All you've got to do is to trace him on the passenger list. There aren't that many people on board—surely!"

"Well," Jennings said slowly, (and it was then that the uncanny feeling began to creep over me), "it may interest you to know that there is no one named Robinson among the passengers or among the crew. Moreover, we have checked your description against every man on the boat, and there is not—one soul—that—it fits!"

Social Hall,
Sunday, November 15th.
12:00 M.

All yesterday we must have been pressing hard upon the heels of summer, and today we have sailed full tilt into blazing sunshine and sub-tropical heat. I cannot help feeling sorry for you, Davy, back in New York, where the November blasts must be whistling around the corners and where, I'm sure, neither of the two trees in your block has a decent leaf left to cover itself.

The officers look very smart in white uniforms and all the experienced travellers have put on cotton suits or frocks. There are even more fresh faces about and everything looks quite bright and picturesque. And I have just recaptured something of my childish faith and devotion by going to a church service on board ship. The captain read a beautiful bit from Job about "drawing out Leviathan with a hook and binding the sweet influence of the Pleiades." Then we sang a hymn about "those in peril on the sea" and I put up a special little prayer for you, Davy boy—and one for us both. It was all very charming and simple.

So now that I have regained my balance, my sober common sense and (let us hope) my sense of humor, I can speak more calmly about last night's development.

We have all been questioned again about Robinson; the ship has been searched from bow to stern; Daniels and Mr. Burr have themselves examined every male passenger who might possibly correspond to our description; but Robinson has not reappeared.

There are four possibilities, according to Adam:

(1) He is a stowaway and has not yet been found.

(2) He has fallen overboard.

(3) He is an impersonation.

(4) He is a ghost.

Nos. 2 and 4 seem unlikely because no one called Robinson is registered, you remember, either as a passenger or as a member of the crew, but then I suppose ghosts don't register anyhow—

• • • •

40 minutes later.

I had just got to that point, Davy, when Jennings came into the social hall and asked me if I'd be kind enough to go down and see Mrs. Lambert, as she'd been asking for me. I jumped up at once and—like a fool—left my journal lying on the table, where I had been writing. However, I did have the sense to close it—of that I am certain.

Mrs. Lambert, Betty and Earnshaw were all in the sitting room when I entered. The poor widow looked somewhat rested and refreshed, but Betty was still quite pale and pathetic. Earnshaw, on the other hand, seemed to have recovered his poise and self-possession, which is very admirable seeing that, from a material point of view at least, he is really the hardest hit of them all. He has lost his employer, his job—and both he and his girl have probably been done out of a legacy by the old man's sudden death.

Acting as spokesman for the party, he explained to me that all three of them had planned to leave the boat at Georgetown, where, after going through the necessary formalities, he would arrange for Mr. Lambert's cremation. They hoped to get back to America on the next boat.

It was at this point that Mrs. Lambert interposed with, "But, Miss Llewellyn, I really wanted to talk to you about Betty. The poor child was promised a holiday—it's bad for her to stay cooped up here all the time and, naturally, she's a bit shy about appearing alone in public after what has happened. You are the only girl on board whom we know and who is anywhere near her age. I was wondering if you would be so kind—"

"Oh, Aunt Mabel," interrupted Betty, a trifle petulantly, "there's really no point in bothering Miss Llewellyn this way. I can hang around with Jimmie."

"I'm going to be pretty busy," interposed Earnshaw, "with Mr. Lambert's papers until we get to Georgetown. I shan't have a minute to spare. You must get some fresh air, Betty."

The girl pouted in a manner not very flattering to myself, but I assured her that I should be delighted to have her company.

"I'll call for you at 1:30 today," I said, "and we'll go to lunch together. I haven't any friends on board the ship and it will be swell for me to have company. And you've no idea how flattered I am at Mrs. Lambert's saying that we are anywhere near the same age!"

I said good-bye and Earnshaw came out of the stateroom with me. When we reached the corridor he took my hand in his and pressed it, saying, "You *are* a brick, Miss Llewellyn. The poor kid's frightfully upset by all this and she seems worried about something, though she won't tell Mrs. Lambert or me what it is. You are just the person she needs. It *is* good of you."

We talked for a while longer about the strange disappearance of Mr. Robinson and the possibility that the poison might have been administered in the first round of drinks. These two facts, Earnshaw told me, had been imparted to him that morning by Mr. Jennings. They had, he added, temporarily upset the only self-respecting theory which he had worked out for Mr. Lambert's death. Then I remembered my journal and he seemed most interested. In fact, he said he was thinking that later on, when he was less busy, he was going to put some things down on paper himself. Then we must compare notes.

As he stood there talking to me, I noticed for really the first time what an awfully attractive fellow he is. With his small dark moustache and thick black hair he really might easily double for John Gilbert. And then there's something frank and genuine about him which I like a lot.

Just as I was about to leave, he added:

"As I said before, Miss Llewellyn, I shall be busy until we get to Georgetown sorting out Mr. Lambert's papers. There are an awful lot of them. And since you are so kind about the whole wretched business, I'm wondering if you would give me some advice about a little personal problem of my own. I'll be working all day, but—could we have a talk some time later on this evening? I'll look for you then."

I gladly promised to meet him any time he was free. Then I remembered my journal again and dashed back to the social hall as fast as my still somewhat invalidish legs could carry me.

Now, I distinctly told you, Davy, that I left the manuscript book on the writing table *closed.* Well, you can imagine my consternation when I found it lying where I had left it—*open,* with two or three sheets of ship's note-paper lying on the section where I described the two bridge hands which were played the night of Mr. Lambert's death (pages 16-17). There were quite a number of people in the room, so my first thought was that somebody had just used my journal as a pad on which to write letters. I was about to return the ship's stationery to the rack and continue writing when I noticed something rather strange.

The top sheet of note-paper had some faint impressions on it which showed that the writer had pressed down fairly hard on his pen or pencil. I held these up to the light, but at first I could make nothing of them except a number of crosses, scrawled at random across the page. Some child had been scribbling, I thought. I looked again and saw the letters A and K followed by a number of crosses.

Immediately the amazing truth dawned on me. Someone had been deliberately copying out the bridge hands from my journal. I could see the sequences quite clearly now—A K x x x and again Q J 10. There was no doubt about it at all.

I turned round to the person who was sitting nearest the table—a large woman dressed in knitted purple.

"Did you happen to see who was sitting at this table last?" I inquired politely, "I think I—er—left my fountain pen here and it's gone."

She looked up unwillingly from a brightly-jacketed romance.

"I believe there was a man there a minute or two ago," she said, "but I didn't notice him particularly. I don't believe he stayed very long."

Stateroom,
Sunday, November 15th.
6:30 P. M.

I escorted Betty up on deck after lunch and we chatted and napped together quite pleasantly. Of course I didn't like to pump her too obviously, but I showed a very lively interest whenever she started to talk about the Lamberts—which wasn't often, as she is a reticent little creature. In addition to the shock of her uncle's death, I think her affair with Earnshaw is responsible for her air of quiet broodiness. Every now and again she opens her mouth as if she is about to be very confidential, then she closes it again or merely makes some casual remark.

But what she did say certainly bore out the truth of Mrs. Lambert's statements. She told me that Uncle Alfred thought nothing in the world too good for Aunt Mabel, who (like her predecessor) before her marriage, had been an actress, but who had turned out to be a good housekeeper, made her husband as comfortable as possible, stayed home at nights, and raised no objection to his having Jimmie live in the house and making the place into a second office when there was any important job on hand. She also told me that Mrs. Lambert had tried her best to reconcile her husband with his son by the first wife (Mrs. Clapp's nephew, incidentally), who, when last heard of, was running a cattle ranch somewhere in the Argentine.

At tea-time Betty went down to keep her aunt company and her place was immediately taken by our Adam, who had been hovering round us all the afternoon like a fish hawk over a shoal of herrings.

"Anything fresh?" he asked at once.

I immediately retailed to him the scanty items that I'd gleaned from Betty. Then, rather shamefacedly, I told him how I had left my journal in the social hall this morning and asked him if it was he who had opened it.

"Heavens, no," he replied, helping himself to sugar, "I was in the bowels of the ship at that time—still looking for Robinson and Jennings. I'll swear we saw everyone on board except three old ladies who were seasick and there's no one who even remotely resembles our inglorious fourth. Those who were sunburnt didn't wear glasses and those who had thick brown hair were too old or too fat or too skinny. It's the most amazing thing."

"I don't like to think about it," I said, "especially when the shades of night are beginning to fall. Oh, look, quick—quick—there's a whale."

We rushed to the side of the boat and saw a thin fountain of water coming up at regular intervals.

"Thar' she blows," sang out Adam, as a number of other passengers flocked towards the rail with little squeaks of excitement.

Then there was a sudden upheaval of water, an enormous tail was shot into the air, and I got a really front-row view of Job's leviathan. I shouldn't care to try him out with a hook, Davy; I know that much. I also know that, for the first time on the trip, I really felt that we were in mid-ocean and very, very far from home!

As soon as the thrill of my first whale had subsided, we got back to business once again. Mr. Burr, who is an ardent reader of detective stories, explained to me (quite gratuitously, I might add) that all self-respecting crime analysis was divided into three leads—Motive, Means and Opportunity.

"Now," he said, "I suggest we take everybody one by one and put down what we've got against them under these categories. The Means, of course, was strychnine, which is, I suppose, more or less obtainable by any adult person who has set his mind on getting it. So we can leave that out. Let's concentrate on Opportunity and Motive—now, here's a piece of paper and a pencil. We'll be perfectly hard-boiled and scientific. You can begin with me if you like."

Here are our notes as we scribbled them down:

Adam Burr. Opportunity: Slight during the first game of bridge, since he was sitting opposite Lambert, but plentiful during the second game when he was sitting next to him. Motive: Possible business rivalry?

(Adam then insisted on giving me a write up—and this is his own handiwork entirely.)

Mary Llewellyn. Opportunity: Abundant during both bridge games. In the first she hovered affectionately around the old man's chair and in the second she sat next to him. Motive: None; but it's quite possible that she did it, since the least likely person always does in the best mystery stories!

Daniels. Opportunity: Plentiful during both games. It was at his suggestion that Lambert took the rickey, whose natural tartness probably masked the bitterness of the strychnine. Motive: None apparent as yet.

Wolcott. Opportunity: Plentiful while watching the play during both games. (Was it a coincidence that he should have left the room just before Lambert's final collapse?) Motive: None apparent, but neither of us likes him or his behavior.

Jimmie Earnshaw. Opportunity: Though he came into the room after the first game, M. L. is positive he stayed talking to her by the couch and never went near the bridge table. It is hardly conceivable that he should have been able to flick a strychnine pellet into the right glass from a distance of about eight feet. Motive: None apparent unless he has purloined the petty cash or forged his employer's signature. He doesn't look that type (M. L.) You never know with these sheiks (A. B.)

Betty Lambert. Opportunity: It is possible that she slipped something into her uncle's glass when she went over to kiss him good night. But, if we are to take his remark about a stiff neck as denoting the first symptoms of the poisoning, then both she and Earnshaw must be exonerated. It is conceivable, however, that Mr. Lambert really did have a stiff neck quite apart from the strychnine, and that he was not poisoned until the second round of drinks. Motive: None apparent.

Mrs. Lambert. Opportunity: None. Both M. L. and A. B. are certain that she did not approach the bridge table during the entire course of the evening. Motive: Only such as one might get in cheap romances or the tabloids. And then, of course, she inherits something in the neighborhood of a cool million.

Daphne Demarest. Opportunity: Fairly plentiful during the second bridge game although she was sitting opposite Lambert. (But what was an intervening table with those Olympic arms?—This from Adam.) Here again, if Mr. Lambert was poisoned during the first game, she is exonerated. Motive: Remote possibility through her connection with Mrs. Clapp, who is a relative in-law of Lambert.

Smoking room Steward (who, for your information, rejoices in the name of Sam Bumstead). Opportunity: More than anyone else. Motive: Absolutely none.

All other passengers (except Robinson, to be dealt with later). Opportunity: None. Motive: Query.

After we had tabulated these findings, we sat back in our deck chairs and had a long talk about Robinson. Both of us felt inclined to believe that he would probably turn out to be the guilty party, otherwise, why should he have given himself a false name and then completely disappeared? Beyond this point, however, we agreed to differ. For Adam believes that the man is actually Robinson and that he is hiding somewhere on board the ship. I, on the other hand, cannot make up my mind whether he has gone overboard (as Robinson) or whether he is someone else who impersonated Robinson for the evening.

If he is an impersonation, it is extremely unlikely that he is anyone at our table, since most of them were neither in or in and out of the smoking room the whole evening. And if not one of our crowd, it would be idle to speculate as to his real identity since he could easily have been any one of the two hundred men and women on board the ship.

Yes, *women,* Davy, I say it advisedly. His voice, as I remember it, was squeaky. His tan must have been false. And he was gambling on his knowledge that no one notices a person on the first night out—anyhow, why shouldn't he be a woman? And he was so inconspicuous that I can't even remember the color of his eyes behind the spectacles, or the shape of his nose.

But if he *was* the murderer, Davy, how did he know that, by playing solitaire at a nearby table, he would be invited to join the Lambert party?

How did he know that Daniels would conveniently order a rickey and that he'd be able to get out of the room before Lambert collapsed?

How did he know that everything would play into his hands so easily and so simply?

And, above all, how has he managed to conceal his identity when the whole ship has been turned upside down looking for him?

Riddle me this, Davy darling.

Stateroom,
Monday, November 16th.
2:30 P. M.

Somewhere in this journal, Davy, I said that I was *enjoying* this easel. My God! I actually did say that—I wrote it down in cold blood and I am ashamed to say that I probably meant it.

But now—now that this second hideous tragedy has occurred, I can only say that I wish I had the wings of a seagull so that I might leave my stateroom this instant and fly as far as possible from this horrible ship. Davy, if I ever get back to you, never, *never* let me set foot on a boat again. Do you remember how we used to quarrel about the ideal setting for a murder story? I always said it was a houseparty out in the country somewhere, preferably in England, where you knew it must be one of the guests. You said it was a boat, where you didn't know your shipmates, but where you did know that one of the people brushing past you, sitting in the same room with you, perhaps eating at the same table, must be the murderer—because *no one* could escape. And where at any time you might catch a glimpse, when you least expect it, of that dark side of his nature that allows him—that prompts him—to kill.

Davy darling, as usual you are right. Nothing could be worse than this—nothing *could* be. It's not that I'm fearful for my life, exactly; it is just the horrible uncertainty, the suspicion of everybody; it's the inhumanity. I keep forgetting the tragedy in the situation for Mrs. Lambert, for Earnshaw; all I can feel is the horror.

And all my superstitious Welsh ancestors seem to be rising up around me with mocking eyes and pointing fingers, saying: "Fancy a Llewellyn daring to take a boat that sailed on Friday the thirteenth!"

But, at this point—in case you are anxious, dearest—I feel I should tell you that I personally am all right. In fact I have just waked up after about ten hours of drugged sleep. Don't worry about me, Davy. My body is safe and well—but mentally, morally and spiritually, I don't think I shall ever be quite the same again.

When Mr. Lambert was killed it was, of course, horrible, but after all he was almost a total stranger to me, and he was an old man with a weak heart who had not so *very* many years to go, anyhow. But when a young person is killed—someone who had all the best of life ahead—and killed in such an unthinkably terrible way—well, Davy, then I feel it's time for me to take to my bed, pull the covers up over my head and never face the wicked world again.

And that's where I am now—at two-thirty in the afternoon! I haven't even got the spirit to get up and go out on deck. My heart is sick, Davy, and there's nothing for me to do but fall back on this journal—blessed anodyne—as a relief for my pent-up feelings.

Now I suppose the best thing is to stop dwelling on my own private emotions and begin at the beginning—or where I left off last night.

There was dancing on the deck after dinner. The night was calm and still, but with a hint of menace in its stillness. The stars were bright—suspiciously bright—and perhaps it was just my imagination, but an atmosphere of restlessness and feverishness seemed to hang about the ship like a miasma. It was stiflingly hot and every now and again one would see people casting anxious eyes seaward as though they were expecting a storm to break at any minute. Even the sailors appeared restive as they did their odd jobs about the deck. The air was vibrant with anticipation.

But the orchestra on board is really quite good and, although I hadn't intended to dance during the trip, I promised Adam one sedate and careful turn around the floor. Just as we were about to start, however, Daniels came up to us and said:

"Do you happen to know, Miss Llewellyn, if Miss Demarest cares to dance?"

Adam smiled down at the little Cockney and said, "Of course, Daniels, *all* women like to dance, or at least, they like to be asked. Just march straight up to her, grasp her firmly around the knees and—off you go!"

As Daniels trotted meekly towards the large-limbed lady of his affections, something must have hit my funny-bone because I started to laugh and laugh—

"Oh, I can't dance," I cried weakly, at last. "I must sit down, oh—oh, my incision!"

And it was lucky I spoke when I did, Davy, for at that very moment the ship must have run into a terrific rainstorm. I say *rain,* but it was just as though some mischievous angel had opened a trap door in heaven and thrown bucketful after bucketful of water on the ship. I have never seen such wetness in my life. It came down like cats and dogs—lions, tigers and elephants—scrambling, tearing, roaring! And all so suddenly that all the dancers who were not under cover became drenched to the skin before they could so much as run across the deck.

And then came the thunder and lightning. I have read my Conrad—I have often heard of tropical downpours, but I never imagined they could be anything like this. The lightning seemed to rip the sky into fragments and the thunder crashed around the boat is though we had suddenly run into a heavy bombardment from an enemy battleship. Then the sea started to swell the symphony—and within a few minutes of being in the middle of a still, summer night we found ourselves tossed violently about till I know I felt like a cowboy trying to ride a steer.

It was fearful, yet fascinating, Davy. I sat there watching it all for about twenty minutes and feeling for the first time in my life that I was not an over-civilized young woman, but a tiny cosmic atom in the grip of the elements.

Then some officer shouted to me to go inside and I reluctantly got up and made my way to the smoking room. Adam had deserted me as soon as the storm broke, saying that he must go down below to see that his porthole was properly shut. Apparently he has a horror of damp sheets.

There was no one I knew in the smoking room except Earnshaw, who was sitting alone at a side-table with a plate of sandwiches in front of him. He wore a grey lounge suit and looked tired after his day's work.

"This is my dinner," he said, pointing cheerily at the sandwiches. "Want to come and share it?"

I sat down.

"And now, how about something to keep the damp out? Isn't it a marvelous storm? I got caught in it and had to change my clothes. Which, I think, indicates a double brandy. What's yours?"

"Brandy sounds good to me."

While we were waiting for the drinks to be brought, we stood by the window and watched the lightning. The rain had now stopped almost as suddenly as it had begun and one or two hardy, mackintoshed figures were venturing out on deck, either to get cool or to watch the still mountainous waters.

"How's Mrs. Lambert?" I asked when we sat down to our drinks.

"She seems a little brighter tonight, poor soul, but she won't like this weather. Luckily Betty sleeps in the stateroom next to her suite, so if she needs anything in the night—but she seems more resigned now—and less frightened, thank heaven."

At this point Adam came into the room and moved towards us as though he were going to come to our table. I shot him a warning glance, remembering that Earnshaw had asked me specially for a tête-à-tête earlier in the morning. Adam left the room looking quite unreasonably aggrieved.

"Are you feeling very sympathetic this evening, Miss Llewellyn?" asked Earnshaw as we sipped our drinks.

I nodded, doing my best to look middle-aged and friendly.

"That's good. I've wanted so badly to talk to someone about Betty and—er—myself. I'm in a terrible predicament and I can't make up my mind what is the decent thing to do. You see, Miss Llewellyn, I—I love Betty and I've asked her to marry me."

"Splendid," I said enthusiastically. "She's a grand girl and you're very lucky, that is—*if Barkis is willin'!*"

The young man looked ruefully down at his hands and then pulled out a cigarette. Incidentally, he omitted to offer me one.

"Here's the story," he said, as he inhaled deep puffs of smoke. "I'd been seeing a good bit of Betty lately—before we came on this trip, I mean. I've been living with the Lamberts while we were working out the details of this Rio contract. Mr. Lambert thought that, by cutting prices to the bone, we could underbid all our competitors. I was round at the house a lot figuring like mad and Betty was always in and out. The old man was quite fond of me and one day he asked me if anything was going on between us. I told him frankly that I'd fallen in love with his niece. Although the most unsentimental of people, he was quite surprisingly decent about it—far decenter than he has ever been to his own son—and said that he'd do all he could to help me, on one condition. The condition was that I shouldn't propose to Betty until after the Rio contract was all sewed up and safe in the bag. If we pulled it off, he said, he'd give me his blessing and a very handsome wedding present."

At this point Adam came into the smoking room again, looking around, and seeing no one besides ourselves whom he knew, walked disconsolately out once more.

"That elderly boy friend of yours is a nuisance," said Earnshaw petulantly. "Am I boring you, by the way?"

I hastily and emphatically assured him of my interest.

"Well, that was all very well," he continued, "but I didn't bargain for Betty's coming on this trip with us. It was Mrs. Lambert who arranged that and—well, it was very sweet of her—but you can imagine how difficult it was for me. The inevitable happened the very first night out—the night Mr. Lambert died. We went for a tour all round the ship and finally we landed in a secluded nook, where—well, never mind about that, but I lost my head completely and told Betty that I adored her. To my surprise I found that she—er—loved me too. We became engaged—secretly of course—then and there. I was absurdly happy until—until—you know the rest."

Earnshaw paused in his story to light a fresh cigarette. This time I asked him for one. He passed his case apologetically.

"But," I said, "I don't see that there's anything so tragic in that, Mr. Earnshaw, you love each other—you—"

"Oh, but everything's so different now. Two days ago I had a good job with Lambert—enough to keep a wife on—but I am not a member of his company. I was hired by Mr. Lambert personally as his private secretary. With his death my job dies too and, of course, he didn't leave me a cent. I radioed the office at once to ask permission to go to Rio and carry through the deal. Today I had their refusal, and a kind but firm intimation that my services were terminated. I'm thirty-four years old, out of work and have only a few thousand dollars saved. Betty's people are wealthy and socially ambitious. She is only twenty—popular and pretty. I ask you, Miss Llewellyn, wouldn't it be pretty inexcusable to hold her to an engagement which was entered upon against the wishes of her family? It may be years before I can keep her in what is usually known as the manner to which she is accustomed, even supposing I *did* manage to find another job. You are a girl and you know how women feel about such things. Now what ought I do?"

He looked so pathetic, so distraught and so handsome that I instinctively moved towards him and put out my hand. The ship was still rolling pretty badly and a sudden lurch almost threw me into his arms. I clutched at his sleeve to steady myself.

"It's the ship, not the brandy, Mr. Earnshaw," I laughed. "I'm sorry, but if you want to know how one girl feels, I can easily tell you. In three months I'm going to be married myself. I'm going to marry a man who earns forty-five dollars a week. He's a far better journalist than I am, but I can earn twice that much. Now, if he lost his job or got a cut or fell sick, I'd marry him the instant I set foot on shore and work my head off to keep him. Wild buffaloes couldn't drag me away from him. Now, if Betty loves you—and if she's the girl I take her for—she feels the same as I do."

I hadn't realized it, Davy, but all the time I was making this impassioned outburst, I must have been hanging on to the sleeve of his coat. You may imagine my embarrassment, therefore, when I looked up and saw Mrs. Lambert standing at the table by our side. She had obviously dressed in a hurry and wore a long coat buttoned up to the neck. She nodded to me politely but, I thought, rather disapprovingly. Earnshaw sprang to his feet as soon as he saw her.

"Why, Mrs. Lambert, I thought you were in bed. Is there anything I can do?"

"Why, yes, Jimmie, I was in bed and so was Betty—at least she came in over an hour ago to wish me good night. When I woke up not long since, I suddenly remembered that the poor child has always been scared to death of thunder and lightning, so I called out to her. She didn't reply. I sent the stewardess in to see if she was all right. But she wasn't there at all. Her berth was untouched. I waited a bit and then I began to get worried, so I slipped on a few clothes and came up to look for her."

An anxious frown passed over Earnshaw's forehead. "She told me quite distinctly that she was going to bed, and that was some time ago," he murmured.

"Well," said Mrs. Lambert, and there was a decided snap in her voice, "it may interest you to know that she is sitting out on deck at this moment with a man—his back was turned so I couldn't see who it was. I naturally thought it was you. Then I happened to catch a glimpse of you in here with Miss Llewellyn. Do you by any chance happen to know whom she's with?"

We both shook our heads.

"In that case," said Mrs. Lambert with the rather aggressive importance of a self-appointed chaperone, "I'm going out to tell her that it's after eleven o'clock and high time she was in bed." And with these words she turned her back on us as if we were in disgrace and marched off to starboard.

Earnshaw looked at me with a wry little smile.

"Oh, Betty!" I murmured.

But the words were hardly out of my mouth, Davy, when we heard a sound that froze the blood in my veins and fixed the smile on Earnshaw's face into a horrible grin.

It was a desperate, human shriek, rising clear and piercing above the noise of the engines and the sound of the waves.

And the ghastly thing about it, Davy, was that it did not seem to come from anywhere *on* the ship. It was as though some wailing Banshee in flying round the vessel had uttered this solitary cry of despair to the winds of heaven and then passed on. For a few seconds we stood rigid, staring at each other in mute horror. The silence which followed that shriek was one of the most tense and terrible moments in my life. I shall never forget it.

But it did not last long, for almost immediately there was a succession of very human, very feminine screams—this time from the starboard side of the ship—and a wild voice, coming nearer and nearer cried:

"Help—help—Betty—!"

Earnshaw sprang towards the door, but before he had got half way across the room Mrs. Lambert appeared, her hair flying in disorder, her face livid with terror.

"Betty—thrown overboard—stop the ship," she gasped.

Earnshaw and I brushed past her and dashed out on deck, where a group of sailors and passengers had already assembled.

And then, Davy, I saw it for the first time and my heart seemed to go cold and dead like a stone inside me. It was Betty's beautiful orange shawl, floating in the air a few yards from the ship, bobbing playfully and wantonly up and down as it was lifted by the breezes. Lightly—almost laughingly it floated—as though the following winds were driving it along to keep pace with the ship—as though it mocked for a moment those cruel dark waters below. Then it began to drop downwards.

I caught one glimpse of Earnshaw's face as he recognized the shawl. In the twinkling of an eye he had thrown off his coat and reached the rail. Three stalwart sailors rushed forward to stop him.

"No, no, sir—it's madness—with this sea!"

Before they could close in on him, Earnshaw's fist had shot out and caught one of the sailors on the point of the chin. The man rolled over as though he had been hit with a hammer. Then, still struggling with the two others, Earnshaw climbed the rail and, well, I don't know what happened exactly, but I do know that I stood there waiting with sickening apprehension—waiting for the splash which would tell me that he had joined Betty.

But one of the sailors must have caught him by the hair or the collar just as he jumped. An officer, who had been shouting orders through a megaphone, joined the group and the next thing I knew was that they were dragging the still struggling Earnshaw back on to the deck.

"It'd be suicide, sir—sheer suicide," cried the officer. "We'll stop the ship. We'll do all we can. Here, hold on to him, boys."

Meanwhile Mrs. Lambert was standing perfectly still, moaning helplessly. There was a terrible racket and hubbub. Then, suddenly, I heard a sound which reminded me of the noise that goes on inside one's head when the dentist starts drilling a tooth.

"They're putting the engines in reverse, turning her round—stopping the ship," shouted an officer in reply to a query from one of the passengers.

"There's a woman overboard—"

By this time I had gone up to Mrs. Lambert and done what I could to calm her. The officer joined us and led us away from the crowd.

"Please, madam, please, try and collect yourself." He shook her arm almost roughly. "It's a serious thing to stop the ship this way. Can you tell us exactly—did you really see the young lady go overboard?"

Mrs. Lambert stared into his strained, anxious face with dull, unseeing eyes. For a moment I really began to fear that the shock had unhinged her reason. Then suddenly and quite coherently she spoke:

"He—threw—her—overboard," she said slowly. "I saw them there talking together. Betty was laughing. He was wrapping her shawl round her. They seemed to be saying good night so I went away. Just as I turned the corner coming back, I heard that shriek—that awful, ghastly shriek. And then a splash—." She shuddered. "I hurried forward and saw Betty's shawl floating out over the sea. I ran to the rail and saw—or thought I saw—something—down there in the water. Just for an instant, then—then it was gone!"

She covered her face with her hands.

"But the man, Mrs. Lambert? Didn't you see him?" The officer's voice was low and stern. "Do try and collect yourself."

The widow gulped and looked up at him with wide, horrified eyes.

"Yes, yes, I saw him," she cried wildly. "He was hurrying down the deck, away from me. He had an overcoat on and a hat pulled down over his eyes. But when he reached that door—the one there with the light above it—he had to turn. It was then that I caught a glimpse of his face. He was wearing steel-rimmed spectacles—clean shaven—and his face was very tanned. In fact, I could swear that—"

She gulped again, then her voice came quite clear and distinct.

"—that he was the man who was playing bridge with my husband the night he was murdered. The man who called himself—Robinson!"

I didn't hear any more, Davy. A stewardess came up and took the poor soul down to her cabin. But nothing in heaven or earth could persuade Earnshaw to move. He stood still, towering above the two British sailors at his side, straining his eyes over the ocean, which, now that the ship's powerful searchlights had been turned on, was as light as the floor of a ball-room.

The horrible grating noise of the engines had begun to die down and the ship seemed to have come to a complete standstill. Apparently it had been made to double back on its tracks and I suppose we were now somewhere near the spot where Betty had been thrown overboard.

I saw Daniels go up and question one of the officers.

"No, sir, there's not one chance in a thousand of picking her up; she probably got caught in the screws right away. But we have to do all this for the log, sir, a mere formality—"

I turned away feeling sick, Davy, as you may well imagine. The idea of Betty down there in that cruel, dark water—the thought of her soft young body caught by those merciless, grinding screws. And here we were all standing around like so many dummies, impotent—powerless to help. "A mere formality!" It was too much. For one moment I felt the awful tragedy of the situation as strongly as Earnshaw must have been feeling it—poor little Betty who was afraid of thunder and lightning!

The deck presented a strange spectacle, crowded as it was with officers, sailors and passengers, the latter in various stages of dress or undress. The sudden stopping of the ship, the noise of the engines going into reverse and the frantic runnings to and fro had caused a number of the more nervous-minded to get the idea that we were about to founder. On all sides one heard the reassuring words:

"No, no, madam, there's no danger. It's only a woman overboard!"

Only a woman overboard, Davy! That was all! And a number of people who hadn't known Betty were actually standing in little groups, talking and exclaiming as though this were an unexpected thrill in their blasé careers—an exciting incident to be stored up as a delicate titbit for their friends when they got home.

And all the while the searchlights were shooting great ribbons of light out over the sea, and eager eyes were scrutinizing the waters—all to no purpose. Occasionally a hopeful cry would go up when a streak of foam, a whitecap, or a whirlpool assumed for a moment the likeness of a human face or form, but the excitement would soon die down again into broken murmurs of disappointment.

At some point or other, Davy, it dawned on me that I had not noticed Adam among the crowd. I suppose I've become so used to having him tag along that I almost take it for granted that he will be somewhere around. But, after looking carefully at every bald head on deck, I realized that not one of them belonged to Mr. Burr. He was nowhere to be seen, nor, with the exception of Daniels, could I find any members of the captain's table.

Feeling an urgent need for speed or action, I went up to the young sailor whom Earnshaw had knocked down a few minutes earlier. He was standing by the rail holding a lifebuoy in one hand while the other caressed his swollen chin. He might have been posing for a sculptor as he stood there, stripped to the waist, his magnificent muscles taut beneath his smooth, brown skin. In spite of Earnshaw's blow, he looked as eager and alert as anyone on the ship. I felt sorry for him.

Fumbling in my bag, I drew out a five dollar bill and held it out towards him.

"Please don't hold it against him," I said, nodding towards Earnshaw. "She was his—his girl, you know."

The young Britisher flashed me one scornful glance from a pair of clear grey eyes. Then, without deigning to notice the bill, he turned seaward again.

"Blimey, miss," he muttered, "there's nothing I wouldn't do for a bloke as can land a straight left to the point like that one. And if we do see 'is young lady down there, well, 'e don't need to jump in arter 'er, 'cos I'm all ready meself. And I reckon I'd stand a better chance than what 'e would, even if 'e is twenty-five pun' heavier and five inches taller."

And after this, Davy, I felt so utterly useless and depressed that I collapsed into the nearest deck chair and had a good long cry all by myself.

I don't know how long it lasted, but I must have been doing a bit of sniffling, for, all of a sudden, I was conscious of a large hand holding a sensible-sized handkerchief under my nose. Daphne Demarest was standing by my side.

"Cheer up," she said, "though God knows there's not much to be cheerful about. Here—have a cigarette."

I dabbed at my eyes with her handkerchief and returned it. "Is there any news?" I asked.

As if in reply to my question there was a loud blast from the ship's siren, followed by the throbbing of the engines.

We had resumed our course.

"Poor kid," growled Daphne. "She's gone, all right. Her steward and stewardess have been looking everywhere for her, but she's nowhere to be found. From the story I heard it sounded at first as though Mrs. Lambert had a bee in her bonnet, but I'm afraid she was right—after all."

I sighed. "Well, I suppose this means more cross-questioning. Oh, Lord, when will it end?"

"There's one comfort," replied Daphne. "None of the passengers seems to have twigged that it was murder—so far. Jennings told me about it and I suppose the rest of our table will be told too, but they are going to spread the story that Betty was depressed by her uncle's death and—well, had an accident." Daphne flicked a cigarette into the sea. "But I suppose it's only a matter of time before the others realize the truth—oh, blast this ship!"

The *Moderna* was now moving slowly through the waters with a sickening vibration. The shouting and the tumult had died, leaving no sound but the turning of the screws. The decks looked dark and gloomy after the lurid play of the searchlights, and the passengers, seemingly conscious for the first time of their déshabillés, were scurrying towards their cabins. Even the faithful young sailor was slipping his tunic over his naked torso and preparing to go below. The search for Betty had been abandoned—

Only Earnshaw stood where I had last seen him, his eyes still turned seaward—his grey tweed coat lying in a little pool at his side. I was glad I could not see his face.

Then Dr. Somers went up to him and took his arm. For a few seconds they seemed to be deep in earnest conversation. At length I saw the young surgeon lead him away.

Finally I went down to my stateroom, Davy, and got out this journal, but I couldn't write a line. I kept thinking of Betty struggling in the cold, dark water. I tried to sleep, but I couldn't do that either. That shriek seemed to haunt me. I wanted desperately to have you near me, darling, to comfort me, to protect me, to put your arms around me and hold me close, close—

And then I started thinking of poor Earnshaw and how dreadful he must be feeling. I thought about everything so much that my head started to throb and I felt I should be really ill if I didn't sleep. So I got out a little blue bottle—the one Dr. Klein gave me when I left the hospital—and took enough to give me ten hours of blessed oblivion.

But I've had a hunch at last, and it is that somehow this second murder is closely connected with the first; and that somewhere I have the clue in my keeping. I can't find it—I don't know where it is; but I've got it, and before we reach land I've *got* to find it.

Before finally dropping off to sleep, Davy, I decided that this ship should be re-christened.

Never again shall I think of her as the *Moderna.* To me she will always be—*S. S. Murder!*

Monday, November 16th.
Stateroom,
10:30 P. M.

Well, darling, I struggled out of bed in time for tea today and found my fellow passengers playing deck tennis and shuffleboard as though nothing in the world had ever happened. The ship was making good time—the weather was perfect—and no one seemed to be worrying about last night's fearful tragedy. It gave me a little stab at the heart, Davy, to realize how unimportant the individual really *is* in the general scheme of things. We come and go, but ships have to stick to their schedules, the public has to be amused, and "the great game must go on." And it would be just the same if it had been you or me instead of Betty.

Adam soon joined me in my little nook on the upper-deck. His round face looked pale—and, if you can imagine a haggard plum, Davy—! But, as usual, he was full of information.

Very cautious inquiries have been made among the passengers who were not in their beds last evening when the tragedy occurred. One woman claims she *thinks* she noticed Betty talking to a man somewhere near the spot where Mrs. Lambert saw her last. But no one, it appears, actually saw her go overboard or heard the splash, though everyone must have heard that ghastly shriek—even the people in the third class. And the terrible fact remains: Betty is nowhere to be found.

"Where did you get to during all the excitement?" I asked him at length.

Adam looked at me closely and cleared his throat before speaking.

"Well, I thought that it would be a wonderful opportunity for me to make a little personally-conducted search for our old friend Robinson. There are certain spots on board ship where no one thinks of looking in the ordinary way—bathrooms, lavatories and such-like indelicate places. I thought perhaps he might pop into one of them for temporary concealment. I wanted to try and catch him red-handed while everybody else was safely up on deck. I even hung around certain corridors. But, unfortunately, I didn't see or hear anything at all suspicious."

"Well," I said, "we at least know now that Robinson was in a definite place at a definite time. This fact will probably be helpful in eliminating some people."

"It's not so helpful as it might be," replied Adam disconsolately. "Almost all our particular little playmates say that they were in bed or in their cabins at the time. But it clears you at any rate—and me."

"How come?" I asked suspiciously.

"Well, you were in the smoking room with Earnshaw when it all happened. And you can take your Bible oath you saw me come in and out several times—at least twice!"

"Oh, yes, of course, I did see you about ten minutes before the cry—but," I added maliciously, "that doesn't prove a thing. And now my conscience tells me I ought to go down to Mrs. Lambert's suite and see if there's anything I can do."

Adam gave a twisted little smile; then he said inconsequently,

"Well, well, my dear, even though you refuse to establish my alibi, I hope you aren't going to refuse to be my partner in the shuffleboard tournament next week. I put our names down."

"Sorry," I snapped, "but even shuffleboard is too strenuous for my stitches. I'll see you at dinner."

With this exhibition of bad temper, Davy, I made my way to Mrs. Lambert's suite. You can well imagine that I did not relish my interview!

I found Earnshaw pacing up and down the little sitting room like a tiger in a cage. He was in his shirt-sleeves, unshaven and hollow-eyed. He looked up at me as I entered with pathetic eagerness. I suppose the poor devil is still hoping against hope and against reason.

I said and did what I could. It wasn't much. Then I went into the bedroom adjoining. Mrs. Lambert seems really sick and a nurse from the ship's infirmary has been sent to look after her. This second tragedy has given her an air of quiet dignity and I found myself more truly in sympathy with her than ever before. It must have been an *awful* shock! She spoke with real feeling about Earnshaw, telling me how she had done everything to help things along. She also told me that Betty had been nervous and frightened yesterday and she wondered if, perhaps, it had anything to do with the anonymous letter she had received.

"Anonymous letter!" I gasped.

"Yes, didn't you hear that they found one in her bag? Mr. Jennings has got it."

"What—what did it say?" I asked, trying hard not to appear too eager in my curiosity.

"Why, it was just a printed note from someone, and unsigned. It said that the writer knew for certain who it was that killed Mr. Lambert and, if Betty would be on the starboard side of the ship—on B deck at 10:30—he would meet her and tell her everything. That's all. She did say something about a rendezvous, but, of course, I advised her not to keep it. I can't imagine why she went against my wishes. It's a complete mystery, but I suppose she thought she was safe, poor child—poor child!"

At this point the nurse intervened with a warning look. I made my excuses, saying lamely that it was time for me to go and dress for dinner.

Our table tonight was in anything but a merry mood. We alone of all the passengers know the actual facts, such as they are, of the two terrible tragedies. Most of us either mistrust or dislike each other, and this is hardly conducive to sprightly conversation. A pathetic little ripple had barely got decently started when the captain rose to his feet.

There was an immediate silence in the dining saloon. Not the tinkle of a glass or the clatter of a fork broke the silence. The passengers at the other tables were obviously expecting something pretty lurid. About fifty pairs of eyes were turned toward the skipper in eager anticipation.

Captain Fortescue made a very sensible little speech, calculated to restore confidence among the passengers, to give the murderer a false sense of security, and to impart no knowledge that was of any possible value.

He told us that a distinguished business man had died of heart failure on the first night out. His niece, despondent over her uncle's death, had gone overboard last night. It was very regrettable—very sad—and he was sure the whole ship joined him in sympathy with the bereaved widow and friend. He wished to say, however, that Mrs. Lambert and Mr. Earnshaw had most particularly requested that none of the ship's activities should be interrupted on their account. They realized that many passengers were taking this trip for reasons of health or holiday. It was by their express desire, therefore, that deck sports, bridge tournaments, and other recreations should go on exactly as usual.

A little murmur of appreciation and sympathy ran round the room, as the—

. . . .

Stateroom,
Half an hour later.

Davy—Davy, *darling,* the most amazing thing has just happened. I'm still all of a doodah about it, but—thank God there is a good strong lock on my door!

I was sitting up in my berth writing this just now. It was about eleven o'clock and the ship was reasonably quiet. I had just got to the part where the captain began to make a speech when the thought suddenly flashed through my mind that there must be a mouse in the cabin. I heard a faint rustle on the floor—just a teeny, weeny little mousey noise.

Well, Davy, you know I loathe cockroaches, I abhor bats, centipedes and spiders, but I don't object to mice in the very least. Consequently I paid no attention whatsoever, and kept on writing.

Then, just when I got to the sentence, "—ran round the room, as the—" there was a little puff of wind and something white moved across the floor. At first I had the wild idea that it was a rat—horrors, a *white* rat at that! This was too much! I jumped out of bed and saw lying in the center of my tiny rug a folded piece of paper—ship's stationery.

I picked it up very gingerly and noticed at once that it had some printing scrawled almost illegibly across the page. It was as though some right handed person had tried to make the characters with his left hand in order to avoid recognition of his writing. The result was an untidy mess.

Holding the sheet to the light, I read (with some difficulty) as follows:

> UNLESS YOU WANT TO GO THE WAY OF BETTY LAMBERT YOU ARE ADVISED TO MIND YOUR OWN BUSINESS AND TO DESTROY THAT JOURNAL.
>
> ROBINSON.

At first, Davy, I felt inclined to laugh. The whole business seemed so positively preposterous. Gradually, however, the full significance of the letter began to dawn on me. Within the last few minutes this fiend—this creature who calls himself Robinson—had crept up to my door and slipped the paper into my stateroom. My head must have been actually within two feet of his hand, with only a thin piece of board in between. He knows about my journal, my detective activities, and he knows me for an enemy. He even pays me the compliment of treating me as a person to be seriously reckoned with!

A sudden feeling of panic overwhelmed me. I rang the bell for my stewardess and asked her if she'd seen anyone hanging around my room. She said she had seen no one—nor had the steward Trubshaw, who she also consulted.

Nevertheless, Davy, someone has approached my room within the last half hour because I *know* the note was not there when I came to bed. For the first time I really feel that I myself am involved in this business. I am no longer just an interested spectator looking on from a safe distance. I am one of the actors in a terrible human drama and, unless I am careful, I may be playing a more important part than is comfortable.

And that makes three anonymous letters to date in this chronicle, Daphne's—Betty's—and now mine.

Perhaps Robinson has a weakness for the fair sex!

At any rate—as I said before—thank God for a good strong lock on this door!

In the future I shall trust *no one* and I shall guard my journal as I would my jewels!

On Deck,
Tuesday, November 17th.
11:45 A. M.

In spite of all the excitement of last night, Davy, I slept remarkably well and woke up feeling more like a sane mind in a sane body than I have for some time. I suppose one reaches an emotional pitch beyond which it is impossible to go, and as I have experienced almost every sensation in the world during the last few days, anything that ever happens to me in the future will seem just an amusing anti-climax.

And I'm sure I was perfectly calm and self-possessed when I presented myself at the purser's office shortly after breakfast this morning and showed him the billet-doux which Robinson slipped so romantically beneath my door last night.

Jennings jumped up from his chair as soon as he saw it.

"Let's go to the captain with this, Miss Llewellyn—right away if you don't mind. He's got the letter which was found in poor Miss Lambert's bag, and I know he'll want to compare the writing. Personally, I believe it's the same."

He went so fast along corridors and up companionways that I was quite out of breath by the time we reached the captain's quarters. As we stood outside the door, waiting to be admitted,

I could have sworn I heard voices inside the room. I must have been mistaken, however, because, when we entered, Captain Fortescue was seated at his desk, alone.

Who wouldn't be the skipper of an ocean-going liner, Davy? I never saw such good, solid comfort in all my life. The cabin was furnished with a number of deep "squushy" arm chairs, several bookshelves filled with detective stories, gorgeous purple curtains covering an opening in the rear, a thick carpet, and cheerful pictures on the walls. Altogether there was a homely touch about the place which makes me feel quite certain that the female contingent from Ealing is very much on the job.

Captain Fortescue gave me a cordial greeting as I came in, and Jennings immediately produced the anonymous letter, briefly explaining how it had reached me. After the captain had read it, he got out a folder from one of the desk drawers. It contained the slip of paper which had been found in Betty Lambert's bag after her death. For a few moments they compared them in silence.

"No doubt about it, sir," exclaimed Jennings at length, "you don't have to be a handwriting expert to see that they were both written by the same person."

Accepting their unspoken invitation, I looked over Jennings' shoulder and studied the two letters. Even from that distance I could see that the writing was identical in both cases.

The captain then asked us all manner of questions about the time and the circumstances of the letter's arrival. When I had told him all I knew, he got out a plan of the ship and we started to study the positions of the various occupied staterooms. By a strange coincidence, Davy, almost all the people who eat at our table are on the same deck as myself and have their cabins literally within a stone's throw of each other!

So there wasn't anything very helpful to be got out of that.

"I think, Miss Llewellyn," said the captain at length, "that I had better tell one of the stewards to keep an eye on your cabin after this. You have a lock on the door, of course?"

I nodded.

"Well, you can't be too careful." He gave me a nice twinkling smile. "What's this journal, by the way, which our friend Robinson refers to so particularly?"

I quickly explained how I kept this record of the case from the very beginning, adding that, while I had written it all over the ship, I had mentioned the fact only to the people who were most intimately concerned in the tragedies. I also related the little episode that occurred when I left the book in the Social Hall.

As soon as I had finished, the captain smiled at me again, this time quite paternally.

"Of course, Miss Llewellyn, it's hard for me to remember that a young and pretty girl like you is also a well-known and accomplished journalist, but—"

Well, here was my opportunity, Davy. There's no need to tell you that it's impossible to get anywhere in our line of business if you don't have a good bit of brass in your composition, so I blurted out:

"Oh, Captain Fortescue, won't you please give a girl a break? Let me send an account of all this to my paper. I'll promise to be awfully careful. You can censor every word I write. I know it sounds heartless, but it's such an opportunity in my career. I may never get another chance like this one. And then," I cajoled, "they might dig up some information that will be very helpful."

But the captain was shaking his head politely but firmly. "Listen, my dear," he said, "I have a daughter in Ealing. She's about your age and she's ambitious too. You must forgive me if I talk to you just as I would talk to her. I can't let you do this—for your sake as well as mine. I can't allow it. You see, we really have no inkling as yet how or why these two unfortunate people died. We have no right even to hint at anything so terrible as murder—that is, to the world at large. Whatever our own private views, we must keep them to ourselves until we know something more definite."

I sighed and then smiled at him in as daughterly a manner as I could. "I suppose you are right," I assented meekly.

"I can promise you one thing, however. If we *do* get to the bottom of this terrible business, I'll do all I can to help you get what you Americans call a scoop. But—"

He glanced at the chronometer on his desk.

"If I promise this, I want you to do something for me in return. I've got forty minutes to spare before I have to make my tour of inspection. I want you to let me read that journal of yours. Will you?"

I blushed like a gawky schoolgirl.

"Oh, I'm awfully sorry," I faltered, "but it's in the form of—er—private letters. There are things in it that are intended for—for one person only. However—if you are really serious and think it would be helpful, I could read it to you. I won't leave out anything that's important—only the personal parts and perhaps some of the descriptions."

The captain nodded assent and Jennings jumped politely to his feet.

"Can I get it for you, Miss Llewellyn?"

"Oh, no. It's locked in my trunk. I won't be a minute."

I tore down to my stateroom, found the manuscript book, and quickly returned to the captain's cabin. Without wasting a moment I sat down in the "squushiest" of the arm chairs and started to read. Jennings and Captain Fortescue both produced pencil and paper and made copious notes throughout my recital. They listened very attentively.

Now you can call me fanciful if you like, Davy, but I am perfectly certain that twice, when I lifted my eyes from the page, I saw the purple curtains behind Captain Fortescue's chair—moving! They were heavy curtains and there wasn't a breath of air in the room, but something was moving them. I watched them whenever I had the opportunity and I am positive that I was not mistaken.

When I came to the end, the captain jumped up from his seat and exclaimed heartily:

"Capital, Miss Llewellyn! It's as good as Conan Doyle or Mrs. Rinehart. I got so thrilled that I almost forgot it had all actually happened on my ship. I'm very fond of detective stories, as you can see for yourself—" he waved a hand in the direction of the nearest bookshelf—"now I suppose I must try—indeed we must all try—to put our reading to good account."

"Talking of reading and mystery stories, Captain Fortescue," I said as casually as I could, "I wonder if you could explain to me these lines which were written by the greatest American mystery writer—perhaps the greatest one the world has ever known!"

The captain looked at me with a puzzled frown, but I kept my eyes glued on the still-moving drapes. Then I quoted Poe's marvelous lines:

> "'And the silken, sad, uncertain
> Rustling of each purple curtain,
> Thrilled me—filled me—with fantastic terrors,
> Never felt before.'"

"I'm afraid poetry is rather beyond me, Miss Llewellyn," replied the skipper, as his eyes followed mine in the direction of the curtains.

"Oh, all right, if you don't want to tell me who's behind them," I said pertly. "Just as long as you know he's there—or, perhaps it's a she. Fie, Captain Fortescue!"

He smiled, but not very convincingly, then his face became more serious, as he added:

"Miss Llewellyn, I started talking to you just now as if you were my daughter; do you mind if I go on in that way a minute? You are a very clever young lady, but I advise you, for the present at least, not to know too much. And what knowledge you have is best kept to yourself. Don't trust anyone and don't ask too many questions. If you are in any difficulties you can always come to me. We will count on your cooperation and you can count on ours. We may seem to be rather backward and slow-moving, but we are not going to leave a stone unturned—we are forging full steam ahead in the way that seems best to us. Isn't that so, Jennings?"

The purser nodded.

"And don't forget," continued the captain, "that somewhere in the Atlantic Ocean, not so very far behind us, is the body of a girl, like yourself, who was killed, perhaps, because she knew too much. In a locked stateroom on E deck there is the dead body of a man—and—and somewhere on the ship there is this Robinson—somewhere—"

But here, Davy darling, I interrupted him with an exclamation, jumped up from my seat and almost ran out of the cabin.

I had suddenly found myself with an Idea—a brain wave! It couldn't wait. I had to be alone to think it over.

And it seemed staggering at first—staggeringly simple. My

one and only original contribution to this case, Davy! It was the captain's last remark that put it into my head.

Can you guess what it was?

Oh, well, it will have to keep for a while because there is the gong for lunch and I am starving.

A bientôt chéri.

Stateroom,
Tuesday, November 17th.
6:30 P. M.

Before I get back to the subject of my Idea, Davy, I must tell you that Mrs. Clapp has taken me to her bosom at last. The unpleasant dinner incident is forgiven and forgotten, and I think we shall be the best of friends in the future.

After I left the captain I decided that I would start my campaign of suspicion and mistrust by avoiding my old friend Adam for a while. Consequently I stuck by Daphne after lunch and finally joined her and Mrs. Clapp on deck.

The ex-Marcia Manners is really a remarkable person. She has a flavor to her like a rare old vintage or the tang of early fall apples. She's impetuous, temperamental and a trifle peppery, but one of the most entertaining women I've ever met in my life. I could make a whole volume out of the anecdotes and experiences she told me this afternoon. In fact, when I get to knew her better, I'm going to ask her if she'll let me write her biography—a nice quiet job for me after we settle down to married life, darling.

She and Daphne have a strange but rather touching relationship. They met each other during the War while Daphne was nursing and Marcia Manners was "entertaining." When young Mr. Clapp died last spring, his widow was so broken up that she turned to Daphne for professional help as well as friendship. They have been together ever since, and for all her starry past and triumphs, the older woman seems utterly dependent on her English companion. In fact, my dear, Daphne Demarest is no fool, and she leads Mrs. Clapp by the nose in a thoroughly accomplished manner.

After tea, I began to work on my private plan.

Now, Davy, I told you that it was when the captain made his last remark that the Idea suddenly came to me. He was talking about Mr. Lambert's body and then in the same sentence he spoke of how Robinson might be in hiding. Well, the whole ship has been combed for him—if he is a living, sentient person he must be *somewhere.* He cannot materialize and disappear at will. He has to eat and sleep. The question before the house is—where is he?

Now do you see what I'm driving at, Davy? Can you think of the one place on board this ship where a stowaway might be safe—the one place where nobody goes and where no one would think of looking in the ordinary way?

Davy, Davy, *Davy,* say that you see it too. Please say that you do—

Yes, darling, yes! The empty stateroom where they put Mr. Lambert's dead body after it had been embalmed by the surgeon. (You remember they are keeping it for a more detailed autopsy at Georgetown.) Of course the door has been locked all the time, but skeleton keys, I suppose, would open it; and while one can't imagine enjoying life in that particular room, one would be safe there, I should think.

And now, I suppose, you will tell me that I am completely crazy.

And that is what Jennings probably thought when I outlined my scheme to him about an hour ago, though he was awfully polite about it. You see, I decided that I must let someone else in on it and he seemed the most obvious person. He's so quiet and reliable—so sane. And then, I knew I should never have the courage to carry this thing through by myself. And there are obvious reasons why it would not be advisable to pick on Burr, Daniels or any of the male passengers.

Being a purser, he naturally remonstrated at first after I had told him of my plans and vowed him to absolute secrecy.

"I really don't see why you need to do this thing yourself," he said. "I think your idea about Robinson's hiding place is pretty horrible, but I suppose it's reasonable. No one else has thought of it as far as I know. I can probably get the keys from Dr. Somers without much fuss. But—why not let me examine the room by myself? It's not at all a job for a young lady."

"Mr. Jennings," I cried, "will you kindly stop being the chivalrous English gentleman. I'm not a young lady. I'm a journalist. And you might as well try and argue a duck out of the water—a cat away from a mouse—as attempt to persuade a newspaper reporter to stay away from the scene of action. Besides, the captain has promised me a scoop if we get to the bottom of this business. This is my one and only brain-child to date and I want to be in at the death. Also, I'd like to go in the middle of the night, because we might catch him asleep. I think it would be more reasonable and less dangerous than during the day."

Finally he gave in. He is young—too—and adventurous. I think the idea of the scoop appealed to him, and I know he likes me. Perhaps I over-persuaded him. I hope not, because I'd hate to get him in trouble. Anyway, it was decided that he should tell no one of our plans except my steward, who would call me at 1:50 A. M. tonight—or tomorrow morning if you want to be exact. Then I am to join Jennings at about 2:00 A. M. and we are going off together to explore the temporary morgue where Mr. Lambert's body lies. He will provide a revolver and two flashlights. It was also arranged on his urgent plea that I should go to bed directly after dinner in order to be rested and refreshed for the expedition. I don't anticipate much sleep *after* it's over!

Now don't worry about me, darling. I'll be safe as houses with Jennings to look after me. He's frightfully protective and maternal. . . .

The steward has just brought me a little note—this time, thank God, it's not anonymous.

> M. L.—Why have you:—
>
> "Divorced old barren Adam from your—ahem! And taken the daughter of the stage to spouse?" Am I what Voltaire would call "the squeezed lemon"? If not, *please* join me for a cocktail before dinner.
>
> Hopefully,
>
> A. B.

Have you noticed, Davy, how poor Mr. Burr is always suggesting a fruit either to me or to himself? In some previous incarnation, I think, he must have been a market gardener.

Well, there's just time to accept this invitation to cocktails if I hurry up and dress. Before tonight is over I shall probably need all the artificial stimulants I can get.

Wednesday, November 18th.
In my stateroom,
About 3:00 A. M.*

I'm writing this partly to keep awake and partly to keep sane, so if you ever see it you must bear with me. Somehow I think that if I force myself to go over the horrors that I've experienced since I wrote gaily (oh fool! fool that I was!) about needing artificial stimulants—if I can face it all again, and put it down in black and white, then I may be able to exorcise this feeling of impending doom. At least it should keep my mind in the past instead of the present and the even more ghastly future; and I'll try to be coherent. But if you knew what may be waiting for me—now—outside my very door! Davy, tell me this isn't possible! Tell me I'm going to wake up in a little while and find it all a hideous nightmare. I'm fairly gibbering now, with terror, and I'm afraid to look in the mirror for fear my hair is turning white. No, I *will not* look! What wouldn't I give to be back at home, listening to Aunt Caroline stumping towards the bathroom with her heavy, reassuring tread! How many years of Paradise wouldn't I forego to have your arms about me, and

* This section, obviously written under the stress of emotion, was almost illegible.—Q. P.

calm this wild beating of my heart against the steady pound of yours. . . .

• • • •

Later.

I feel better now. The thought of you made me cry, and that relieved me. Then I tried to sleep—but, no! There's nothing for it but to get on with my story and tell it the best I can—quietly, at first, because I was simply sleepy, when Trubshaw called me at ten minutes to two: sleepy, and disinclined to go through with my ridiculous determination. If I hadn't made such an issue of accompanying Jennings I could have stayed safe in my bed. No one will ever know how fervently I wish all this could be a bad dream—a grisly chimera which I might forget tomorrow and ever afterwards.

But what I tell you now I can never forget, I think—if, indeed, I live to remember it. And since it is quite possible that I may never see you to tell the story with my own lips, I must write it down quickly and trust that these words, at least, may reach you safely.

When Trubshaw's discreet knocking finally woke me, at 1:50, I lay still for a moment, collecting myself, and cursing my "nose for news." Then I heard the steward's whisper through the door.

"Mr. Jennings is ready," he said. "Ready when you are, Miss. Is there anything I can do for you, Miss, before you go?"

Nothing warned me. Instead, I felt a pleasant flicker of excitement, with only a rather invigorating tinge of fear. I slipped on a dress and tennis shoes and made my way to the purser's office.

I found Jennings calmly smoking a pipe in his room with two

cups of coffee on the table at his side. He greeted me cheerfully, but his cherubic face seemed less pink than usual and there was a serious look in his eye which belied his casual air.

"Sit down and have some coffee, Miss Llewellyn," he said, pushing a cup towards me and lighting my cigarette. "We can take our time about starting. There's not a soul waiting for us—unless it's our old friend Robinson! But I must confess I'm a bit skeptical even about him."

I took a sip of coffee, but to my surprise I found that my teeth rattled so against the edge of the cup that he evidently heard the noise.

"Look here," he said paternally, "why don't you back out of this business now? I can easily go alone and search that stateroom. There's absolutely no need, for you to come along too."

"N-nonsense," I chattered, "I'm c-razy to g-go!"

"Well, there's no hurry. Here—let's have something to help the coffee down."

He produced a bottle of three-star brandy from a cupboard on the wall and poured out two stiff measures. After I had taken a few gulps I felt decidedly better—once more keen to get on with our adventure.

"You haven't told anyone about this?" I asked anxiously.

"No. I don't like doing this without the captain's permission, but you made me promise and I've kept my word. I had some difficulties in getting the surgeon to give me the keys to the stateroom without telling him exactly why I wanted them. He seemed to suspect me of the most sinister intentions. And you may be interested to know that you were quite right in your supposition. Although the ship has been searched several times for Robinson, no one has been in that stateroom since Somers locked it up last Saturday. Of course, I don't see how Robinson could get in and out, but there's a remote chance that he might be hand in glove with some member of the crew."

"Whereabouts is this stateroom?" I inquired. "It seems a funny place to put a corpse—surely the neighbors might object!"

Jennings raised his eyebrows and took a sip of coffee before replying. "It's not the usual procedure, Miss Llewellyn. But then, this whole business is rather unusual, isn't it? When anyone dies on board ship we generally bury them at sea—as quickly as possible. If there is any objection to that, the body is put in the isolation ward or the hospital. But, it so happens that one of the pantry boys reported a suspicious-looking rash just after we left the harbor. The little rascal wanted to get to Rio, so didn't say a word until we were out to sea. Dr. Somers is keeping him isolated for observation. Then the ship's hospital is in constant use. We couldn't keep a body there for ten days. That's why Captain Fortescue decided on an empty stateroom."

"But," I exclaimed, "it isn't *healthy*, Mr. Jennings! A dead body right in among the passengers—ugh—!"

The purser gave me a twisted smile, though inwardly, I am sure, he was cursing me for an interfering woman.

"Oh, come, Miss Llewellyn, it isn't as bad as all that. Mr. Lambert's body is right down on E deck, No. 213 to be exact—in a section of the ship that is at present quite unoccupied. Since the trade slump we've been running very light and there are lots of cabins that we never need. A number of our stewards have been dismissed and we are keeping the unused sections of the boat shut up to save heat, light and service. This stateroom is a long, long way from your own—or from anyone else's for that matter."

Involuntarily I gave a little shudder. Then I picked up my tumbler and drained the last drop of brandy.

"Let's go," I said with decision.

Jennings rose to his feet. Then he took a revolver from his desk drawer and handed me a flashlight.

"Are you sure you still want to come?" he asked seriously. "The ship's rolling pretty badly and you may get bumped about in transit."

"Lead on, Macduff," I [mis]quoted* gaily, and together we started off on our journey into the bowels of the *Moderna.*

At first it was quite fun, Davy. The passages were all lighted, and we caught several unofficial glimpses of the night-life on board an ocean-going liner. One stray reveller evidently mistook me for his errant lady-love and wanted to start a fight with the stalwart Jennings. We heard nocturnal squabbles between husband and wife; we also heard horrible noises which proved—if further proof were necessary—that the ship was rolling pretty considerably and to the intense discomfort of a number of its passengers. Stewardesses were running to and fro with basins and pursed lips.

By and by we left the first class behind us. Corpses, apparently, travel third, Davy—an ironic reflection for rich passengers like Mr. Lambert. And now our journey became somewhat more precarious. We passed down very narrow passages where grimy, half naked engine-room hands stood about in little groups, feverishly inhaling a few puffs of cigarette smoke before going to wash the caked sweat from their bodies. We caught an occasional view of the engines themselves—those huge, smooth giants which were carrying us relentlessly forward irrespective of storm and stress. We traversed evil-smelling areas which reminded me of the garbage cans of yesteryear, and we saw pale shadowy forms hurrying upwards from below the water line for a breath of pure air. It takes all this varied humanity to get a huge liner to

---

**Note.* The letters between the brackets are mine.—Q. P.

its destination, Davy. How little of it we realize as we sit and sun ourselves on the upper deck.

I say a "huge liner." In reality the *Moderna* is only about 15,000 tons. Yet it seemed miles long to me last night. I thought we should never reach our destination. At last we came to a heavy iron bulkhead which Jennings rolled back with a harsh, grating noise. Closing this behind us, we stepped into the musty atmosphere consequent upon closed ventilators, shut portholes and the lack of proper cleaning and care.

Up to this point our journey had at least been warm, well-lighted and full of life; but now we had emerged into a dark, airless region, empty and silent as a vault. And not only was it cold and cheerless, but there was a darkness in the atmosphere—a sense of staleness and decay which was almost as oppressive as actual putrescence.

"Don't be afraid of the gun," Jennings murmured in a terrifying stage whisper which was meant to be casual. "The first chamber is loaded with blank—so, even if it *did* go off by accident—"

"I'm not afraid of anything except the cockroaches," I shuddered, as several ghostly shapes, large as fifty-cent pieces, scudded noiselessly away before our advancing feet.

But as soon as I spoke, I realized that I was lying in my teeth, Davy. I *was* afraid of something else. I was afraid that we were being followed. Distinctly, as we progressed, I heard faint noises in the dark distance behind us—noises which were independent of the weather or the creaking of the ship. I plucked at Jennings' sleeve.

"Did you hear that?" I whispered. "It sounded as though someone else had just pushed back that door."

"Rats," he answered and, although I could not see his face, I felt sure he was grinning reassuringly.

"That's worse than anything," I muttered as we crept onward.

Soon after we had passed a bend in the corridor, the purser began flashing his light on the numbers of the rooms. Suddenly he stopped.

"Number 213. Here we are."

He produced a key and turned it in the lock.

Then, as the door opened, Davy, my nostrils were immediately assailed by the sickening-sweet smell of formaldehyde—of the embalming fluid which is supposed to arrest decomposition and all its attendant horrors. And, at this moment, I realized that here was one of the things, without my knowing it, had terrified me most about this expedition—*the odor of death.* It now rushed out at us like a tangible presence; it invaded my hair, my clothes, my whole body; it was almost overwhelming.

But I had hardly braced myself to follow Jennings into that dreadful room, when the door suddenly swung shut with a resounding crash. We staggered back. For a moment we stood in the corridor, speechless and immovable.

"My God, was that the ship or was it—was it something inside that room?" I whispered fearfully.

"We'll soon see," muttered Jennings between clenched teeth and gripping his revolver firmly in his right hand, he kicked the door open again and started to fumble with the electric switch. There was a click but no responding illumination.

"Damn it! They've taken out the bulbs," he muttered, turning his flashlight towards the ceiling and then around the room. "But it must have been the rolling of the ship that closed the door. There's no one here."

Holding my handkerchief to my nose, I entered the room after him and we proceeded to examine it. A fair sized cabin, it would normally have held about six third-class passengers. But now only one berth was occupied, and, try as I would to prevent it, my eyes kept returning to that white, shrouded figure, rigid beneath its covering sheet. There were heavy curtains at the foot of each set of berths. We pulled them back. There was nobody behind them. Outside, we could see the waves dashing against the porthole. The ship was still staggering and shuddering beneath their blows. I noticed that the Thing on the bed had been strapped in place to prevent its rolling on to the floor. A wise precaution. Suddenly, for no particular reason, I began to think of that most ghastly of all ghost stories—"The Upper Berth." A strange, uncanny sensation of unreality began to sweep over me.

But just at this moment there was something more tangible—or more audible—to worry us. Jennings' bent back straightened with a jerk and he stood in a listening attitude. At last he had heard it too. At last he realized that we actually had been followed and that the noises which I had heard earlier were not merely—rats!

No rat in the world ever made that sound. They may do queer things, but they don't *sneeze!* And I had distinctly heard a sneeze in the passage.

We both moved hurriedly to the door at the same moment and almost bumped our heads together as we reached the passage. There was a flicker of light just around the bend and I caught a glimpse of a white figure, quickly disappearing in the other direction.

"Wait here," snapped Jennings, as he started to run towards the light.

For a moment I stood there,—just outside that terrible stateroom, too dazed to move. I had left my torch in the cabin and it was pitch dark in the corridor. The silence was broken only by the faint whisperings of insects,—the occasional scampering of rodents, and the gulp-gulp of waves against the porthole. Jennings was lost to sight. I was alone in the very entrails of the *Moderna.*

And as I stood there, Davy, I began to be conscious of a feeling of blind, overwhelming panic. I had been frightened before, but it was nothing compared with this new feeling of helpless and abandoned terror. Without clearly knowing what I did, I re-entered the stateroom and started to battle with a new idea which had suddenly crashed through my bewildered brain. A crazy, fantastic notion which was so staggering that it actually made me feel safer in that room—alone with a dead body—than I had felt outside in the passage.

Supposing Jennings himself should turn out to be Robinson!

Supposing he had brought me to this isolated part of the ship where I could scream until I was black in the face and no one would ever hear me—supposing, I say, he had brought me here to do with me as he had done with Betty Lambert. And if he was Robinson, then there was nothing of which he was not capable.

And though I knew of no particularly good reason why he should be Robinson, there was also no earthly reason why he should not be, as well as any young or youngish male on board. In my heated imagination I could see those smooth pink cheeks covered with grease paint to give the appearance of tan; those clear blue eyes masked behind steel-rimmed spectacles and that blond hair darkened to a chestnut brown.

Of course my first thought was to turn and flee—to get away as far as possible from this horrible place. Then I remembered that maze of corridors—those innumerable turns. I had a vision of myself wandering round and round—lost in the bowels of the

Moderna. My sense of direction had completely deserted me. I could only stay where I was and wait—and hope.

I jumped up, flashed my light on the door and fastened the bolt securely from the inside. At least he could not get back into the cabin until I was calmer.

All this must have taken about three seconds of actual time. In an effort to regain my composure, I sat down again waiting for footsteps, waiting for anything to break the monotonous roar of the waves which seemed to intensify the awful stillness and solitude of that cabin.

Awful stillness? But was it so awfully still after all? I was beginning to have uncomfortable doubts about my solitude. Somewhere, somewhere in this very room there was a movement. I could swear that there was life other than my own. Or was it just nerves—my heart's tumultuous beating that I heard?

Was it the measured breathing of a living being, or was it—another wild idea struck me—was it, perhaps, the corpse?

What if that shrouded form on the bed were not Mr. Lambert's body at all but—but—

I turned my torch on to the opposite berth with a trembling hand. For a few seconds I stared at that awful whiteness. But, despite the flickering and dancing of my light, I could see no ripple, no faint undulation of the covering sheet. It was as still as death itself.

But I must make sure. True, I had not the courage to pull back the sheet and gaze at what it concealed. But I had hands. I could feel where I dared not look.

Balancing my electric torch on the washstand so that its light was turned away from the figure on the bed, I moved slowly across the room. But, just as I reached the other side, Davy, the ship gave one of those long, trembling shudders that ships give under stress, seeming to falter in her progress as if frightened by what lay just ahead, and throwing me off my balance so that I clung on to the ironwork to support myself. Then there was a thud. My flashlight had fallen on the floor and gone out.

The room was in total darkness.

I didn't scream, Davy; please always remember that I didn't scream—at least, not then. I simply put out my arms and groped blindly about to find my bearings. And then—oh, Davy, shall I ever forget it?—my hand touched something soft—something soft and yielding.

It was human flesh!

In the darkness, I thought, I must have unwittingly removed the sheet from the body and now, it seemed, I was holding Mr. Lambert's hand in my own. But, before I had time to take in the full horror of this contact, I suddenly felt that those fingers—those fingers, which I had imagined to be dead—were slowly closing around my own. My hand was held in a vise-like grip.

It was then, Davy darling, that I thought I must go mad. I opened my mouth to scream, but no sound came except a strangled sob. I suppose I tried to move my hand away but my muscles refused to obey the dictates of my brain. My senses were numb—my legs seemed to have turned to water—my body was limp and powerless. I only knew in a hazy way that I was going to faint. I hoped that oblivion would come soon.

Apparently it did—

Exactly what happened after that I shall never know, for I did not recover consciousness until I awoke to find myself here in my own stateroom alone, on my berth, with my door shut but of course unlocked. The first thing I did was to lock it, quietly. And no sooner had I turned the bolt than I heard—oh, Davy, this is the part that freezes my blood so that I can scarcely write.

I heard Adam Burr's voice outside my door speaking my name. His voice was quiet, but penetratingly hollow. At the sound—Davy, am I going mad?—doubts and fears came rushing to the surface. What on earth was he doing there at that hour of the morning? It was all I could do to keep from screaming aloud. I pressed, my hand against my mouth, shutting the sound in.

"Jennings has gone for a stewardess," the voice went on. "They ought to be back shortly. Can't I—"

"No, no!" I said, almost sobbing. "Please go away. I don't want *anyone.* I don't want to open my door again tonight. I can't—"

His voice broke in. It sounded strange and far away—or was it that my senses were leaving me again? He must have asked me a question, because suddenly he spoke my name sharply.

"Miss Llewellyn, are you really all right? You wouldn't like me to call Dr. Somers?"

"No, no," I repeated, "just leave me alone—please."

"All right, my dear, just try to get some sleep. No one shall be allowed to disturb you."

There was another colloquy outside my door a little later when Jennings and Trubshaw came back with the stewardess, but I would not let anyone come in. I assured them that I needed nothing and then I heard them all tiptoeing away down the corridor.

Yes, Davy, they tiptoed away; but all the long time I've been writing this, someone has kept tiptoeing back again continuously. The corridor outside my room is haunted with the sound of footsteps. That is one reason why I've been sitting up writing to you instead of taking Adam's advice to "try to get some sleep."

Now, darling, once again I see through the porthole that there is a "grey mist on the sea's face and a grey dawn breaking." The idea of new day is giving me back my sanity. There have been no footsteps for the last half hour and I am beginning to feel safe again—safe, at least, behind my locked door. It's like a release from suffering, Davy, this sudden sense of security after the agony of fear. I feel a little as I did when I came out from under the ether three weeks ago—shaky and sick, but free from the cruelty of pain.

Tomorrow, perhaps, I shall have more courage and be able to laugh about it all. So good night at last, my very dear.

On deck,
11:00 A. M.

And good morning,—oh, blessed morning, Davy darling! In this clear, unclouded sunshine, surrounded as I am by laughing crowds of gaily-dressed people, by all the carefree bustle of a ship at play, the terrors of last night seem not only unreal and fantastic—but more utterly ridiculous than anything that ever I have been concerned with!

Will my insatiable reporter's instinct always hound me into such foolhardy exploits as last night's expedition to Room 213? Will the irrepressible Irish strain in my somber Welsh blood continue to persuade me into crazy deeds of derring-do? If so, may the outcome be always an object lesson, as last night was; may my essentially feminine and hysterical makeup always betray me. Then perhaps in time, before you give me up altogether, I may learn to check those impulses.

But already, you see, I've recovered, physically and mentally. Joy cometh with the morning: my curiosity has been satisfied, and Mary is—to all intents and purposes—herself again.

But now, I imagine, you will be anxious to hear all about what happened last night after I passed out of the picture, and why Adam Burr had left his virginal couch to play sentinel outside my door in the wee small hours of the morning. I've just had it from Jennings and believe me it's some story, my dear, but it's too bad I should have missed it all by fainting.

My stewardess brought me some tea and toast at about nine o'clock, and I dressed as quickly as I could because I wanted to have it out once and for all with Mr. Jennings. I found him in his office, looking far more damaged than I after the exploits of last night, but he seemed very much relieved at the sight of me and perked up considerably when I told him that I was none the worse for my experience.

After I had told him all that I've just told you (omitting, of course, my absurd suspicion that *he* might be Robinson), the purser proceeded to give me his version of what happened after he left me to follow, moth-like, after the disappearing light.

"I shall never be able to forgive myself, Miss Llewellyn," he said frankly, "for leaving you alone like that. I suppose I was a bit wrought-up myself, but when I saw that light, I really thought we might have discovered something at last, so I gave chase for all I was worth. I kept catching glimpses of a white figure in the light of my flasher, but I never got near enough to see who it was. But one thing I did know—the johnny I was chasing was just as familiar with the geography of the boat as I was. He led me a merry little dance, but I finally cornered him in one of the unused bathrooms. You'll never guess who it was."

"I'm past guessing anything," I said.

"It was Trubshaw—"

"My steward!"

"Yes. The wretched fellow was terrified out of his wits, but he wouldn't give me any explanation of his presence except to say that he was there in your interests. Well, this riled me a bit, as you can probably imagine, so I just marched him back to Room

213 at the point of the gun, determined that he should tell his story in front of you. I thought that possibly you might have told him to follow—"

"Good heavens, no," I exclaimed. Then remembering my mistrust of Jennings, I shut my mouth and waited for him to continue.

"When I got back to Room 213," he went on, "you can imagine my surprise to find that the door was locked. I listened a minute or two and, hearing noises inside, I banged for all I was worth, threatening to shoot the damned thing down if it wasn't opened at once. I called your name but you didn't answer. It was terrible.

"Then all of a sudden, I heard another voice—the door was thrown open and I saw a man supporting you in his arms—"

"Oh, my God! Who on earth was it?"

"You may well ask, Miss Llewellyn," replied Jennings, with a sly little smile. "I don't know who I'd expect, but it certainly wasn't the person I saw. It was Adam Burr—! His bald head was gleaming in the light of my flash-lamp and he was almost staggering in his efforts to support you and unlock the door at the same time. He looked so funny in his embroidered bathrobe—doing a sort of strong man act."

"But why on earth was he there at all?" I asked incredulously. "I've never heard of anything so—so perfectly incongruous—to be locked alone in a stateroom with a corpse and Adam Burr!"

"Well," said Jennings, "before asking Burr for any explanation the first thing to do—obviously—was to get you back to your stateroom."

The purser then went on to describe how he and Trubshaw carried me through dark corridors and up innumerable companionways. (I can't help being glad for their sakes that I still have to gain eleven pounds to reach my normal 120!)

"Mr. Burr came along, too," continued the purser, "and—"

At this moment there was a knock at the door and Adam entered, looking very much the worse for wear and tear.

"Ah, we were just talking about you," said Jennings cheerfully. "Perhaps you'd like to come in and tell the story of your life."

Adam looked at me haggardly. "Thank God you're all right," he groaned.

"And what have *you* got to say for yourself, Mr. Burr?" I inquired archly. "Chasing a girl all over the ship that way—locking her into an empty stateroom? Are we going to have an explanation?"

Adam turned from one to the other of us and twiddled his thumbs. "Well," he said at length, "Jennings has heard it all before, but—if you insist—it's really quite simple—

"I'd been worried about you, Mary Llewellyn, for the past two days. You'd been avoiding me purposely and you've obviously had something on your mind. Yesterday I spoke to your steward about you. Trubshaw looked after me the last time I took this boat, so we are old friends. He told me about your anonymous letter. Well, the long and the short of it is that I promised him something—something pretty substantial—if he'd keep me in touch with your doings. You see," he added apologetically, "we've lost one girl already on this trip—and—I happen to be rather fond of you, my dear. Fellow post-operatives and all that! But I won't get sentimental. Last night he came to me and told me about your—er—projected expedition with Jennings. I offered him—"

There was an angry noise from the purser. "He shall hear about this from me," he spluttered.

"Oh, no he won't," replied Adam suavely. "I told you last night that you are not going to make trouble for him, poor fellow, because if you do, it will mean awkward questions for you, John Jennings. You yourself might have some difficulty in explaining what you were doing alone with a young lady at 2:30 A. M. in the unoccupied parts of the ship. Now, don't interrupt me any more."

Adam came over and sat beside me; then he continued:

"Well, I decided to follow you. Trubshaw had a flashlight and claimed he knew the way. I'll admit there was a double purpose in my plan. I wanted to keep an eye on you, my dear, and, at the same time, to be in on any excitement that was going on. Well, we got to the corner without your suspecting that we were behind you. Then, after you got into the room, I was suddenly seized by an attack of sneezing. Trubshaw turned and fled, leaving me in complete darkness. I slipped past the door of No. 213 and heard Jennings go thundering along in the other direction. That gave me my opportunity to see what was going on in the stateroom, so I crept up to the door, slipped in and hid behind the curtains. I sensed at once that you were in a very nervous state, Miss Llewellyn. I decided, therefore, that I would not frighten you by announcing my presence until someone else was with you. I thought you'd just sit down and wait until Jennings came back. Everything was all right until you started to walk towards me. Then the ship gave a roll and your flashlight fell on the floor. Apparently losing your balance, you fell against me and clutched hold of my hand. I did not mean to scare you, but—well, the next thing I knew was that you were lying cold and limp in my arms and Jennings was uttering the most horrible threats from outside the door."

"Well," I said, "you are the first man that's ever scared me into unconsciousness, but I've no doubt you acted with the best intentions. The road to Hell—"

"Exactly," said Adam, "and I think our expedition of last night was a good example of what we shall let ourselves in for in the next world if we don't mind our own business in this. Now, is everything forgiven and forgotten?"

"Certainly."

Then we shook hands all round and Jennings produced some stuff called *Amer Picon* and we all took an apéritif, pledging each other to silence and secrecy as to the details of last night.

As Adam and I left the purser's office, he whispered in my ear, "I didn't tell Jennings that it was you who locked the door, my dear. But I think I know why you did it—"

"Oh, thank you," I breathed fervently. "It was a wild impulse on the spur of the moment. He's such a nice boy and—"

Here I heard my name called from the purser's office. Bidding Adam wait for me on the upper deck, I reentered and found Jennings sitting where we had left him, a mischievous smile playing about the corners of his mouth.

"I thought perhaps you might be wondering why I—in my official capacity—did not take steps with regard to Mr. Burr's extraordinary behavior last night?"

"I've got past wondering about anything on board this ship," I replied.

"Well, has it ever occurred to you," continued the purser, "that Adam Burr might be a villain—after all?"

"It has occurred to me, though, on the whole, I'm inclined to think that he is a nice, old fashioned gentleman with practically no vices except a slight and perfectly innocuous tendency toward being a 'sugar daddy.'"

Jennings smiled, then he started to laugh, rather foolishly. Finally he spluttered out:

"You know, I almost had him arrested last night, but—when Trubshaw and I were carrying you back to your cabin—we had just reached a bulkhead—Burr started to push it back for us—there was a puff of wind—the embroidered robe was blown open—and—and—well, he clutched at it with frantic modesty—but, Miss Llewellyn—"

Here Jennings broke off and cleared his voice. Then he continued:

"At that moment I saw something which will establish his innocence once and for all—something that makes it impossible for me to believe evil of him. Miss Llewellyn—"

He lowered his voice as if to impart some scandalous impropriety,

"*—he wears—a—nightshirt!*"

On deck.
Wednesday, November 18th.
5:00 P. M.

So now, my dear, my confidence in Adam is completely restored and we are back on the old basis. I am reinstated in my former position as safety-valve and he is once again the father confessor and maiden aunt. It was Jennings' account of his sleeping apparel that did it, Davy, for try as I will, I am utterly unable to visualize a villain who wears a nightshirt!

But I'll come back to Adam later on. Meanwhile, I must tell you that I went down to see Mrs. Lambert after lunch. She is much calmer now and was holding quite an animated conversation with Earnshaw when I entered. Apparently she feels she would like to offer some sort of reward for information leading to the arrest of the criminal. In fact, she has suggested this to Captain Fortescue, but he is still unwilling to let the passengers know definitely that there is a cold-blooded murderer in their midst. The voyage has only just begun to take on some semblance of gaiety and relaxation, which he is naturally loath to disturb in any way.

Earnshaw, on the other hand, looks drawn and haggard. Even his dapper little moustache appears quite wilted and droopy.

Several times I noticed that Mrs. Lambert was looking at him in a peculiar way as if she were afraid that he might be contemplating something desperate. I found him, nevertheless, extraordinarily controlled and reasonable, despite his air of dejection.

When I took my leave, he walked a little way down the corridor with me and I told him of my adventures of last night, omitting, of course, my various suspicions of the persons concerned. He listened with absorbed interest. When I had finished he said:

"That was a splendid idea of yours, Miss Llewellyn. I've spent a lot of time lately on this Robinson hunt, but I never thought of looking in that stateroom. It was a long shot of course and apparently didn't lead to anything except—well, I'm bound to say I think Mr. Burr's presence there was decidedly fishy!"

"Neither you nor Mrs. Lambert is particularly fond of Mr. Burr, are you?" I asked innocently.

"Oh, I've got nothing against him," he said hurriedly. "Nothing whatever. He was a business rival of Mr. Lambert's—but he seems a harmless old thing. Nevertheless, I hope you are taking care of yourself. When I think of what happened to Betty—I—You keep your door locked at night, I suppose?"

"Invariably; and the captain has told someone to watch my room. Don't worry about me."

He held out his hand and I saw him smile for the first time since Betty's death; smile so almost tenderly, in fact, that I felt my nerves tingle a little bit, just as Betty's might have done. But really only a *tiny* bit, darling.

"And you should take better care of yourself," I added, "you look quite worn out." Then I disengaged my hand which seemed to be still in his.

After this I went up on deck, where I was soon joined by Adam, who came fussing up to me like a freight train on a siding.

"Well, have you forgiven me?" he asked. "Have I proved at last that, though I am a bald-headed old prune, your safety is very near and dear to me? If I have, there's a piece of news you might be interested to hear. It concerns yourself, incidentally."

Of course, Davy, no one in the world can resist that kind of thing, so I quickly assured Adam that I was all ears.

"Well, we have some information about Betty at last. It's not much, but it's something. I went to see Jennings after lunch and started to tell him once again what I thought of him for taking you down to that filthy place in the middle of the night. Of course, John Jennings and I are old friends—but there are limits to what one will put up with, even from friends. Finally, he admitted that he had received instructions from the captain himself to let you have your way in everything, because—because apparently you are involved in Betty's death more than you think."

I sat up in my deck chair with a jerk. "Involved! What on earth do you mean? I was talking to Earnshaw in the smoking room when the poor child—"

"Oh, no. I don't mean you are under suspicion. No, no. It would take a man—or at least a far stronger woman than you—to throw an able-bodied girl like Betty over that high rail. But, it appears that she left a message for you on the night that she died."

"A message for me! I never got it."

"No, unfortunately it was given to the steward at about nine o'clock and you never went down to your stateroom again. It happened this way, apparently, though no one knows about it yet—that is, none of the passengers except you and me."

"But, why wasn't I told? Surely it's *my* business if the message was for me."

"Don't be impatient, my dear. I'm telling you now. Well, as

I was saying, or rather, as Jennings was saying an hour ago—Trubshaw, who is the Lamberts' steward as well as yours, happened to pass the door of their suite at about 8:15. He heard an argument going on inside and suddenly the door was thrown open and Betty rushed out with tears in her eyes. He heard her parting words: 'I don't care what you say, I'm going to do it' or something of the sort. The steward is positive of that. Then she went straight to her own stateroom and locked the door. About three quarters of an hour later she rang for Trubshaw. She was lying on the bed in the dark and her voice still sounded very tearful. Then she said that she wanted to see you just as soon as ever you came down to your stateroom. She gave him a dollar and made him promise not to tell a soul. At the same time she asked him to get in touch with you at whatever hour you appeared, as it was *very urgent.* It's too bad you never got the message—you might have saved the poor kid's life. She was never seen after that, except by her aunt at eleven o'clock, just before she was murdered."

"How frightful!" I exclaimed. "I expect she wanted to ask me to go on that date with her. But it's no wonder Mrs. Lambert was worried and got up to look for her. Incidentally, was she able to throw any light on the earlier incident?"

"Oh, of course, Mrs. Lambert was terribly upset when the subject was brought up. She blames herself for not being more sympathetic with her niece. Apparently she had asked Betty what she was going to do with herself that evening and Betty said that, since Earnshaw was busy, she was going to keep a date which she had on deck. Mrs. Lambert asked if the date was with you, and Betty finally confessed that it was with a man. Her aunt remonstrated pretty strongly, pointing out that it wasn't exactly the thing for her to make herself conspicuous with strangers so soon after her uncle's death. At last she (very foolishly) forbade her to go and Betty flung out of the room with the words which Trubshaw overheard."

"But the man?" I cried excitedly.

"That's the silly part of it. Betty wouldn't tell his name or anything about him. Of course most of it was explained in the anonymous letter which was found after her death—when it was too late. But Earnshaw was in the room at the time, and if he'd had any red blood in his veins you'd have thought he'd have insisted on her staying with him instead of letting her go and get thrown overboard by the murderous Robinson. But then, I always did think he was a bit of a gigolo—"

"Gigolo nothing," I exclaimed indignantly. "How on earth could he have realized the danger? Besides, he was awfully busy working on Mr. Lambert's papers. He told me so himself."

"But that didn't prevent him from spending quite a long time with you later in the evening."

"Nonsense. He only wanted to talk about Betty. He was head over ears in love with her and he probably thought she was safe in bed. You are a silly, suspicious old man, Adam Burr. You're simply jealous because Earnshaw is the most attractive man on board—"

"More attractive than the uniformed Jennings? More attractive than the young man you write your journal to? More attractive than—*me?*"

Of course there was no answer to such foolish questions. "Um-m-m," whispered Adam in my ear. "And I'm inclined to think Mrs. Lambert agrees with you. She's no chicken, of course, but (if you will excuse my mixed metaphors) there's many a good tune played on an old fiddle. He's been very attentive since she became a rich widow—very consoling."

I laughed in spite of myself. Really, Davy, the man is more of an old woman than Aunt Caroline herself.

"Caesar's wife!" I cried, "I'm ashamed of you, Adam Burr. When it comes to a question of virtue you are as cynical as a Paris concierge. You mistrust Earnshaw simply because his dark hair and moustache make him look like the handsome Villain of the piece. But apart from the fact that he had a perfect alibi in both cases, may I remind you that our particular villain is clean shaven—with brown hair and spectacles? As a budding young detective I am not interested in Earnshaw. I am interested only in Robinson."

"Well, that lets me out," said Adam cheerfully. Then he added in a serious tone: "And, as a matter of fact, the authorities are inclined to agree with you about Robinson. They are convinced that he is an impersonation—probably one of the passengers in disguise—and that he and he alone is responsible for the murder of both Betty and Mr. Lambert."

I gave a slight shiver. "In other words, every time I sit down by a man—at table—on deck—or in the smoking room, my neighbor may be Robinson. That's a pleasant thought!"

"Well," replied Adam flippantly. "Here's an idea to cheer you up. Why not turn tonight's fancy dress dance into a Robinson party? Make everyone dress as our mysterious 'thirteenth chair' and give a prize for the one who looks most like him. We will be the judges. It's more than probable that Robinson himself would get fourth place the way Charlie Chaplin once did at a Charlie Chaplin party. What are you going as, by the way?"

"I'm going as a newspaper and pray to heaven it won't be windy. And now, if you've no more to tell me, I want to take a nap—in preparation for tonight and in reparation of last night."

Adam scratched his bald pate. "You are not going to take a

nap, my dear. You are going to scribble in that infernal book of yours. And I have some more news too. What d'you think? Mrs. Clapp—the inimitable Marcia Manners—has promised to give a turn tonight. But, not a word, mind. Jennings told me as a profound secret."

"Oh, good," I said, rising from the chair. "If she's anything like what she used to be, it will be a marvelous treat. Worth our passage money for that alone! Well, I'll see you at dinner."

Then I made my escape and fulfilled Adam's prophecy by writing all this to you, Davy darling, when I ought really to have been sleeping.

But there's time for a nap too.

So here goes!

On Deck.
Thursday, November 19th.
9:30 A. M.

Well, Davy, I really felt the depression was over when I saw the passengers decked out in gala array for the fancy dress dance last night. After the terrors of the past few days, the long faces and the mournful expressions, it came as a distinct relief to see everybody looking gay and festive again. And the Veuve Clicquot to which Adam treated our table at dinner was a great help in reviving our spirits. The ship was magnificently decorated and the authorities are evidently doing all they can to make us forget the two unsolved tragedies.

Our old friend Wolcott has reappeared at last after an indisposition of several days' duration. He was dressed as a medieval monk—a costume which admirably suited his oily smile and unctuous suavity. Throughout the first two courses he did nothing but say *"Pax Vobiscum"* to every remark that was made, until Daphne, a magnificent Britannia, said that she would stick her trident into him if he said it again. Silvera, in an obvious endeavor to accentuate his pseudo-Spanish origin, was dressed as a toreador, and very dark and dashing he looked. I found myself pitying the bull every time I caught the dangerous gleam in his cruel, handsome eyes.

Little Daniels had blossomed out as some sort of swashbuckling Don Juan or pirate—a costume which only served to enhance his diminutive stature and to accentuate the size and splendor of his Britannia, about whom he fluttered constantly like a hen who has hatched a turkey's egg.

Some famous psychologist has said that any self-chosen fancy dress is the embodiment of one's suppressed desires. If so, that gives one a good line on Adam, for he appeared as a very hirsute cave man with a huge mop of horse-hair covering his bald head; an indeterminate garment hiding his pendulous tummy and those spindly legs stained in a manner which hid their whiteness and exaggerated their spindlyness. His line was to say to every available female: "G—rr, grr—I'm Adam, won't you come and be my little Eve!"

Mrs. Clapp was in plain black evening dress, as usual, though we were given to understand that she would change later for the monologues which she had promised.

Since you are always so sweet and sympathetic about clothes, darling, I may as well describe my own simple costume, which was designed not so much for its beauty as to enable me to refuse dances without going into too many details about my late lamented appendix. For my dress I had sewed a number of old newspapers on to a slip. On my head I wore a saucy little cap cut in the shape of an ink bottle. My swan-like throat was embellished with a necklace of fountain pens intertwined with ticker tape, and my waist was festooned with rosettes of typewriter ribbon and blotting paper. I was a lovely object, as you may well imagine.

There was dancing in the social hall after dinner and it was fun to watch it, if only to see Britannia ruling over her ardent Don Juan—or to watch Adam, the primeval man, hunting out the youngest passengers of the female persuasion and hugging them to his padded chest. Even Wolcott came over and asked for "the honor" of a dance, which was promptly refused. Silvera stood moodily in a corner, smoking a cheroot and scanning the proceedings with smouldering eyes.

After people had amused themselves by bursting a vast number of balloons and hurling multi-colored streamers in their friends' faces, there was an interval. I was just about to risk my dress on the windy deck when Jennings announced that Miss Marcia Manners, the famous actress, had kindly consented to give two monologues.

We hurried into the dining hall, where a rough and ready stage had been erected. Adam found me a front seat and we eagerly awaited the appearance of Mrs. Clapp—the strange, dark woman who had once held princes and potentates spellbound by her magic art.

Now, Davy, I have seen Cornelia Otis Skinner. I have listened entranced to the performance of Ruth Draper, but I have never imagined that a monologue could be quite as good as this. In a sense it wasn't really a monologue at all, because, in some subtle manner, one got the impression that the stage was full of people. Without their actually saying a word, one knew exactly what the others were doing and thinking through the superb acting of Marcia Manners.

In the first sketch she was a woman, presumably of forty, who whimsically announces that she has decided to divorce her rich husband. Her friends come to her and beg her to reconsider this rash decision. One of them explains that she needs her on various committees; another, after tenders of undying devotion, is shown up as anxious not to miss the delightful dinner parties which her darling Agatha gives so charmingly and so regularly. Another "dear friend," after expressing much solicitude, finally is forced to admit that she desires above all things to avoid the breaking up of her pleasant intellectual flirtation with Agatha's husband.

It was a masterpiece of comic satire—a perfect orgy of clever cattiness.

It becomes a bit more serious—even a trifle pathetic—when her débutante daughter enters and points out in the frank, hard-boiled manner of the very young how she will lose caste in her own particular social set if her parents are divorced. She begs her mother to wait, at least, until someone named Harold has popped the question, or until she has landed a job in Lady Queenie's newly established hat-shop. There is no word of regret at losing her mother's company.

After a perfectly charming interlude with her little dog—(Davy, I swear you could see its tail wagging!)—the husband appears. At this point Marcia Manners starts to play the dual rôle, changing from the wife to the husband merely by altering the inflections of her marvelous voice.

Having admitted to several infidelities of which Agatha obviously has had no previous suspicion whatsoever, he implores her to remain with him—at first for the sake of the home, the children and appearances. Finally he tells her that she is the only woman in the world with whom his life would be comfortable, and things are just about to come to a crisis when she calmly announces that she never had the slightest intention of leaving him, but—and these are her final words, Davy—"There comes a point in every woman's life when she wants to know exactly where she stands with regard to her husband, her friends, her children. I thought this was the best way to find out. And now, darling, I do hope you're going to be able to take me to Bermuda next month—it's our silver wedding, you know!"

She received a terrific ovation. People who remembered her in her prime actually stamped their feet with such enthusiasm that I thought we should all be precipitated into the hold—or whatever it is that lies below the dining hall. Even the younger passengers, to whom she was merely a name and on whom a great deal of her gentle irony was doubtless wasted, shouted their appreciation so vociferously that there was no doubt about their sincerity.

After about two minutes she came back for the second act and gave a delightful little piece about an old lady whose income has been cut by the depression and who cannot decide with which of her numerous relatives to go and live. I won't bore you with a long description of it, Davy, but she finally decided on a scapegrace son—the worst proposition from almost every point of view—simply because his socks need darning and he always offers her cocktails and cigarettes as though she were forty instead of eighty-five.

I was just marveling at the remarkable way in which she could juggle her age, her voice and her personality so competently, when a familiar voice behind me said:

"My God, to think that anyone who can act like that should have been fool enough to quit the stage and marry a man with the name of *Clapp!*"

It was Earnshaw. He was staring at the empty stage with shining eyes. Dressed in everyday clothes, he had obviously just come up from his stateroom especially to see Marcia Manners act. It was equally obvious that he had not been disappointed.

"Oh, Mr. Earnshaw," I said, "wasn't she grand! I'm so glad you didn't miss it. How about a breather on deck now the dancing is beginning again?" I turned to Adam. "I know you're dying to dance, Adam, and there's a blonde little apple over there that's just waiting to be picked!"

"Grand!" echoed Earnshaw, as the cool breezes from the ocean fanned our heated faces. "Grand is the word! And to think," he added reminiscently, "that I once imagined that I could act! That's the first time for two days that poor little Betty has been out of my head, even for a minute. But she'd make you forget anything, that woman!"

I gave him a sympathetic smile and sat down in the deck chair with much rustling of paper. Earnshaw lifted a fragment of my dress and studied the market reports in the financial columns that went to make up my sleeves. "What's this costume meant to be?" he asked listlessly.

"A newspaper. But don't be alarmed if those quotations show that stocks are going down. They may be years old for all I know. I gathered them up from the office before leaving."

He smiled wearily. "You are a reporter, aren't you?" he asked politely, though his eyes were looking out over the ocean.

"I prefer to be called a journalist, but I hope I smell as sweet by any other title."

"Oh, yes, of course, I remember now. Someone told me—I think it was Jennings—that you are keeping a journal about everything that has happened so far on board ship with regard to—er—Mr. Lambert's death and—"

"Quite right," I replied, "but it's a very haphazard sort of affair. I'm writing it to amuse myself and to amuse a friend of mine—the man I told you about the other night—it lays no claim to being either exact or scientific."

"Amuse" was an unfortunate word, Davy, when you consider to whom I was speaking, but Earnshaw apparently missed its significance for he bent eagerly towards me, saying:

"You know, Miss Llewellyn, I've been so frightfully upset lately that I've been almost out of my mind. I haven't been able to think clearly or coherently, but I do have—or at least I think I have—a theory—quite a workable theory too. As far as I know, nothing has happened yet to disprove it. It concerns Mr. Lambert's son, the one who is supposed to be in South America, but of course I can't say anything definite until I've thought it over a bit more and tested out certain aspects of the case. I was wondering if sometime we can go through your journal together and see if there could possibly be anything in this little idea of mine."

I did not reply, Davy, because at this moment we heard something which made us both stop speaking and hold our breath. The orchestra had stopped playing a few minutes earlier and I had noticed that a couple had come out on deck and taken the chairs a little way from us, just behind an awning, where we could not see them. Being unobserved, they apparently did not realize that they could be overheard. The first sentence was enough to rivet our attention.

"It can't go on. I can't stand it!"

The voice was Mrs. Clapp's; the tone agonized. But the reply was inaudible and obviously came from someone who was not trained to make the voice carry across large theatres. Then Mrs. Clapp's voice continued:

"But, darling, I thought that you would always stand by me. Whatever my faults in the past, I never imagined this could separate us."

Though both Earnshaw and I were straining our ears, we were

still unable to distinguish the voice of the second speaker. Then Mrs. Clapp spoke again:

"You are the only one I've ever really cared for. The only person who understands about Alfred and what I went through with him. The only person—"

But at this point the orchestra struck up again and we could not hear any more. Earnshaw had risen quickly from his seat in a vain attempt to see who the second speaker was. When he returned to me, he whispered excitedly:

"I couldn't see who she was talking to, but the conversation was very, very interesting, Miss Llewellyn. It all fits in with this little theory of mine about which I was speaking just now. It may not surprise you to know that young Lambert's name was Alfred."

"And so was old Mr. Lambert's," I whispered back, as I saw Adam marching towards me, waving his arms supposedly in imitation of a gorilla.

"I must have my newspaper," he cried alcoholically. "The safety-valve even of primitive man—"

Earnshaw rose, excusing himself politely, and I went in to watch the dancing for a few moments with Adam before going to bed. Mrs. Clapp, looking about thirty years old, was waltzing around with Jennings. She had kept on her stage dress, of shimmering silver lamé and had seemed to put off her sorrow with her sombre mourning. She smiled gaily to right and left as people called out their congratulations on her performance. It was incredible that she should be the same woman who had gone through the emotional scene which we had overheard on deck a few minutes before.

Daphne was sitting in a corner with Daniels, her trident and helmet discarded, looking rather a hot and wilted Britannia. Mr. Wolcott had given up dancing and was making his way towards the smoking room with three slightly tipsy-looking business men. Silvera was nowhere to be seen. The party had undoubtedly lost a good deal of its pep. It was stiflingly hot in the social hall.

"Let's go back on deck," I said to Adam. "Your fevered brow needs cooling and if I don't get into the fresh air at once, you'll have to act up to your costume and carry me off in a fainting condition."

We went out on deck and took the two seats which Earnshaw and I had just left. Adam lit my cigarette and for a few minutes we gazed up at the starry heavens without speaking. The night was calm and the motion of the boat was hardly perceptible.

"We ought to be seeing the Southern Cross in a day or two now," he remarked idly. "We get to Georgetown on Sunday."

"Thank heavens," I replied. "It will at least be a brief respite and we'll have solid ground under our feet for a while. I'm so sick of all this battle, murder and sudden death—" Then I told Adam about the conversation which Earnshaw and I had just overheard.

"Wait a minute, wait a minute, hold your horses, my dear," he cried, when I had finished enlarging on Mrs. Clapp's third monologue. "There's one little point you ought to remember, before you enter all this into that diary of yours. Marcia Manners' husband—the late lamented Clapp—was also named Alfred. She is, was or has been Mrs. Alfred Clapp. I'm quite positive about it."

"Ye Gods!" I cried, "there seem to be a perfectly indecent amount of Alfreds in this business. And what a horrible name it is too!"

But I did not finish my remark, Davy, for at this moment two people came out and occupied the chairs where Mrs. Clapp had been sitting earlier in the evening with her unknown companion. You can imagine my surprise when I realized that they were Daniels and Wolcott, both of whom I had seen a few minutes before very differently engaged. These two arch-enemies were now occupied in earnest discussion.

Whatever your opinion of eavesdropping, Davy darling, you must admit that almost anything was justifiable after our terrible experiences on board the *Moderna.* All's fair in love and murder, so both Adam and I pricked up our ears and listened for all we were worth. Fortunately the orchestra was playing very softly.

Mr. Wolcott's voice was speaking: "You haven't a scintilla of evidence against me, Daniels, not a scintilla." (He was evidently rather proud of his long word.)

"Oh, I haven't, haven't I?" the little Cockney replied pugnaciously. "I could make things so hot for you, Wolcott, that you'd want to follow Betty Lambert overboard if I started to tell all I know. One word from me and the passengers of this ship would tear you limb from limb."

"Nonsense, Daniels. You are exaggerating." Even in the distance I could hear a slight tremor in the oily tones of Wolcott. "You know quite well there's nothing you can do and, for the sake of the line, you wouldn't do it if you could. A scandal of the sort you suggest would ruin the reputation of the ship. Heaven knows it must be bad enough now!"

There was a long pause before Daniels replied. "I'll admit it doesn't suit my book to tell what I know about you just at present. In fact I might forget it—on one condition. Now there's a little proposition I've been thinking over. It's dirty business but—"

At this point the orchestra began to play louder and we could hear only fragmentary snatches of their conversation. It was perfectly maddening, Davy, because I distinctly heard my own name mentioned once or twice—and then I caught Daniels' voice:

"She's keeping a journal of the whole affair—even the game of bridge—you've got to do it, Wolcott—it's the only way."

And Wolcott's: "Too dangerous, Daniels—Miss Llewellyn—a newspaper reporter—crime—horrible."

And then we heard no more because the dance was over and a number of people came out on deck. Adam and I looked at each other questioningly and then I looked at my watch. It was 11:30.

"Bed time," I said. "Good night, Adam. I'll see you in a jigsaw puzzle."

Then I fled. I was too tired to talk over these new developments.

But before going to bed, Davy, I made a decision which I have just carried out. There are altogether too many people interested in this journal of mine. Well, it is now reposing in the captain's own private safe. I took it there this morning and I'm not going to let it see the light of day until I wrap it up and send it off to you from Georgetown. Neither Earnshaw, Adam, nor Jennings will persuade me to produce it again. I have not said anything about this move of mine to a single soul, but as I finish each installment I'm going to take it up to Captain Fortescue and give it into his own hands for safe keeping.

And that, Davy darling, is that!

On Deck.
Friday, November 20.
2:30 P. M.

At this point of the trip, Davy, I cannot help wishing that Aunt Caroline had adhered to her original intention and come along with me. I need a woman badly: someone in whom I can have complete and absolute confidence. Daphne is too close to Mrs. Clapp and Mrs. Lambert is too close to her sorrow. As for the other women on board, they have held themselves very carefully aloof from all murderous complications and there's not a nickel's worth of brain amongst the lot of them anyhow. But there are moments when I feel I shall go mad if I have to spend the rest of my "holiday" hating and suspecting everyone around me.

And then there are so many currents and cross-currents involved that I cannot help thinking that the *Moderna* will soon start to turn round like a spinning top and be sucked under the ocean in a gigantic whirlpool. And it's less than three days before we get to Georgetown. After that, the murderous Robinson will probably become a myth, and the ghosts of Mr. Lambert and Betty will wail over the Atlantic—unavenged throughout eternity.

How I dither on! Let me come back to the facts which I

learned this morning from Adam, most indefatigable of snoopers. One thing he maintains quite definitely. The authorities hold the theory (this through Jennings) that it was unquestionably Robinson who murdered both Mr. Lambert and Betty; that he is an impersonation; that he is either a passenger or a member of the crew; and that no one, as yet, has provided any decent suggestion as to his motive. Radiograms have been sent to police headquarters in New York, but no information has come to hand.

The possibilities surrounding Robinson's identity are so numerous that it's no good even considering them. There are over a hundred men on the boat and I still maintain that "he" might easily have been a woman. The funny part of it is that the people who could not possibly have been Robinson are about the only ones who have acted suspiciously so far. I refer, of course, to Daniels and Wolcott, whose conversation last night is still puzzling Adam and me.

We were talking about these matters in the smoking room this morning when the two of them came in together, as friendly as possible, and started to play bridge with a couple of the passengers—a Mr. Hirsch and a fellow called Stutton, who never speaks a word to anyone. They played for about half an hour and then Wolcott broke up the game and left the room. After about ten minutes he came back and joined Daniels. They talked together for a while in low tones and then sauntered over towards the bar and invited two other men to play. By this time our curiosity was thoroughly aroused, so Adam and I asked permission to stand behind their chairs and watch the game. Daniels and Wolcott were partners and I noticed that, after the first rubber, they managed to cut out together again.

There was nothing unusual in the game itself. One thing,

however, struck me quite forcibly. On the night of Mr. Lambert's murder I distinctly remember Wolcott's saying that he did not play bridge—or, rather, that it was only the psychology of the game that interested him. Now I noticed that he played remarkably well, better by far than little Daniels, who made so many mistakes that his partner's white goatee wagged constantly and a gentle "tut, tut" followed almost every hand.

"What stakes are you playing?" asked Adam, after Daniels had failed to make an obvious little slam, and gone several hundreds down.

Wolcott gave a pious smile and leered at me. "I always prefer to play for love," he said unctuously. "Bridge is such a noble game that it should never be commercialized."

We watched for a little while longer and then strolled out on deck. There the initial rounds of the various Deck Sports tournaments were in full swing. Rubber quoits were flying about in every direction; noisy couples were screaming excitedly over deck tennis, and a shuffleboard block almost hamstrung me as I walked towards the ship's rail.

"Beastly sorry!" called Daphne. I might have known that only she could have been responsible for such violence. Smiling, I acknowledged her apology.

"Oh, Miss Llewellyn," cried Mrs. Clapp, who was dressed in white tailored silk and, through some trick of light and shadow, looked sixteen instead of sixty, "you must enter the shuffleboard contest. Daphne and I are anxious for your blood. We've beaten two couples already!"

"I'm sorry," I answered, "but I lost all the blood I can stand before coming on board and I could no more wield one of those ferocious implements than I could—"

I paused, reflecting that the conversation was beginning to

take on an almost sinister turn. But Mrs. Clapp did not seem to notice it. She merely turned back to the game and "shuffled a board" with almost as much vigor as Daphne had done a few minutes previously. Marcia Manners is undoubtedly a remarkable woman, Davy. Her success last night has given her a jaunty, rejuvenated air and she is as different as she can be from the sable-clad, negligible old lady she seemed when I first saw her. And there is fire in those dark eyes, just as there was fire in those words I overheard last night.

What *was* she talking about and—to whom? So far both Adam and I have been utterly unable to figure it out.

And what is the secret between Daniels and Wolcott? How much do they know? And why have they suddenly become such friends and so keen on bridge? And why, oh why, is everyone so interested in my journal—now safely reposing in the captain's safe, thank Heaven!

Then there is Daphne. Is she just an ordinary overgrown Englishwoman with a simple soul, large feet, and the strong right arm of a trained nurse? Or is she—as Adam puts it—"not at all the type of iron horse that I should like to see beside *my* bed of pain!"?

Adam and I discussed this and various other problems as we gazed seaward over the unending stretches of the Atlantic.

Then we went down to lunch.

Stateroom.
Friday, November 20th.
6:30 P. M.

While I was at lunch the steward brought me a message—"Mrs. Lambert presents her compliments and would Miss Llewellyn be so kind as to take tea this afternoon, etc." Of course I said that I would be delighted, and presented myself at her suite at 4:30. I hesitated for a moment at the door because I saw that Dr. Somers and the nurse were there too. It was Earnshaw who bade me enter.

Mrs. Lambert was lying on the couch in the sitting room, fully dressed in a long and rather becoming black gown. Her hair had been carefully fixed but there was no make-up on her face. She looked her age and then some. On the other hand, her appearance is considerably improved by the fact that she must have lost at least fifteen pounds since she came on board.

"Well, Miss Llewellyn," said Dr. Somers, with the youthful heartiness that will one day develop into a perfect bedside manner, "how do you think our patient is looking?"

I took Mrs. Lambert's hand and told her how glad I was to see her up again. The nurse, a brisk, efficient young woman, smiled at me as though I had paid her a personal compliment.

"Yes, yes," continued the doctor, "and I'm packing nurse off too. There's no more need for her either. Fresh air and plenty of food from now on, Mrs. Lambert; that's my last prescription."

The widow gave a wan smile. Then Dr. Somers turned towards Earnshaw, whose pale cheeks were in striking contrast to the ship surgeon's healthy tan.

"And you, Mr. Earnshaw—the same applies to you too. I shall have you on my hands as a patient if you don't get out and about more. Try and work up some interest in the activities of the ship. Play deck tennis, shuffleboard, bridge, and take your mind off your troubles. I'm serious, man. You look all in."

Earnshaw promised to be a little more considerate of his health and then tea was brought in. The surgeon refused to take a cup, and when the nurse had collected her things, they both took their leave. The atmosphere of the sitting room seemed to grow cold and chilly without their professional cheerfulness. For a while no one spoke, but after Trubshaw had passed the teacups, my hostess did her best to be polite. I admired her effort just as I admired Earnshaw's charming manners, but they could not make me forget the terrible bereavements which they had both suffered.

It was Earnshaw who finally broached the subject which was apparently uppermost in everyone's mind.

"Miss Llewellyn," he said, "I told you last night that from the beginning I have had a theory about the death of Mr. Lambert and Betty. I did not mention it to anyone before, but since Mrs. Lambert seemed so much better today, I decided I would discuss it first with her. She has agreed—"

"I have agreed," interrupted Mrs. Lambert, "to let him tell you all this on one condition. I hope you will forgive me for bringing up the matter of your profession—but you are a journalist—and there are certain details, certain intimate family matters—which I would not wish to have made public. In deference to my husband's memory—I'm sure you will understand."

"Of course, I will treat it as confidential," I replied earnestly. "Only, don't you think, Mrs. Lambert, that if this theory is going to be of any help in solving the terrible riddle of your husband's death, you ought to tell the captain, or someone in authority? He's the nicest man—so discreet."

Mrs. Lambert passed a hand wearily across her forehead. "You shall help us to decide what is best," she said. "But when you've heard what Mr. Earnshaw has to say, I think you will agree that it's the sort of thing that should be kept in the family as far as possible."

"Yes, but why—"

"I know what you are thinking, my dear, but you've been so kind all through this dreadful time. And then, I have a feeling you'll be able to help us. Jimmie spoke of a journal—a sort of record you are keeping."

I nodded my head without speaking. Then Earnshaw's voice broke in again. "Miss Llewellyn," he said gravely, "Mrs. Lambert was right in saying that some rather intimate family history was involved. I don't want to be long-winded, but I'll have to go back a bit—if you don't mind?"

He fumbled for a cigarette and offered me one. I prepared myself to listen.

"You know, of course, that Mr. Lambert had been married before. His first wife was a Miss Felicia Manners—sister to the Mrs. Clapp who sits at our table. She was a woman of about the same age as Mr. Lambert, and for the last ten years of her life she suffered from some disease of the spine which confined her almost entirely to her room. Mr. Lambert was good to her—

very kind and considerate—but in many ways he was a man far younger than his years. His zest for life was amazing. He loved dancing, golf and the theatre, everything where there was movement and excitement. There were many people who said that he neglected his invalid wife. The chief of these was his son, Alfred Junior. I have often heard the old—er—Mr. Lambert say that his son's face was like the voice of conscience. I never met Alfred Junior, so I can't say to what extent either of them was justified. In fact, I didn't even know Mr. Lambert himself till after he became a widower, and by that time his son had gone abroad."

At this point Earnshaw got up from his seat and threw his cigarette out of the porthole. It was evident that he was coming to the part of the story that was not so easy to tell. When he resumed his narrative, he kept glancing towards Mrs. Lambert, who was lying back in her chair with her hand covering her face.

"You may or may not believe it, Miss Llewellyn, but Mr. Lambert's interests in the theatre took an extremely practical turn. He put up the money for two of New York's, most successful comedy hits—'Watch my Dust' and 'Face the Footlights.' I believe he did extremely well out of these two productions, though in one or two others he was not so successful. It was through his interests in the stage that he met the present Mrs. Lambert. He—er—helped her—"

At this point Mrs. Lambert sat bolt upright and looked me squarely in the face.

"As one woman to another, Miss Llewellyn, I may as well tell you there was nothing between us at that time but friendship. If you want the honest truth, I *do* believe that Mr. Lambert started to care for me before his first wife died, but I took nothing from him—that is, nothing but what I had the right to take. He saw that I got one or two parts in his various shows, but I had to work for them the same as everyone else. He admired my work. There was no reason at all why his son should have objected to our friendship."

Right or wrong, Davy, I believe she was speaking the truth. Otherwise I saw no reason for what seemed like a mass of irrelevant detail. I can imagine few things less interesting than the extra-marital infidelities of poor old Lambert.

"The long and the short of it is," continued Earnshaw, "Mr. Lambert quarrelled very bitterly with his son. Even before his second marriage Alfred declared that he would have nothing more to do with his father. He left home and went to live in Paris with his aunt, Marcia Manners. When she made her ridiculous marriage to young Clapp, a friend of her nephew's and about his own age, (who died last spring, by the way, of tuberculosis) Alfred Lambert got disgusted again and went off to South America. Nothing has been heard of him for quite a long time—that is, unless Mrs. Clapp has heard. I know Mr. Lambert didn't."

Here Mrs. Lambert interposed with: "And you *must* believe me, Miss Llewellyn, when I tell you that I did all I could to heal the breach between father and son. I urged my husband to write—to send money—. He even offered a pretty substantial allowance, but the letters were all returned marked ADDRESS UNKNOWN. The boy never made a move towards reconciliation. I understand he referred to me, even after my marriage, as 'the woman my father lives with.' A business associate of my husband's saw him in the Argentine not so very long ago and told us that he still spoke very bitterly."

Earnshaw lit another cigarette and turned towards me. "Now perhaps, you are beginning to get a glimmering of my theory, Miss Llewellyn; and at least you will see why it's not the kind of thing one would wish to tell the authorities. Now here's another point which is important—" He drew some papers out of one of the drawers of the small writing table. "Here is a copy of Mr. Lambert's will. The original is with his lawyer in New York, but there is something extremely interesting about it. The bulk of his property goes to Mrs. Lambert. Alfred Junior is not mentioned, but the money is left to Mrs. Lambert in trust for the duration of her life, to go, at her death, to the nearest male relative who bears the name of Lambert. Betty's father, Mr. Lambert's only brother, is the executor. He is an old man and has no male children—now, do you see what I'm driving at—if Mrs. Lambert were to die, young Alfred would inherit every penny of his father's money!"

There was a little cry from Mrs. Lambert. "You oughtn't to say it, Jimmie. You oughtn't even to think it. I'm sure that he's utterly incapable of anything so terrible. Besides, we aren't even sure that he is still alive himself."

"Do you know anything about him?" I asked.

"No," said Earnshaw, "the strange part of it is that neither Mrs. Lambert nor I has ever set eyes on young Lambert. But—and remember this—there are, or there were, three people on board this ship who knew Alfred by sight. One of them was his father, one of them is Mrs. Clapp, the other—" and here I caught a glimpse of steel in his eyes—"was poor little Betty!"

"Good God!" I exclaimed, "if your theory is correct, it would at least explain what to me has always been the most unreasonable, as well as the most terrible part of this whole business. The murder of Betty struck me, apart from being particularly brutal, as being utterly and absolutely pointless unless—!"

Earnshaw squared his jaw. "Exactly," he muttered, and I noticed that the knuckles of his clenched fists were quite white. "And there's another point which everyone has either forgotten or completely overlooked. Mrs. Lambert is quite positive that there was something wrong with the sherry which she had the night Mr. Lambert was killed. Isn't it just possible—I hate even to say such a thing—but might not Alfred Lambert—as Robinson—have tried to get rid of two people at the same time? Remember there were *two* obstacles between himself and Mr. Lambert's money."

"Then if that is true," I exclaimed, "Mrs. Lambert is not safe for a single moment. Oh, I don't want to frighten you," I added quickly, as the poor widow stirred uneasily in her chair.

"Well, of course," continued Earnshaw, "there's been the nurse, and the doctor was always in and out, but even so—I know we shall both be glad to reach Georgetown. But in the meantime, something has got to be done. Now, Miss Llewellyn, let us suppose, just for the sake of argument, that Alfred Lambert came on board this ship disguised as Robinson. He hangs around his father until he gets invited to a bridge game. He has the poison ready. He slips some into his father's glass and some into Mrs. Lambert's—"

"That would have been difficult," I interrupted, "I don't remember his ever leaving the bridge table."

"Now that's exactly where you can really help us," cried Earnshaw enthusiastically. "I imagined you recorded everyone's movements that evening. That journal of yours would bring out just such points."

"I'm not so sure," I said doubtfully. "It was some hours afterwards that I wrote it and naturally I recorded only what I could remember. And then it's more or less in the nature of a private letter—"

Here it suddenly occurred to me, Davy, that I had been a little bit over-frank in this chronicle about the Lambert ménage; that

I had expressed my opinion pretty freely about Mrs. Lambert's exact age and I had not always been as kind as I might have been even about poor little Betty. I couldn't possibly let them read it. I couldn't even trust myself sufficiently to read it out loud and expurgate where necessary.

"I'm sure I'll be glad to answer any questions which I can," I said at length. "But first I'd like to hear more about your theory—especially where Betty is concerned."

"All right," said Earnshaw. "I'll go on with my supposition. Young Lambert has been successful as far as one of his victims is concerned. He probably hopes that everyone will think Mr. Lambert was poisoned during the *second* bridge game for which, of course, he had a perfect alibi. He discards the disguise of Robinson and either takes another, or keeps himself concealed somewhere in the ship. From now on we can only draw on our imaginations. Let us suppose that he meets Betty by accident and she recognizes him. Perhaps he is a passenger, perhaps an officer, perhaps he is a member of the crew or staff. He knows at once that recognition spells danger. Betty has only to put two and two together and it's all up with him. He writes her an anonymous letter giving her a rendezvous. And here comes another point which is important. At one time, while Betty was a mere school girl, she admired her cousin tremendously. When I first met her, she was always singing his praises. I believe there was a tenderness on his side too. That may account for the fact that she did not tell Mrs. Lambert about her suspicions or about the rendezvous. At any rate, as we all know, she went to it and met—her death—poor child!"

Earnshaw paused for a moment and cleared his throat. Then he continued in a husky voice.

"Mrs. Lambert came up to look for her that night while

you and I were talking in the smoking room. She saw her sitting with a man, whom she afterwards recognized as Robinson. Young Lambert must have been desperate. Perhaps Betty had just said she would tell all she knew. Perhaps—oh, we have no idea as to what passed between them, but he had to act fast—before he was seen and his identity disclosed. And then—the cruel devil—"

Here Earnshaw's voice broke down completely and there was a long moment of silence. We were all thinking of that dreadful night when a single cry rang out across the sea—

"But what can *we do?*" I cried at last.

"The first thing is to protect Mrs. Lambert," replied Earnshaw soberly. "If my theory is correct, she is now the only person who stands between Alfred Lambert and his father's money. He is a murderer, he is more desperate than ever—"

"Yes, of course," I rejoined, "but if neither you nor Mrs. Lambert has ever seen young Lambert, how are we going to identify him? Isn't there a photo—or something?"

Earnshaw shook his head. "No. But there are one or two things that may be helpful. Remember that Mrs. Clapp knows young Lambert by sight. Someone might broach the subject tactfully. As you know, she did not approve of Mr. Lambert. She has not come forward as yet to offer a word of sympathy or regret. Neither of us could approach her on so delicate a matter. She's a difficult woman, I imagine—artistic and temperamental. But she seems to like you. I wonder if it would be possible—"

I thought hard before answering. "I'll see what I can do," I said at length, "but we'll have to be frightfully careful. Remember Mrs. Clapp is young Lambert's aunt and, from what you say, I gather she was very fond of him."

"And then," continued Earnshaw, "I'd hoped we'd get some

help from your journal. Betty might have said something to you—something, anything that would give us a clue—however slight—as to the identity of Robinson."

"There's no need to go through my journal for me to tell you that," I replied. "Betty was very reticent with me. She mentioned young Alfred Lambert once, but she spoke as though he was on a ranch in the Argentine."

"He's *supposed* to be," sighed Mrs. Lambert.

I was now warming up to Earnshaw's theory very decidedly. Indeed, it seemed to me like the only really constructive piece of thinking that anyone had done so far.

"But don't we know *anything* about young Lambert?" I asked. "His age—height—something to go on?"

"Well," answered Earnshaw reflectively, "we know he's under thirty and over twenty-five. And I have an idea, from something Betty once said to me, that he's fair and smooth shaven." A tinge of color spread over his pale cheeks and he passed his hand reflectively over his dark chin. "In fact, she made some not altogether flattering comparisons at one time. I imagine he had a schoolboy complexion. Betty never liked my moustache."

"All the Lamberts have baby skins," said Mrs. Lambert absently. "Alfred—my husband—hadn't a hair on his body. At least—," she paused and looked a trifle embarrassed.

Earnshaw hurried to the rescue. "There are probably fifty young men on the ship to whom such a description applies," he said.

"But my recollection of Robinson is that he was older," I answered. "Between thirty and forty, I should have said."

"Well, we can't tell. Remember Alfred has lived on a ranch, and then, one can play almost any kind of trick with make-up. I never saw him myself, but—"

"I remember thinking Robinson was about thirty," said Mrs. Lambert, reflectively. "His back was turned toward me most of the time, but I know he struck me as being awfully healthy looking. So nice and brown—just as though he'd spent his whole life in the open air."

Well, Davy, we discussed the whole matter a little while longer and finally it was decided that we should keep our own counsel for the time being and not tell the authorities. I am to broach the subject to Mrs. Clapp as soon and as diplomatically as possible to see if I can tell from her manner whether she knows anything of young Alfred's whereabouts. I don't expect to get very far because she's so clever that she could make me believe anything she wanted. However, I'll do what I can. But I am not very optimistic.

After a final plea from Mrs. Lambert for tact and discretion with regard to publicity, I took my leave and came in to write this all down on paper as quickly as possible.

It may look fine in black and white, Davy darling, but it doesn't tell us who Robinson is. And who knows that he may not strike again before we do find out?

Stateroom.
Friday, November 20th.
10:30 P. M.

Heavens, Davy, what an evening! Talk of cheap melodrama. I shall never forget it. And there's so much to tell you, my darling, that I feel I ought to write in shorthand unless I want to sit up all night. But my Gregg is a bit rusty and I shouldn't sleep anyhow, so I may as well try and get it off my chest, even if it takes me into the wee small hours.

It all started after dinner when I strolled out on the promenade deck by myself to smoke a post-prandial cigarette and think a few pleasant thoughts for a change. It was a heavenly time of the evening, midway between sunset and nightfall and the boat seemed to be plowing its way peacefully onward towards a new world where there is no depression, no Sunday column, to write, and, above all, no crime or fear or suspicion. I had just succeeded in forgetting about the Lamberts and was thinking about our wedding day, our brand new apartment and your nice rugged face, darling, when I suddenly became conscious that someone was standing behind me.

I turned round to find myself looking into the dark, sombre eyes of Señor de Silvera. He looked so lonely and so forlorn that

I thought I'd cheer him up with a little Spanish conversation. I proceeded, therefore, to inform him very totteringly that it was a nice night, that the sea was calm and that we should reach Georgetown in a very few days.

"Muy bien," he said politely, and then continued in execrable English. "Miss spiks well. We will spik togezzer, no?"

Don't be jealous, darling, when I tell you he's about the youngest and handsomest president of a corporation that I've ever seen. He's intelligent, too, even if his conversation is more reminiscent of a "First Spanish Phrase Book" than anything else. He is married, he tells me, therefore he is sad. But he is glad, because he is going to his wife. He is bored. He likes not the trip. He was, I am sure, just about to inform me that the cat is on the mat and that the pen of his aunt is in the garden, when Daniels and Wolcott came up and joined us, both eager for bridge.

I asked Silvera if he would like to be my partner. He assented willingly enough, so we all went into the smoking room and started to play. No sooner had the first hand been dealt than Adam came in and started to "kibitz" behind my shoulder. We had decided on a tenth of a cent a point between Daniels and me, and a tenth between Daniels and Silvera. The pious Wolcott still steadily refused to play for money, and even objected to being carried by Daniels. His objections, on this latter score, however, were completely overruled by the little Cockney.

For a while, all went well. I got moderately good hands and Silvera was magnificently if monosyllabically polite every time I made a contract. Wolcott played brilliantly, and as soon as the luck began to go his way a little, he and Daniels quickly retrieved their losses and were well on the plus side. Silvera's temper did not improve as we began to go down and he kept growling to Burr in Spanish about his cursed luck at cards. Judging from their bewildered expressions, I should say that neither of our opponents understands any language other than his own.

Now for the excitement, Davy darling. Hold your breath for a moment and read what follows very carefully. Our opponents were one leg on rubber game and we were sitting like this:

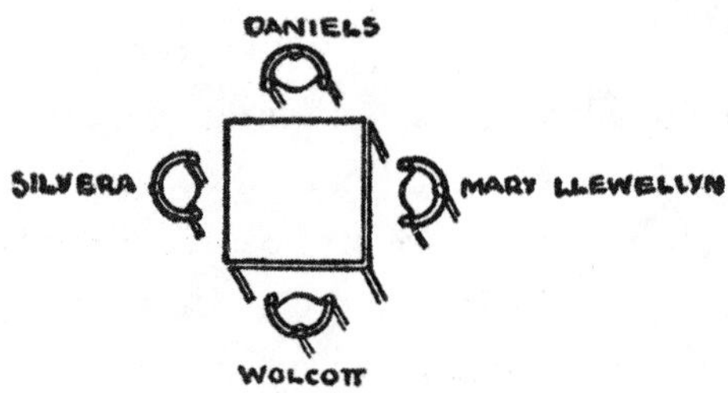

Wolcott dealt and bid a spade. My hand was pretty rotten—nothing but a king of diamonds and a queen of clubs. Silvera bid two diamonds and Daniels supported Wolcott's spades. Finally Wolcott got the bid for four spades and Silvera doubled. Daniels and I passed.

I wasn't particularly interested one way or the other, but suddenly I noticed a puzzled expression come over Adam's face. He kept looking from one hand to the other and started rubbing his chin so vigorously that I thought he must be breaking out in a rash.

I was so busy staring at Adam that it was some time before I noticed Silvera's face. The others were apparently waiting for him to lead, but instead of looking at his cards, he had laid them down on the table and was glowering at Wolcott with an expression of incredible ferocity. His eyes were gleaming like a trapped tiger's and his upper lip had come away from his teeth in a manner which made one think he was just about to bury his fangs in the old man's jugular vein. There was a moment of uneasy silence, broken only by the sound of Adam's footsteps as he hurried tactfully to the door, closed it and turned the key. Sam Bumstead, the steward, was temporarily absent. The other passengers were playing the races in the social hall. The five of us were alone in the smoking room.

Then, in the twinkle of an eye, I saw Silvera raise his hand above his head and bring it down with a crash on poor old Wolcott's left wrist. A pack of cards, identical with those we were using, fell to the floor in wild profusion. For one awful moment, Davy, I thought the Brazilian had performed the old western trick of pinning his opponent's hand to the table with a knife.

But, physically at least, Wolcott seemed none the worse for this act of violence. He sat perfectly still, rubbing his wrist gently and staring with mild astonishment at the cards which lay at his feet. Silvera towered above him, beads of perspiration shining on his forehead.

Then came the big surprise, Davy, and I knew for the first time how Balaam must have felt when his ass turned and answered him in the Bible. Silvera had, throughout the trip, talked either in Spanish or broken monosyllables. Now he burst forth into a torrent of almost perfect English:

"Ah—so! You are cheating after all, Mr. Wolcott! I fancied I saw you conceal the pack of cards about your person. And I thought it strange the way your luck turned so suddenly. Your anxiety during the past few days to play with Mr. Daniels—an indifferent player at best—was, to say the least of it, a trifle odd. You are a rogue, sir—I shall inform the authorities. I shall—"

There was absolutely no doubt about it, Davy. Wolcott had had an extra pack of cards hidden up his sleeve, though why on earth anyone should want to cheat at one-tenth of a cent a point was completely beyond me—especially when it was the cheater himself who had declined to play for money. The old man blinked stupidly at Silvera, but did not say a word in his own defense. Instead, I heard him mutter, in a pathetic little whisper: "I told you it was dangerous, Daniels."

This remark seemed to inflame Silvera more than ever and his voice became so high-pitched and his manner so threatening that I was certain he was about to resort to personal violence. It was Adam who finally saved the situation, and for the first time I realized that he has a hidden strength and virility which certainly is not obvious to the naked eye.

"Un momento, Sr. de Silvera," he cried. *"Tengo algo muy importante que decirle. Estos señores no hablan Español."*

The Brazilian turned flashing eyes towards Adam, and a spirited conversation ensued. When it comes to talking Spanish, I am a weak sister, as you know, Davy; but I can follow a conversation well enough, and I think I caught the general drift of what these two were saying.

Apparently Adam started to tell him that he knew exactly who he (Silvera) was. He also knew exactly why he was going to Rio and how he hoped to win the Harbor Construction contract for his company. He, Burr, was frank to admit that he was after it too. Adam then went on to point out that Silvera, wishing to travel incognito, had posed as a Spaniard (which he wasn't) and pretended not to speak English (which he did perfectly). Only the four people in the room knew his secret and Adam gave his guarantee that if Silvera would forget this unfortunate incident, the rest of us would forget his extraordinary lapse into English and any other irrelevancies which had cropped up during the trip.

At first Silvera listened to Adam with obvious astonishment. Gradually, however, I saw the dark color mount to his cheekbones. His voice was tense and sibilant as he said in Spanish:

"There is nothing disgraceful in my traveling this way, Mr. Burr. I am doing it for business reasons only. If it were officially known that I am returning to Rio so prematurely, the other construction companies would realize the magnitude of the contract and underbid me before I had a chance to look the situation over. As for my English—if I choose to keep to myself during the trip, that is my own affair entirely."

Adam gave him a searching look. "Naturally, señor. You did not wish Mr. Lambert to know who you were. I can well understand that. And since you unfortunately found yourself at our table—well, what better disguise could you adopt? And having started the pretence of not speaking English, naturally you had to continue it."

"It's my own business," repeated Silvera angrily.

"But the new breakwater is my business, too," replied Adam. "A cable to Rio—a little hint as to your movements—" He waved his hand airily.

The anger died out of the Brazilian's eyes. He turned to Wolcott. "I shall forget it," he snapped. Then he rose, strode to the door, unlocked it and left the room.

A number of people began to filter in after the door was open. Daniels, Wolcott and I were still sitting in our seats, staring stupidly at each other like wax figures in a shop window. It had all been so quick and so utterly unexpected that we seemed to have been holding our breath for about five minutes. At length Wolcott bent down and slowly began to pick up the cards. Adam was smiling at Daniels in an elfish manner which made his ears stick out.

"I think it'll be all right as far as Silvera's concerned."

"Adam, you linguist, you shaper of human destinies, you big executive," I whispered. "May I ask you if you are going to give *me* an explanation of all this or are you going to set a price on *my* silence the way you did with Silvera? If anyone's been cheated it's me. I'm nearly eighty cents down, and—"

"Mr. Daniels is going to explain to both of us," said Adam in a dramatic stage whisper, as a fat woman bore down on our table with the obvious intention of taking the Brazilian's place.

Daniels gave a little nod. "Come into the purser's office," he said, ignoring the large lady.

"I want to save the hands," remarked Adam, as he picked the cards carefully from the table.

"I'm not sorry about losing mine," I said. "It was pretty punk."

Wolcott did not move from his chair. He looked old and dazed. Adam and I followed Daniels into the purser's office and closed the door. It was unoccupied. We all fumbled for cigarettes.

"Well," piped the little Cockney at length. "What do you want me to say?" He looked perkily around. "I apologize for myself—and for Wolcott."

"We don't want apologies, Daniels." There was a steely timbre in Adam's usually fatuous voice. "What I want to know is why that last hand was identical with the one which was played on the night Mr. Lambert was murdered—the one which, unless I am much mistaken, Miss Llewellyn copied down and put first in her journal."

Here Adam spread the cards out on the purser's desk. "Look, Mary. You haven't your journal with you, but you do have your memory. Isn't this hand familiar?"

Davy, he was right. I haven't consulted my journal, but I'm sure that he was right. I had been holding the cards held by

Daniels himself on that fatal first night out. Wolcott had Mr. Lambert's hand and Silvera held the cards and was sitting in the position occupied by—Robinson!* Having copied out that hand so carefully I shall never, never forget it. There was no question but that the cards were the same in the essentials. Whether or not we held the same rags, of course, I could not say.

On me, at least, the effect of this announcement was electric. I had suspected nothing. In the smoking room I had simply been too dazed to think of anything except to hope that no one had a gun handy. Adam, from his point of vantage as onlooker had seen and remembered—a remarkable feat when one came to consider it. Realizing that there must be some method in all this madness, he had saved the situation as far as Silvera was concerned, and now he was hot on the trail of Wolcott and Daniels.

But Daniels did not look in the least perturbed. He was blinking his funny little eyes and smiling in a way that showed he was quite master of the situation.

"Well," he said, looking amusedly from one to the other of us, "now that you have literally laid your cards on the table, Mr. Burr, I suppose I must do the same. If you'll pardon my saying so, Miss, you have caught me by the short hairs. I suppose I've got to admit that it was me that copied the two hands from Miss Llewellyn's diary the day she so—er—carelessly left it in the social hall. All that I can say is that I did it with the best intentions."

"Mr. Daniels," I fumed, "that is the most preposterous thing I've ever heard in my life. What right have you—a private manuscript—and who *are* you, anyhow?"

At this moment the door opened and Jennings came in. He looked surprised to find us holding a conference in his office and

---

*See page 16—Q. P.

the cards on the table must have made the scene similar to one of those old-fashioned pictures—"Gambler's Ruin or the Road to Hell."

"Mr. Jennings," squeaked little Daniels on a falsetto note, "these two have got me in the dock. Now they are asking me who I am. Will you do me the favor to tell them? Yes, yes," he continued as Jennings hesitated, "you can tell them the truth."

The exposure of Daniels as a double murderer would, I am sure, have surprised both Adam and me less than what we now heard.

"Mr. Daniels," replied Jennings calmly, "is a private detective who has been in the service of our line for the past five years. Before that he was at Scotland Yard. He went over to America on the company's business and is now going to Rio for the same reason. Although he is a valued and trusted employee, he has been traveling as an ordinary first class passenger because—well, perhaps I had better let him tell you that himself."

I gasped. Funny, chirpy little Daniels an ex-Scotland Yard detective. It was incredible!

"You look surprised, Miss Llewellyn," said the little Cockney. "Nothing should surprise an American journalist. Yes, I'm a detective all right, though perhaps not the type that you get in your lurid American thrillers. Captain Fortescue was specially anxious for me to travel as an ordinary passenger because there's a number of international card-sharpers who work this South American trip. Last time the *Moderna* went from New York to Rio a party committed suicide on board under very suspicious circumstances. A young man he was. He'd been heavily fleeced—"

"And Wolcott?" asked Adam.

"Right the first time," said Daniels, grinning. "I recognized Wolcott at once as one of the bunch. Someone must have tipped him off as to who I was, because he wouldn't touch a card until the night of the fancy dress party. Then, he must have thought I was—er—otherwise occupied, because he inveigled two of the wealthiest men on board into a game. They were just sitting down to play at five cents a point when I called him out of the room. I had an idea—"

"But what's all this got to do with the murder of Mr. Lambert and Betty?" I asked impatiently. "Surely the solution of that mystery is more important than the conviction of an old card sharper—"

Daniels blinked at me and gave a knowing smile. "Naturally, Miss Llewellyn," he said gravely, "I have devoted all my energies on this trip to the Lambert case. I have, if I may say so, been more busy than you and Mr. Burr. And, I might add—about equally unsuccessful. Captain Fortescue thought I should get further by continuing to mix in with the passengers as one of them. I'll admit I haven't got very far, but your journal has helped me considerably from several points of view—"

"My journal! Then it was you behind the curtain that day in the captain's cabin."

He nodded. "Perhaps I'd better apologize, Miss Llewellyn. But I'd also like to express my admiration, if you'll allow me, for the clear way in which—"

"But you had no right," interposed Adam, "to read it in the social hall without Miss Llewellyn's permission. That was ungentlemanly and—"

"I'll admit it," said the little Cockney a trifle shamefully, "but I'm sure Miss Llewellyn will accept my apologies when she hears my reasons. I did evil, so to speak, that good might come. We were all looking for this party who calls himself Robinson. None of us remember much about him. He was a pretty ordinary person in every way. There was only one thing that stood out in my mind—the badness of his play at bridge. Why, he was even worse than me!"

Daniels paused, almost as if he were waiting for a burst of applause. We all looked at him stonily.

"Well, Mr. Burr," he continued, "a man may disguise his face, his voice, his figure and his manners, but it is just about impossible for him to disguise his game of bridge. I decided that if I could get Robinson into a rubber—if I could put those same hands before him—he would probably make the same mistakes as he made before. But, you may see my difficulties. I'm not a conjurer. I'm not even a bridge expert. I'm no good at sleight-of-hand or any other parlor tricks. Then suddenly, luck played into my hands!"

"Wolcott!" I exclaimed excitedly.

"That's the ticket. I caught him sitting down to play bridge for high stakes. I have a good bit of information against him which—well, that's neither here nor there. At any rate, perhaps I used a certain amount of—er—persuasion. Finally he decided, though much against his will, to put his card-sharping abilities to good use. We went over the two hands and he pointed out that, in each instance, there was just one possibility of making a fatal error. Robinson made the mistake both times. Well, Wolcott arranged two packs of cards and we have been trying out those two hands on all the people we could get hold of. We wanted to see if anyone would lead the jack of clubs the way Robinson did. Silvera was our latest—er—victim, but unfortunately Wolcott wasn't feeling very well and must have bungled things. Or, perhaps, that Spaniard is especially keen-sighted."

"But wouldn't Robinson remember the hands?" asked Adam, and I could tell that he was fascinated by Daniels' little scheme.

The detective shook his head. "If Robinson murdered Mr. Lambert," he said sagely, "he had a good deal more important things to think about that night than the play of the cards. But it is possible that it might be sort of instinctive with him to make the same mistakes, if you see what I mean."

"And no one has made them yet?" asked Adam excitedly.

"No one so far; we haven't had a chance to try many people, but we're hoping to get our opportunity at the bridge tournament tomorrow night. The only trouble is that every man is supposed to play with a woman and I shan't be able to partner Wolcott."

"Oh, let me help," I cried excitedly. "I think it's a marvelous idea. Not conclusive, of course, but it will at least give us something to go on and help to eliminate a number of people."

Adam gave me a paternal smile which gradually changed into a severe frown. "No, Mary," he said grimly. "This is a dangerous business. And if Wolcott were found out again, you'd be involved in a nasty scandal. I can tell you a better idea. Daniels will arrange for you to be Wolcott's partner and then, just before the tournament starts, you must say you have a splitting headache and retire. I imagine Jennings can arrange for Daniels to take your place."

The purser nodded. "We're short of ladies anyhow," he remarked as he lit his pipe.

"But I shall have to go down to my stateroom and miss all the fun," I said querulously. "However—I'll do anything you say to help."

Burr's proposal was eagerly agreed to by little Daniels. In the meantime he and Wolcott will carry on the good work of trying to lure any possible Robinson (male or female) into a game, and I am to go round cracking up the bridge tournament and getting everyone to sign up for it. So—if Robinson is a first class passenger, he won't escape our toils.

Needless to say, Davy, my evening was so full I didn't get a chance to talk to Mrs. Clapp on the subject of Alfred Lambert. And as I have a hard day ahead of me tomorrow I'd better say good night now, darling.

I blow a kiss to you across the waters—

On Deck,
Saturday, November 21st.
Noon.

We're in the tropics now, Davy, and no mistake. For the past few days it has been warm, but today is a real scorcher—far too hot at least for the emotional scene which I have just been through. There's not a breath of air and the *Moderna* seems to be stationary—"as idle as a painted ship upon a painted ocean." Actually we are making very good time, it seems, and the passengers are all excited over the fact that a record run has just been announced. I say "excited." As a matter of fact they are lying listlessly about, too hot and lazy to do anything but bore each other.

But I, my lord, have not been idle. Directly after breakfast I decided I must make good my promise to Earnshaw and Mrs. Lambert by interviewing Mrs. Clapp as soon as possible. I hunted around, but I could not find them on deck or anywhere else about the ship. I was told that they have been knocked out of the shuffleboard contest, undoubtedly to their great chagrin, but Daphne (partnered by Daniels) is still a possibility for the deck tennis championship. I made my way to the courts on the upper deck. Daphne was nowhere to be found. As their opponents were waiting for them, anxious to play off the semi-finals before the afternoon heat, I finally volunteered to go and get Miss Demarest from her stateroom.

Accordingly, at about ten o'clock, I knocked at the suite occupied by Mrs. Clapp and her companion. Hearing a noise that sounded like "come in," I opened the door and entered. I must have been mistaken, Davy, because neither of them could possibly have wanted me or anyone else at that particular moment. Mrs. Clapp was lying on the couch half-dressed in a mauve peignoir and obviously in one of her tantrums. Daphne was standing by the porthole, crying. I say she was crying, my dear. As a matter of fact she was making a noise like a young elephant with a toothache. It must have been one of her snorts that I mistook for permission to enter.

I was just about to state my mission and beat a hasty retreat when Mrs. Clapp sat up on the couch with a theatrical gesture and commanded rather than said:

"Don't go, Miss Llewellyn. Stay here and try to teach this ridiculous young woman some sense. Apparently I am incapable."

Daphne had paid no attention when I entered. Hearing Mrs. Clapp's voice, she turned and faced me. Her nose and eyes were red, her face was streaky and her hair was all at sixes and sevens. Honestly, Davy, she looked perfectly fantastic and even more enormous than usual.

"No bad news, I hope?" I said hurriedly.

"*Bad* news!" snorted Mrs. Clapp. "Preposterous news, comic news, tragic news—call it what you will! Miss Demarest has just informed me that she intends to get married—in Georgetown of all places!"

Daphne blew her nose into a sopping handkerchief.

"Why, that's delightful," I said fatuously. "I suppose it's Mr. Daniels. I wish you every possible happiness, Daphne."

"Happiness, Miss Llewellyn? How can you talk of happiness when the granddaughter of an earl marries a common little Cockney nobody of half her size? Why, Mr. Daniels won't even tell her his profession—if he has one."

"I can assure you, Mrs. Clapp," I said chuckling inwardly, "that he has a very reputable profession. Far more so than mine!"

"I don't care who he is or what he is," said Daphne fiercely. "He's rippin' to me. I like him—"

"You like him, my dear Daphne," said the great actress in withering tones, "because he is the first man who has ever made a fuss over you. He's courted you with cheap presents and mash notes as if you were a servant girl. Look, Miss Llewellyn."

She pointed to a small table which contained about six unopened boxes of chocolates, a geranium in a pot (cut flowers being unobtainable presumably in mid-Atlantic), and a nondescript mother-of-pearl box with a hideous effigy of the *Moderna* on the lid. This latter article was obviously designed for trinkets, though a more useless possession for the tweed-clad Daphne would have been impossible to imagine.

But there was something incredibly pathetic about the little collection, Davy. One could see how Daniels had tried by his gifts to show this plain, large-boned woman of thirty-five that to him she was a young girl, feminine and desirable. One could see how Daphne, accustomed as she must have been to making a fuss over other people all her life, appreciated these little tributes more than a younger or prettier woman might have done. To her, I felt sure, they were neither comic nor pathetic, even though their giver did not come up to her shoulder and was never too sure of his vowel sounds or aspirates. The marriage may not have been made in heaven, but at least it was more suitable than Mrs. Clapp's last effort. To my mind the actress was the very last person who had the right to mock at any misalliance.

"Well, Daphne," I said with forced cheerfulness, "if Mrs. Clapp won't come to your wedding in Georgetown, I'll be delighted to give you away and act as maid of honor."

Mrs. Clapp snorted again. "You probably think, Miss Llewellyn, that my objections are purely selfish. I feel I stand *in loco parentis* to Daphne. The night of the fancy dress she and Mr. Daniels were making themselves very conspicuous. I reasoned with Daphne; I pleaded with her. I know men. I've been married myself several times—and—"

"And as you know very well," interrupted Daphne with some heat, "you are perfectly capable of marrying several times more. Then where would I be! Look at this trip. When you first came on board you swore you'd never look at a man again. You wore all your deepest mourning. You didn't even ask me to give you face treatments. Now you use a pot of cold cream every night. You've got out your Paris frocks, and you make yourself look perfectly stunning—"

Mrs. Clapp preened herself and her ill temper began to disappear visibly. Daphne, you remember, is no fool.

"You can't blame me for wanting a home of my own," she continued, seizing her advantage. "A fat lot of good it's done me to be the granddaughter of an earl. I never got a penny out of it, let alone a husband. Daniels isn't any Beau Brummel, but he'd never want a great hodge like me if he was. And he's not so common as you make out, Marcia. His father was a dentist! And I love the little box he gave me and I love him—even if his name is Percy!"

She started to sniff again and I almost felt like joining in, Davy. It ought to have been funny, but there was suddenly something so child-like and defenceless about Daphne that the situation was robbed of its humor and became merely pathetic. And yet, I can understand why the sophisticated Mrs. Clapp, who is genuinely fond of her, wants to save her from making a fool of herself. There's a great deal to be said for both points of view.

"Daphne, dear," said Mrs. Clapp a little more gently, "why won't you trust me more? I'll give you all you want. You'll have heaps of opportunities to meet interesting people in South America. Indeed, I am sure a great many men of your own class and—er—size would think you a very fine figure of a woman. Don't snap up the first man who offers—"

"Nonsense. You know I'm a fright," snapped Daphne, blowing her nose again and recovering her self-possession with extraordinary rapidity. "And don't start to tell me I'm a noble character. I've heard it all before. And I'm going to marry him, Marcia, so that's that, tantrums or no tantrums. And now I'm going to play off the tennis semi-finals. We'd have won the shuffleboard yesterday if you hadn't been flirting with that brown-faced young man from the third class." Then she added crossly, "Talk about snapping men up. Who has a chance with you about?"

At first I thought Daphne must be pulling the old lady's leg, Davy, but she was obviously in earnest. Indeed she was just about to stalk out of the room when I remembered that it was her swain who was waiting for her on the upper deck. As her nose was shining like the Pole Star, I begged her, in the name of womanhood and decency, to fix herself up a bit. She retired to the bedroom without a word and finally left, slamming both doors after her. Mrs. Clapp was not to have a monopoly on tantrums!

When she had gone I was invited quite amicably to stay and have a chat. Like most actresses, Marcia Manners is one of the vainest creatures on God's earth, Davy (not without reason, of course), and I soon had her in the best of humors. We talked about Daphne for a while and then very cunningly I shifted the conversation to Mrs. Clapp's attraction for men and the brown-faced young man in particular. Suddenly I sprung my bolt.

"There's a man on board who reminds me very much of your nephew, Alfred Lambert. I met him once some time ago," I added mendaciously. "I wondered if perhaps—"

"Alfred! On *this* boat!" Her face had gone very pale. "Why that's impossible. He's in the Argentine. And how on earth did you know him?"

My reply was evasive, Davy, but she was looking at me so hard and so searchingly that I felt positive she could see through my little strategy. Her tone, however, was elaborately casual as she continued:

"Talking of Alfred reminds me that I really ought to call on Mrs. Lambert. After all, I am in a sense related to her. She's Alfred's stepmother, though he'd hate to admit it. And I'm his aunt. I haven't even offered her my sympathy yet, though I know she knows that I consider her very well rid of *that* old tomcat. I don't want the wretched woman to think I'm a hypocrite."

"Talking of cats," I expostulated weakly, "I don't think Mrs. Lambert is a wretched woman at all. I quite like her now."

"Oh, she's attractive enough as a person, my dear, but the world's worst actress. The very, *very* worst. And her old noodle of a husband simply used to force her into all the best parts in his shows. It was quite a scandal. Still, I think I'll go and see her. What's happened to the rather nice looking man who was her husband's secretary? The one like John Gilbert or Ramon Novarro or someone? Yes, I'll certainly go and see her."

"That would be very kind," I said. "And you would be just the person to take poor Mr. Earnshaw out of himself a bit. Betty's death has upset him fearfully. The only time I've seen him look like a human being since then was the night of your monologue. He admires you—your acting tremendously."

"Yes, that's a good idea," she said musingly. "I ought to call on Mrs. Lambert. I'd better get out my black again, I think. Have you seen this little model I got from Lelong? It's very suitable."

We talked a bit more, Davy, about nothing in particular, but she resisted my every effort to bring the conversation back to young Lambert. Frankly, I was afraid to press her, as I felt I had already been clumsy in approaching the subject. Marcia Manners is the most kaleidoscopic of people and you never know which of her many personalities she is going to switch on next. Just as I was leaving, I remembered my second mission.

"Have you entered the bridge tournament?" I asked.

"No, my dear," she replied, as she performed some mystic operation on her face before the mirror. "The men are all so hideous on the boat that there's not one I could bear to have sit in front of me for two hours on end."

"How about the man in the third class that Daphne spoke of?" I asked innocently.

Mrs. Clapp looked very red as she removed a thick gelatinous substance from her chin and cheeks.

"Hardly *convenable,* my dear. People would talk. Now I wonder if Mr. Earnshaw—or perhaps it's all too recent."

"Good idea!" I remarked, "and he is certainly easier on the eyes than some."

After this I took my leave with the happy thought that, even if I haven't found out much, I have at least given Mrs. Lambert and Earnshaw a chance to do their own probing with regard to the mysterious young Alfred.

But, I almost forgot to tell you the big news. She's offered me

Daphne's job if the marriage really comes off at Georgetown. I told her that I had other plans, in which you are intimately concerned, Davy boy. We compromised on my writing her biography the next time she's in New York. I shall call it, YOUNG MEN I HAVE MARRIED or BETWEEN BOX OFFICE AND ALTAR.

But for all her frivolity and her fickleness with husbands and companions, Marcia is no fool either.

In fact, she's a very clever woman. Never forget that, Davy dear.

Stateroom,
Saturday, November 21st.
6:30 P. M.

By this time, Davy, I imagine you are just about as sick of theories as I am. Everybody seems to have one and they are all different.

But, at least—as the dear little boy said when he saw the "Sign of the Cross"—"there's one poor lion that ain't got no Christian." For I myself have no theory. In fact, I'm in such a fog listening to other people's that I really don't know what I do think about it all. All I know is that everyone seems to suspect someone else, whereas to my mind no one is above suspicion, least of all, perhaps, the most subtle of the theorists. The trouble is that there are too many suspects and all too few tangible clues.

Now, at the risk of boring you I must tell you all about Adam's theory—and a perfectly startling one it is too. We spilled the beans to each other on the upper deck this afternoon.

It was too hot to do anything but talk, so I got gossipy and told him all about my visit to Mrs. Lambert and Earnshaw. After that I gave him a somewhat exaggerated and facetious account of my interview with Mrs. Clapp and Daphne earlier in the day. He listened very attentively, as though he were balancing my words in relation to some ideas of his own. After I had finished he did not speak for several minutes. Finally he said:

"You know, Mary, for several days now I've had a perfectly fantastic notion which I haven't dared to mention even to you—in the first place, because you are such a lioness in defense of your own sex, in the second place, because I don't want you to think me more of a nut than you do at present."

"You're nutta nutta tall," I remarked flippantly. "But what has my sex got to do with it?"

"Nothing has struck you as odd about at least two people on the boat? No? Well, let me explain something in your unsophisticated little ear. You've been in love, I presume."

"Your presumption," I replied, "is perfectly justified, but we didn't come up here to discuss love."

Adam sighed romantically. "Alas, no. But I must remind you that two of our fellow passengers are on the brink of matrimony. Neither of them is what you might vulgarly describe as a spring chicken. Neither of them can be said to exude that strange indefinable something which used commonly to be known as sex appeal. I cannot speak for Daniels' hidden charms, but as a mere man of normal instincts it is impossible for me to understand how any male under six feet ten can possibly be in love with that armor-plated Amazon who—"

"Rot," I said angrily, "just because you are crazy about brainless little nincompoops with nothing but curls or curves to recommend them, it doesn't follow that some men haven't got enough gumption to like a sensible sort of woman, even if she isn't any lingerie ad."

Adam sighed and patted the region of his belt. "I like you, my dear. You have curls, curves and brains, but you interrupt me frightfully, and, like all women, you make things so unpleasantly personal. Look at the thing more judicially. Daniels is a detective, as we know. He comes on board this ship and presumably falls head over heels in love with this great big penniless Englishwoman. Of what does the courtship consist? Billets-doux which she shows round to all and sundry; boxes of chocolate which are so large that no one could fail to see them; compliments which are so loud that the whole boat hears them. But have we ever caught them whispering sweet nothings into each other's ears by moonlight? Have we seen them deliberately trying to escape the public gaze? Have we seen them doing all those hundred and one little things which you and I would be doing if it had happened to us? We have not."

"When the really big things in life happen to us," I protested, "we don't give a damn about the public. And poor little Daniels is far too busy trying to solve two mysteries to have any time for sweet nothings on the upper deck."

"And then Mrs. Clapp," he continued, ignoring my interruption. "Why does she make so much fuss about Daphne's laggard lover? Why does she act as though this young Lochinvar from Scotland Yard had come to steal a pearl of great price? Why does she lay such emphasis on Daphne's womanhood? Why—because I don't believe that Daphne is a woman at all and I don't believe that Daniels believes it either."

He got up and started to pace excitedly up and down the deck.

"Now," he continued, "let's go back to Earnshaw's theory, which fits in admirably with mine. He suspects that young Alfred Lambert is on board this ship. He says that he and Mrs. Clapp are—or have been—friendly. She is his aunt. Now do you see what I'm driving at? Now do you understand Daniels' motive in these preposterous attentions towards a woman twice his size?"

"Yes, yes, I see your idea," I cried, "but you are missing one very important point in feminine psychology, Adam Burr. You are—"

• • • •

Later,
Stateroom.

The rest of that sentence, Davy, will never, never be written. So many terrible things have happened since I started to write it that my views on feminine psychology must pass into the limbo of things unimportant and forgotten.

My hand is still shaking so that, as you will see for yourself, my writing is almost illegible. But let me reassure you, darling—I'm locked and bolted in my stateroom now and there is a grim-faced guard in the corridor outside. And I am still alive and completely unharmed—that's something to be thankful for.

I was just finishing up my last installment at about seven o'clock this evening—in a hurry as usual, as it was about time to dress for dinner. And, as usual, I was sitting on the foot of my berth, the writing pad on my knee and my back to the door. The ship was very quiet. Suddenly I heard a faint noise behind my head and, at the same moment, the awful thought came to me that I had forgotten to slip the bolt. Without daring to move, I lifted my eyes to the mirror above the wash basin. Even in the dim light of my cabin I could see that my door was slowly opening!

The minute that followed was so packed with sensation that it seemed to last for hours, and I could go on describing it for pages. I remember shrinking into myself as I huddled against the side of the narrow berth, back of the door which, silently and relentlessly, was opening to give something entrance into my room. The noise of the engines, even the occasional lapping of the waves against the porthole, seemed to have ceased for a moment, as if the ship itself and the very elements were waiting to listen—watching to see what would happen.

There was a bell at the head of my bed—just out of reach. But I did not dare to move a finger towards it. Some deep-rooted instinct, some sixth sense told me to keep perfectly still because I knew it was important that I should see who was entering my room. This instinct (call it curiosity, if you like) must have been even stronger than the thought of self-preservation.

I was gazing into the mirror, fascinated—like a rabbit watching the deadly approach of a weasel. In the gradual widening space between the edge of the door and the jamb I could still see nothing except the dim outline of the stateroom opposite. And then, suddenly—stealthily—the reflection of a face appeared in the glass; a face pressed, listening, against my door. It became more and more distinct, and then—Davy, even now my head reels when I think of it and my heart thumps so hard that it seems to shake the earth.

In the mirror I saw it was—Robinson!

Even in the dim obscurity there was no mistaking him, though either it was too dark or I was far too upset to take in any details that might throw further light on his identity. But all the things I remember were there—the thick glasses, the thick brown hair, and that *smoothly* smooth tanned face. The features were commonplace enough and yet somehow they inspired a feeling of revulsion and horror that was almost overwhelming. My hands grow cold and clammy as I recall them.

At first I thought he did not see me. He was peering around the room as though looking for something. By now I could tell that he was dressed in a dark suit and wore a black tie. Then I saw something else. It was the dull gleam of blue steel in his hand. Davy darling, he had a revolver.

I am thankful that I was too petrified to scream. I know that, had I done so, I should not be writing this to you. One sign of the panic I felt—one false move towards the bell—and it would have been all over. But as he stood there behind me and I watched his blurred reflection in the mirror, I lived through an eternity.

Then, suddenly, I felt something that was even colder and more deadly than the numbness of my own senses. There was a slight movement in the mirror and I was conscious of the pressure of cold steel against my left shoulder—a horrible, *downward* pressure which told me that his revolver was pointed towards my heart.

At that moment, Davy, I felt positive he was going to kill me as he had undoubtedly killed Mr. Lambert and Betty. A thousand thoughts flashed through my head in the split fraction of a second. I thought of you and asked myself, for some absurd reason, whether you would be left saddled with our new apartment. I thought of Adam and the others on board ship who would try frantically to solve this third mystery. Then I found myself wondering whether death would be painful and began to speculate philosophically as to what would come next. I suppose desperation must have lent me a certain amount of courage, or indifference, for I suddenly heard myself saying in a voice that seemed to come from miles away:

"Please, Mr. Robinson, get it over with quickly. Your pistol is hurting my shoulder."

There was a fragment of a laugh from behind me: a malevolent little cackle. The pressure of the steel was increased until I felt that he must be boring a hole right through me. Normally it would have been agonizing, but I was so anesthetized by the horror of the situation that I did not really feel the pain. The spot is still livid on my skin.

"Don't move a muscle and above all, don't turn your head!" The high-pitched voice, obviously another part of the disguise, was exactly as I remembered it during that fatal bridge party.

I sat perfectly still, but my eyes were still watching him in the mirror.

"I shan't hurt you if you do exactly what I tell you. I want that journal of yours—get up and get it *without turning round!*"

Still I did not move.

"Get up," he repeated.

"Mr. Robinson," I said in a low voice, "my journal is locked in the captain's safe with the exception of these two pages. If you would like to come with me I will be glad to go and fetch it—or, perhaps, you would rather wait."

The pressure of the revolver barrel against my back was somewhat relaxed.

"You swear it isn't here?"

"I swear it. And I'm afraid you've wasted your time."

Once again I heard that ominous little laugh. "I've wasted my time, have I?" he muttered. "Well, it won't be altogether wasted—"

As he spoke there was a click and the cabin was plunged into comparative darkness. He had turned off the lamp behind me. I could no longer see his face in the mirror, but I knew he was there because I still felt, or imagined I felt, the pressure of the revolver on my shoulder.

Then something happened, Davy, the very thought of which makes me feel sick with horror at this moment. An arm was thrown about my neck and I felt my head tilted backward. Before I realized what was happening, I was conscious of warm human breath in my nostrils and a mouth was pressed against mine in the most loathsome kiss it is possible to imagine. And even at the time I know why it was so loathsome.

Davy darling, his lips tasted of *blood!*

Something snapped inside my brain. Let him shoot; let him kill me; let him do anything, but I had to escape from that hideous embrace—from the horror of those vampire lips. I struggled like a fly in a spider-web but the arm around my neck felt like a steel band. I could not cry out. The pressure of the mouth was stifling against mine. Then suddenly, I caught the faint outline of the bell. My arm was close against the button. With all my strength I pushed against it, grinding my elbow into the socket.

I don't quite know what happened next, but suddenly I heard the door slam and realized—with what relief you can imagine—that I was alone. Far in the distance I could hear the peal of the bell. Louder and louder it sounded until it seemed that the whole ship must hear it. Surely Trubshaw would come; surely someone was near at hand to help me. But there were no reassuring footsteps.

I staggered into the corridor. "Steward, steward," I screamed. But still the ever-faithful Trubshaw did not appear. The passengers were busy dressing for dinner and, though two or three female heads popped out of doors for a moment, no one came to my assistance.

At last (and I suppose all this actually took about three seconds of time) my middle-aged stewardess came bustling up.

"Is there anything I can do, Miss?" she said. "Mr. Trubshaw don't seem to be here and I was off duty, but—" Then she gave one look at my bleeding mouth and dishevelled hair—"are you hurt, Miss?"

"A man," I gasped, "did you see a man in a dark suit leave my stateroom?"

"I passed one in the passage just now," she said. "He went into the gents' lavatory—"

"Go after him," I yelled. "Quick!"

The stewardess hesitated a moment while modesty warred with her desire to be helpful. Then, she turned and hurried down the passageway. Within a few seconds she was back.

"He must of gone out the other door," she said shaking her head. "It leads into the next corridor. All the lavatories have two exits."

By this time, Davy, a number of people had appeared from various neighboring staterooms and started to make the usual fatuous inquiries.

"It's nothing," I said. "I bit my lip. Will you send Trubshaw to me, Mrs. Wilson?" As I spoke the steward appeared looking pale and frightened.

"Miss Llewellyn," he gasped, "can you come at once? It's Mrs. Lambert." He drew me aside. "She—she—oh, I don't know, but I think she's *dead.*"

Dressed as I was in the flimsiest of wrappers, I started to run towards the widow's stateroom.

"Trubshaw," I cried. "Go and fetch Dr. Somers. Send him here at once—and Mr. Daniels. I'll do what I can for her. Only hurry, hurry—"

When I reached Mrs. Lambert's suite, I stood for a moment in the sitting room. It was empty, except for a frightened young waiter cowering in a corner, but there was an untouched dinner tray on a side table and all around the tiny escritoire was an untidy mass of paper. The drawers were thrown wide open and everything was in wild disorder as though someone had been looking eagerly for something which he could not find.

With fast-beating heart I went towards the bedroom door and threw it open. There on the floor, lying diagonally across the room, lay the body of Mrs. Lambert.

I was at her side in an instant, my head against her left breast to see if I could detect her heartbeat. But, before I could decide whether or not life was extinct, I saw something which made me recoil.

On her white negligée, just above the heart, was a vivid spot of fresh blood, still damp and gleaming—

At this moment the door behind me opened and Dr. Somers came in, black bag in hand.

"Would you mind taking her feet?" he said after he made a rapid examination. "I want to get her on the bed."

Together we lifted Mrs. Lambert's prostrate body. Then Dr. Somers turned and started to fumble in his bag.

"Is she—is she dead?" I asked breathlessly.

"Dead! Not a bit of it." There was the usual professional cheerfulness in his tone. "She's had a nasty shock, but I think she'll come to in a minute."

"But the blood," I exclaimed. "It looked as though she's been shot—or stabbed."

Instead of answering, the ship's surgeon pulled aside the wrapper and disclosed Mrs. Lambert's firm white breasts. To my intense relief there was no wound or abrasion on their smooth surface.

"The blood probably dropped from your mouth, Miss Llewellyn," he remarked. "You've bitten your lip quite badly. Let me put something on it for you."

"Oh, never mind me," I said impatiently. "I can wait."

Dr. Somers was breaking a small capsule under Mrs. Lamberts' nose. She gave a tiny sneeze and then her eyes opened.

As long as I live, Davy, I shall never forget the look of stark terror in her eyes.

"Robinson!" she whispered. Then she sank back on her pillow.

The surgeon returned to his bag, poured something into a tiny medicine glass and forced it between Mrs. Lambert's closed lips. A faint tinge of color was coming back to her cheeks.

"She'll be all right," he said, "her pulse is strong. Now I want to put some antiseptic on your mouth."

While he swabbed my lips, there came a sound of voices from the small sitting room adjoining. Daniels and Trubshaw were apparently having a heated discussion. I could hear the steward's story quite distinctly.

He had been passing Mrs. Lambert's suite at about seven o'clock, he said, when he met the pantry boy coming with her dinner tray. (She's taken all her meals in her room ever since the tragedy.) He wanted to ask Mrs. Lambert if he could do anything for her, so he knocked on the door, but there was no answer. He tried the door and it was unlocked, so they went in. As soon as he entered the sitting room he saw the mess of papers around the writing desk. Growing alarmed, he knocked at the bedroom door; there was no answer. He pushed it and found it locked. Hearing nothing when he called, he went to get the pass key, opened the door, and found Mrs. Lambert lying on the floor as we had found her. He told the boy to stay where he was. He was running for help when he heard the frantic ringing of the bell and saw me standing outside my stateroom looking, as he picturesquely put it, "like she'd just caught the tail-end of a typhoon with stern awash."

Dr. Somers had now finished painting my lips with mercurochrome, so I went into the sitting room and gave Daniels my version of Robinson's visit. He did not wait till I got to the end before he turned to Trubshaw and asked him if he had seen anyone answering Robinson's description anywhere near the Lambert suite.

Poor Trubshaw went white.

"Y—yes, sir," he stammered, his eyes widening at the sudden recollection. "Just before I got to this room, I saw a gent like that coming away from it, but I didn't think anything of it because I don't know all the passengers by sight anyhow."

"Where did he go?"

"I'm sorry, sir, I didn't notice," Trubshaw said. "He turned the corner—"

Daniels turned sharply to the pantry boy.

"Did you see him too?" he snapped.

"N—no, sir," the kid managed to say; he was shaking with fright. "That is—I saw his back—but I didn't pay no attention—"

Daniels turned back to Trubshaw; he ordered:

"Go up and tell the purser what's happened. The man must be about somewhere. A search should be made at once—now, while the passengers are in the dining saloon."

"And send Miss Bush to me immediately," added Dr. Somers, as the steward left the room. "Mrs. Lambert will need a nurse tonight."

Trubshaw hurried off and Daniels went over to the writing desk.

"Looks as if he's been here too," he muttered. "I wonder if anything is missing."

"Earnshaw could probably tell us," I suggested. "Let me go and fetch him."

Daniels nodded distractedly and I went off to Earnshaw's cabin, which I knew was situated halfway between Mrs. Lambert's and mine. There was no answer when I knocked, so I pushed open the door. It was an inner cabin and therefore almost completely dark, but in the light from the corridor I saw a white figure lying on the bed. I could tell it was Earnshaw because the dark blot of his moustache stood out against the white background of his face. He was wearing an open shirt and cotton trousers.

"Mr. Earnshaw," I cried; but there was no answer.

I must have been in a thoroughly morbid state of mind, Davy, because it flashed through my mind at once that something had happened to him too. As my hand fumbled for the light switch I found myself vaguely wondering what new horror I should see now. The sound of deep, regular breathing greeted my ears like music. Earnshaw was asleep.

I turned on the switch. He stirred and rubbed his eyes. As I moved forward to shake him by the arms I almost upset his dinner tray which lay, untouched, upon a chair.

"Come quickly," I said. "It's Mrs. Lambert—"

He jumped up like a flash. "Good God, she's not—"

"No, it's not serious, but we think there's been a robbery. You're needed."

As we hurried down the corridor I told him in a few words what had happened.

"The damned swine!" he muttered.

"And he must have gone straight from her room to mine!" I rejoined, as we reached Mrs. Lambert's door.

We were greeted by Daniels and Dr. Somers, who informed us that Mrs. Lambert could now talk to us. We were only allowed five minutes, however, as he had given her a strong sedative which would, so he hoped, shortly take effect.

Miss Bush, the ship's nurse, was seated at Mrs. Lambert's bedside when we entered. The widow was propped up on her pillows, still deathly pale, but she gave Earnshaw a brave smile when she saw him.

"I'm sorry to have been such a fool," she said in a low, tremulous tone, "but I've had such an awful shock and—and—"

"Don't distress yourself," said the young surgeon. "The story can wait, if you'd rather."

"No, no," cried Mrs. Lambert fiercely. "I want to tell you now because it may help you to catch that fiend. Ugh—" She turned her head as if to escape some painful memory. Then she continued in a calmer tone. "I was in here reading, just before dinner. I am—at least I was—feeling a little better today. I heard someone in the sitting room and thought, naturally it was the boy with my tray. I got up and opened the door. Standing at the desk was a man in a dark suit. His back was turned toward me, and he was busy going through the drawers of the writing table. Then he must have heard me for he wheeled round suddenly. In the light from the reading lamp on the desk I could see his features quite plainly. There was no doubt about it at all. It was my husband's murderer—the man who called himself Robinson. He looked exactly the same as he did the last time I saw him—just after he had thrown poor little Betty overboard. For a moment we stood staring at each other—then he gave a funny, horrible sort of laugh and raised his right hand slowly and deliberately. In it he held a revolver, which was now pointed straight at me. Luckily I was standing on my side of the door, and I just had the presence of mind to step back, slam and lock it. Then—then I'm afraid I don't remember any more."

This recital had evidently tired Mrs. Lambert, for her head sank wearily back on her pillow. Dr. Somers made a sign that it was time for us to leave. We returned to the sitting room.

"I wonder what he was after," said little Daniels reflectively, as he gazed down at the mass of papers on the desk.

"Let me look," cried Earnshaw.

Daniels moved aside and the secretary started to go through the loose papers in a thoroughly business-like way. There were a number of private letters, bon-voyage telegrams and the like. These he piled carefully on one side. At length he turned and faced us.

"I thought as much," he said. "Mr. Lambert's will is missing. It was in this drawer—"

"Heavens!" cried Daniels, "why on earth should anyone want to steal that?"

Earnshaw turned towards me. "You remember I showed it to you yesterday, Miss Llewellyn? It was only a copy, of course. The original is with his lawyer in New York. It's no good to anyone, but it does at least help to prove the point I was trying to make to you yesterday. This Robinson must be someone who had a vital interest in the disposition of Mr. Lambert's property."

And he appears also to have a vital interest in my journal. In fact he seems to suffer from what Kipling would call " 'satiable curiosity" about quite a number of things.

Stateroom,
Saturday, November 21st.
9:30 P. M.

I drank every drop of Adam's champagne, Davy, and it fortified me sufficiently to get dressed, to make the most of what Robinson had left me in the way of looks, and totter upstairs to play my modest part in the bridge tournament. It was supposed to start at 8:30.

When I reached the social hall I found everything all ready and the dear old ladies were saying, "Can you please direct me to table number eight?" or "I used to play a great deal of whist in the old days but I'm afraid I haven't mastered this new-fangled contract yet." And from the younger people one heard the usual nervous inquiries: "Do you use Lenz or the official system?" "Two forcing bid—you must keep it open," and, "My dear, Culbertson is not a *man,* he's a disease." Judging the skill of the participants by their conversation, I was rather glad I was scheduled to have a headache for the evening. And it wasn't going to take much acting. My interview with Robinson had left me limp as a rag that is temporarily buoyed up on a few champagne bubbles.

I had scarcely time to look around when Adam came over

and pounced on me. After thanking him for his most uplifting present, I proceeded to give him some of the highspots of the afternoon's entertainment.

"You poor dear!" he exclaimed when I had finished. "And Daniels told me that the brute actually bit your lip!"

"Now that I come to think it over, I'm not so sure that he really did," I said reflectively. "Of course I'd like to pose as a martyr, but, as a matter of fact, I probably bit it myself before he started to maul me. I was so petrified I might have bitten my tongue in two without feeling it."

"Well," Adam reassured me, "you look very handsome with that mercurochrome mouth. And there's an idea for you to make a million dollars, Mary. Why not patent the idea of putting up mercurochrome in a lipstick—hygienic, antiseptic and cosmetic all at once—and permanent too!"

At this moment Daphne entered by another door with her partner, the silent Sutton.

"And speaking of cosmetics," Adams continued, "have you noticed our Daphne tonight? All dressed up for the final extermination of poor little Daniels. Where nature fails, art has stepped in. And, incidentally, both she and Mrs. Clapp were very late for dinner this evening. So was Silvera."

I turned my eyes towards Miss Demarest. Indeed she looked, as Mrs. Clapp would have put it, a very fine figure of a woman. Her dress was an epic poem, long and trailing; her eyes and mouth were skilfully made up and she had obviously had the best finger-wave the ship's barber has to offer. I could even detect traces of a facial in the rosy glow of her skin.

I turned again to Adam. I saw that he was giving me what the novelists describe as a "meaning" look. "Did you hear me say that both Mrs. Clapp and her companion were very late for dinner tonight?" he repeated.

I knew exactly what he implied but I chose to ignore it. "I'm not surprised," I replied, "those movie effects take time. They are called forth only by prayer and fasting. Wait till you see Mrs. Clapp. I'll bet she's a knockout. Daphne won't be allowed to get away with a thing."

"If Robinson got into dinner on time, he had to make a mighty quick change," said Adam stolidly.

I could not longer ignore the implication.

"Look here, Adam Burr," I said with some heat, "yesterday you expounded a cock-and-bull theory about Robinson being a woman or Daphne being a man—or something. Well, you can forget it. I've got two things to tell you that will scatter your little brain-storm to the four winds of heaven. In the first place the conversation which I overheard on the night of the fancy dress dance was between Mrs. Clapp and Daphne. Marcia admitted that she was simply trying to persuade Daphne to stay single for her sake—"

"Nice way for two women to talk," muttered Adam.

"Oh, you hundred per cent normal he-man, you," I cried excitedly. "You'll never see anything that isn't an inch in front of your nose. Mrs. Clapp is a temperamental creature who likes to dramatize things. Her emotions aren't really a bit deep so she makes the most of them while they last. I don't believe there was anything in it at all, except the normal desire of an old woman to keep a useful servant attached to her. And no wonder, seeing all the things Daphne does for her."

"Well, Mary, I think I ought to tell you something which I've discovered, though I must admit I'm not very proud of my discovery—nor of my methods."

Adam was blushing and looking down like an old-fashioned débutante. I was not going to say anything to help him.

"Yes," he stammered. "I got—er—Trubshaw to let me have a peep in Mrs. Clapp's suite yesterday—while she and Daphne were on deck. The first thing—the very first thing I saw was a safety razor lying on the washstand in the bedroom. Now—!" His voice had risen to a crescendo of triumph.

I gave him what is usually called *one look.* He winced.

"Mr. Burr," I said at length, "you must have been a widower for a very, very long time. Or you must have lived a particularly sheltered life lately. Haven't you any sisters to explain the facts of life to you? If not, I must inform you that what with sleeveless evening dresses and other modern fashions—women need—er—certain timely aids to beauty which they did not need perhaps when you were a boy. But I would prefer not to enlarge on it, as it is a subject that presents but few attractions."

Adam turned to me with a puzzled, guilty expression, shook himself and said reproachfully:

"You always sound so positive, Mary."

"Well, at least I'm positive of one thing," I replied. "Robinson is a man. That kiss carried conviction. There was strength in that arm. Ugh—! No woman could have done what he did to me. No woman would have wanted to."

Adam smiled at me and patted my bruised shoulder in a manner that was annoyingly pitying and paternal.

"Sometimes," he said, "I don't think you are very subtle, Mary Llewellyn. This afternoon you gave me a long lecture on feminine psychology, now it's my turn to give you the masculine point of view. There isn't a male living who would get any kick out of kissing a girl at the point of a revolver that way. Remember, Robinson is a hunted criminal to whom every second is precious. Presumably he is not a Frankenstein or a Dracula. I believe that kiss was a mere gesture."

"You're not very flattering, Mr. Burr."

He ignored my interruption. "And a mere gesture that no sensible man would make, however much he might want to. I don't mean to detract for a minute from your personal attractions, my dear, but let us look things squarely in the face. A snatched embrace is too high a price for any man to pay who runs the risk of capture and death. A clever woman, on the other hand, might make such a gesture in order to try and put people off the scent. She knows that is the thing which is expected from the villain of the piece—"

"All that I can say, Adam, is that you were not the recipient of the kiss."

He took a long pull at his cigar and then stubbed the glowing butt in a fern-pot. He looked at me quizzically.

"Mary," he said softly, "what would be your impression if I were to kiss you now?"

"Rage," I said sweetly, with some amusement.

"No, no. I don't mean that. I mean your physical impressions."

I turned away. "Come, come, we are getting too analytical altogether."

Adam looked quite embarrassed for a moment, then he stammered out: "Oh, dear, my vocabulary is so weak, but my remark really was quite innocent. Of course, I know my kiss would leave you absolutely cold, but at least you'd get the impression of cigar smoke and Yardley's shaving soap. If I had kissed you before I shaved for dinner, you would have the impression of whiskers. Now, do you see what I'm driving at?"

"Adam," I cried, "I apologize. You really aren't so dumb after all. Of course, I see what you mean, and I never thought of it myself. I'm the only person on the boat who knows what Robinson *smells* like. Let me think. Well, apart from the blood, which was probably my own, I have a hazy impression that he might have smoked a cigarette within the last half hour. There was a suggestion of cold cream or something faintly scented and there were no whiskers. Definitely no whiskers. Oh, and one more thing. I don't believe he smokes a pipe because my boy friend in New York does and I'd know that smell anywhere. Now, do you want me to go round kissing every man on board until I find the right combination?"

Adam chuckled. "That's asking a bit too much, my dear; but no whiskers and cold cream—! Men don't generally use cold cream, you know."

"They do if they are disguising themselves as someone else," I answered. "Or it may have been grease paint. I'm not an expert on smells I'm afraid. No, you can't persuade me it wasn't a man and for all your unflattering and ungallant explanations, it was a man who definitely wanted to kiss me, though who on this ship has that desire I can't imagine."

"Well, my dear," replied Adam softly, "of course I don't want to incriminate myself, but—I can!"

Mr. Wolcott appeared opportunely at this juncture and solemnly wagged his goatee over my hand. "It's a great pleasure," said the old humbug ponderously, "to be playing tonight with someone who really has a feeling for bridge."

For a few moments the three of us stood talking in a corner as we watched the last stragglers take their places. Silvera was playing with the large woman who had burst in upon our momentous game the day before. Jennings had conscientiously volunteered to partner an old whist-fiend with an ear trumpet. Mr.

Hirsch was seated opposite his wife. Then Adam left us to join a vapid young thing with a Greta Garbo haircut.

Wolcott and I were just about to take our places when there was a rustle near the entrance and Mrs. Clapp swam into the room, magnificent in a white satin gown whose startling severity was relieved by a heavy silken fringe. She was closely followed by a tired and handsome Earnshaw. A little knot of people clustered around to pay a final tribute to Fame. Every man in the room strove for a glance or a nod of recognition, and every woman present knew that Marcia had made them all look hopelessly dowdy. Wolcott was swept from my side.

I seized my opportunity for a few words with Earnshaw.

"Any news?" I whispered.

"No," he answered, as he passed a hand over his smooth, dark hair. "There was nothing else missing that I could see and Mrs. Lambert is sleeping soundly. Otherwise, I couldn't have come tonight. I hate doing it, but—well, Mrs. Clapp might drop a hint about her nephew, and I promised her anyhow. I hope you are feeling better yourself, Miss Llewellyn. You've still got a nasty mark on your shoulder."

"I'm not so hot," I whispered. "Look out for men with bleeding lips—I hope I bit the brute."

Then we all took our places and Jennings announced the rules. I dealt the first hand, saw that it was a rotten one, and immediately decided that the moment for my headache had arrived. The purser was summoned; Daniels appeared like magic and the substitution proceeded according to schedule. I was not sorry to get away.

When I came down to my stateroom I saw the guard sitting at an intersection which commands a view of Mrs. Lambert's suite and my cabin. He has the nose of a boxer and a torso like Jim Londos', so if Robinson goes on the prowl again tonight he'll probably meet his match.

None the less, sweetheart, I prefer to trust in the Lord and a good stout lock.

• • • •

Later.

I got undressed after I'd finished writing to you and settled down in bed with a novel—a detective story you gave me by that friend of yours, Quentin Patrick.* I found it very nice and restful after the thrills and horrors of his voyage—pleasant milk and water after a steady diet of highballs. And, as I read it, I couldn't help thinking if your ingenious buddy can make so much out of a synthetic situation in a New York literary agency, what could he not do with a real, red-hot, full-blooded sort of mystery such as we've been having on board the *S. S. Murder?*

Still, I'll admit the book kept me awake and held my attention so that it came as a distinct shock when I heard people coming down from the bridge tournament at about twelve o'clock. Presently there was a little tap at my door. I jumped up in bed.

"Who's there?" I cried.

It was Trubshaw's voice. "There's nothing to be afraid of, Miss. Just a gentleman wants to speak to you—he says it's urgent."

From his tone, my dear, you might have thought I was in the habit of entertaining gentlemen at this hour every night of my life.

"But who is it, Trubshaw? I'm in bed and asleep."

---

*I presume the book to which Miss Llewellyn makes this not very flattering reference is *Death for Dear Clara* (Popular Library, No. 8)—Q. P.

"It's Mr. Daniels, Miss. He says, could you—would you mind giving him a minute. He seems a bit upset, but—he's got a plate of sandwiches for you, Miss."

Well, Davy, I suppose a detective who's in love with another girl is safe enough and I was ravenously hungry anyhow, so I slipped on my wrapper and told Trubshaw to show the gentleman in. I had a shock when I saw his face. He looked so unhappy and perplexed, and so embarrassed at finding me in bed that he was almost inarticulate. In order to put him at his ease, I greeted him with perfect nonchalance and promptly grabbed a sandwich.

"Miss Llewellyn," he stammered at length, "I must apologize—indeed, I must—for troubling you this way: especially as you are probably tired out after your very—er—unpleasant experience of this afternoon. But I've come to appeal to you in the name of the line—you are the only person who can help us."

"What on earth has happened, Mr. Daniels?" I asked. "Here, have a sandwich. It will calm you down. You're all jumpy. Didn't your little scheme work?"

The detective pulled a handkerchief out of his pocket and mopped his face. "Yes," he said slowly, "it worked—in a way. Then again in another way it's caused more of a muddle than ever. You see, someone made both the mistakes Robinson made—led the jack of clubs in the first hand and the jack of diamonds in the second. In fact, as Wolcott has just pointed out to me, this same person led a jack, right or wrong, every time there was a jack to lead; they seemed to have a—er—what d'you call it—fixture on leading jacks, just as Robinson did—but the whole trouble is, I'm absolutely certain *that this person could not possibly have been Robinson!*"

"Good God," I cried, now thoroughly excited, "who on earth was it?"

Daniels shook his head. "Wild horses wouldn't drag the name from me, Miss Llewellyn. It's unthinkable—utterly and absolutely unthinkable. It just doesn't fit. Nothing fits. That's why I'm here."

"Well, you might at least tell me and let me form my own conclusions."

The little man shook his head sadly, then continued: "Miss Llewellyn, you may think I've been idling my time away on board this ship. As a matter of fact I've worked like a nigger. It's been no holiday for me. I know a great many things that are not in your journal. For instance I could tell you—approximately, that is—where almost every passenger on the boat was when Mr. Lambert was poisoned. I have a list of all the people who were up and about when poor Miss Betty was thrown overboard. I have a pretty good idea—though this is a lot harder to establish definitely—which of the passengers might have been in a position to make that attack on you and Mrs. Lambert this afternoon. Of course, I don't say I know about everyone, but at least I have a list of the passengers who have alibis for these times. It's meant a deal of work for me, but it doesn't look as if it's going to help much, because, you see, the person who made those mistakes tonight at the bridge table is on all three of my lists as having a perfect alibi in each instance. Now, do you see how hopeless it is to fit things in?"

"But, Mr. Daniels," I said, "you are ignoring two possibilities, surely. Perhaps Robinson really is not a disguise at all. Perhaps he's a real person still hiding somewhere about the ship—or, perhaps he's not a passenger."

The detective gave me a strange look and his voice dropped

to a mysterious whisper. "That might be true as you say, Miss Llewellyn, but it so happens that Robinson was in the social hall tonight while we were playing bridge. He left a—a message!"

As he said this, Davy, a horribly uncanny sensation began to creep over me. For the first time I began to feel that we must be wrestling with something that was not of human flesh—that the powers of darkness were abroad on the *Moderna.* I shivered and pulled my wrapper more closely around my shoulders.

"Don't be alarmed," said Daniels, as he consolingly passed the plate of sandwiches. "It was nothing very terrifying, but it does give us definite proof that he was in the bridge room tonight."

Here he pulled a document from his pocket and handed it to me. One glimpse showed me that it was the copy of Mr. Lambert's will which had been stolen from his widow's stateroom that afternoon. On the back, in the same crabbed printing which I knew so well, had been scrawled:

I'VE SEEN ALL I WANT.
THANKS * * * ROBINSON.

"Heavens!" I exclaimed. "The man is growing more and more daring. He's positively *fresh!* If you don't catch him before we reach Georgetown, there won't be a soul left on this ship to continue the trip. But how on earth did you get hold of this will?"

"It's the most amazing thing," began Daniels, and then he proceeded to tell me exactly what had happened. It appears that, after bringing me my dinner, Trubshaw had gone up to the social hall to help the other stewards arrange the tables for the bridge tournament. He distinctly remembers moving one of the large decorative fern-pots to make room for a table. He stood by it as the people came in and directed them to their places. He is prepared to swear that at this time there was nothing in the pot except the fern. After the play began, he went below to get his dinner. At ten o'clock he returned to the social hall to help pass the refreshments. At some time or other he took up his old position and noticed, to his surprise, that there was a paper sticking out of the pot. He immediately gave it to Jennings, who in turn handed it over to Daniels. No passenger who was not playing in the tournament came into the room during the course of the evening. Everyone must, at some time or other, have been near the fern-pot. The inevitable conclusion is that Robinson is either one of the players or one of the stewards.

"I showed the document to Mr. Earnshaw," concluded Daniels, "and he has identified it as the one that was lost. He suggested looking for finger-prints, but—I'm not an expert, besides I can't take the prints of everyone who was there tonight. It would cause no end of a pother."

"Well, there's at least one conclusion to be drawn from all this," I remarked between mouthfuls of the last sandwich. "Mr. Earnshaw's theory that young Alfred Lambert is on board this ship certainly seems to be borne out stronger than ever. There's absolutely no one else who could possibly have any interest in the old man's will. Find Alfred and you'll find Robinson—"

"I haven't heard a word of this," said Daniels jumpily. "I knew of young Lambert's existence of course, but—"

"Oh, Lord, and I promised I wouldn't tell. I was forgetting you hadn't read the last installments of my journal, Mr. Daniels."

"That's just why I came here tonight," he said eagerly. "Miss Llewellyn, you *must* give me leave to go through that diary of yours. I may have been all wrong in my deductions so far. Perhaps the party—" here he passed a hand tragically across his brow "—who made those fatal leads tonight really *is* Robinson.

It's frightful to think of, but we at least have something to work on now. If I could get a clue or the least trace of a clue from your journal, I would spend the whole night in sending radios. I could get information that might back up this—this ghastly possibility. I could arrive at the truth before we reach Georgetown. I said a while ago that I knew certain things you couldn't know. Well, you've proved by your last remark that you have certain information which it is my duty to know. You must help me."

Davy, I swear to you that the little man almost threw himself on his knees at this point. He was so worked up that I'm sure he must have burst several buttons.

"Oh, I know what you're going to say," he continued in the same impassioned tone. "Your journal is a private communication. You've talked about me as 'that funny little Cockney'; you've given your frank opinion of everyone on board; you've put in things that have nothing to do with this wretched Lambert business. I know all that. But Miss Llewellyn, this is no time to consider personal feelings. This is a matter of life and death. That journal will never leave my hands. The private parts shall be as sacred as my own dead mother's memory. I will return it to the captain's safe unharmed—"

By this time I was doing my best not to laugh. He looked so comic standing there balancing first on one leg and then on the other like a little sparrow. I almost wanted to throw him some sandwich crumbs.

"Mr. Daniels," I said flippantly. "If you talked this way to Daphne I'm not surprised at her promising to marry you. I believe you'd make a girl promise anything. Of course you can have my journal. I'm only too glad to think that my literary efforts may turn out useful after all. But it's awfully mean of you not to tell me who led those jacks."

He wrung my hand. "Oh, thank you," he said, "I shall never forget this—never. It's been a beastly business, and—"

"And it will be far more beastly for you if you ever tell Daphne what Mr. Burr said about her in my journal," I said grimly. "Married people are supposed to have no secrets from each other, but if that ever leaks out I'll come all the way to England and shoot you. Here are the last two entries, by the way, if you want them, and now I'll wish you a pleasant night reading it."

He picked up the pages and moved towards the door. I called him back. "Since you won't tell me anything interesting, you might at least let me know who won the tournament."

"Miss Demarest," he answered. "They gave her a silver butter-dish with an enamel picture of the boat on the cover. It's very handsome—and very appropriate. Good night."

How's that for a finale, Davy?

On deck,
Sunday, November 22nd.
Noon.

Something seems to be happening at last, Davy, though what it is I don't rightly know. There's an air of suppressed excitement everywhere, quite apart from the fact that we reach Georgetown tomorrow. No one has the vaguest idea what it's all about, but the whole boat seems to feel it.

And the focal point, as far as I am concerned, is little Daniels. I caught fleeting glimpses of him once or twice this morning after breakfast. He was bustling to and from the radio room, but I could not induce him to stop and talk to me. After what he told me last night I was naturally all agog with excitement, but could read nothing from his preoccupied expression. One thing is certain—he is hot on the trail. Where it will lead him remains to be seen.

There are no blue laws on this ship, Davy, and immediately after church service a group assembled on the upper deck to watch the finals of the deck-tennis tournament (mixed)—Daniels and Daphne versus Mr. and Mrs. Hirsch. The latter couple, seasoned old veterans that they are, took the business very seriously and were extremely annoyed at the non-appearance of one of their opponents. They were just beginning to murmur something about winning the championship by default when we caught a glimpse of Daniels in the distance.

"I'll get him, I'll get him," cried various voices.

"No," thundered Daphne, "I will get him." And without another word she marched off towards the scurrying form of her partner, lifted him bodily off his feet and carried him over to the court. This performance was rewarded with a roar of laughter from the onlookers, in which the little detective joined with good-natured but rather feeble comment about being literally swept off his feet. He insisted, however, that he was far too busy to play; but Daphne was adamant. Other things could wait. Sport must come first.

After a few more half-hearted protests from Daniels, the game began. It was an exciting contest. Mr. and Mrs. Hirsch were faultless players and I was told they had waltzed through the earlier rounds of the tournament without any difficulty. Daphne and Daniels, on the other hand, were erratic, but colorful. They had the crowd with them, probably because it was rumored that another type of partnership was in the offing.

During the first set (which finally went to the Hirsches 6-4) the ship's messenger boys kept up a constant chorus of "Mr. Da-a-aniels, Mr. Da-a-aniels." I think at least six radiograms were brought up, and his game began to suffer so badly in consequence that Daphne finally seized the whole bunch of them and handed them over to me with instructions not to let her partner so much as look at the backs of them until they'd won the match. Daniels gave me an anxious glance from the back line.

During the second set things began to get really exciting. Realizing that they were being outplayed by the veteran Hirsches, the English couple adopted entirely new tactics. Daphne stood right up at the net, using all the advantage of her height, caught everything she could get hold of and flicked the quoit back with the wickedest little spin you ever saw in your life. Daniels, in the meanwhile, hopped about the back line like a cricket and gallantly retrieved the very occasional shots which their opponents managed to get past his Amazonian partner.

"The sky's the limit," murmured Adam in my ear as time and time again Mr. Hirsch failed to lob high enough to go over Daphne's head.

"Mr. Da-a-aniels," sang out the ship's messenger and two more radiograms were added to my pile.

"Congratulations seems to be a bit previous," remarked Mr. Hirsch, facetiously, as the second set went to our friends and Daniels stopped for a second to count his envelopes.

"He must be playing the market," said some wag, as they took their places for the final set.

There's no need for me to go into every point of the next game, Davy. Suffice it to say that the Daniels-Demarest household will be enriched by yet another useful article in the shape (doubtless) of a silver cruet or a salad spoon. If Daphne goes on winning things at this rate no one will ever be able to say that she went to her husband empty-handed. Seriously though, she played a magnificent game and I shall always think of her in a gym costume against a background of sea and sky, leaping, running and hurling like something on the Acropolis. She was unique—graceful and strangely beautiful. In fact, if you take her away from her surroundings of undersized men and women, she is a super-creature, a young goddess—a thing to be loved and wooed even as Daniels has (apparently) loved and wooed her. I admire his good taste. After all, it is only a thin, niggardly convention which demands that women should be pretty and reasonably small. I have a distinct presentiment that the angels in heaven will be beautiful in the large, sexless and somewhat athletic manner of Daphne Demarest.

But I am digressing, darling, and though the deck tennis was fascinating, it is not half so thrilling as the latest developments in the great game of hunting Mr. Robinson.

As soon as they had won the championship, Daniels left his inamorata, and came over to me to collect his radiograms. We left the spectators who were thronging round to offer their congratulations and retreated to a quiet corner. There I watched him read his messages with a serious, puckered face. After looking them over he gave vent to a long whistle.

"Well?" I inquired. "Am I to be allowed in on things at this point?"

He shoved the envelopes in his pocket before replying. "Miss Llewellyn," he said seriously, "I certainly owe you a debt of gratitude. Last night I could not believe the evidence of my own senses. Then, as I sat up reading your journal, I began to see daylight. Your account is so clear, and—ah—complete, that I cannot believe that you do not know—that you have not; known all along who is—er—responsible for the deaths of Mr. Lambert and his niece."

"Mr. Daniels!" I exclaimed. "You are either flattering or insulting me. I have no more idea who Robinson is than the man in the moon. It wouldn't surprise me if he were Captain Fortescue—yourself or—or—the ship's cook! I'm waiting for you to tell me."

He shuffled his feet and looked around him apprehensively. "No, no, not yet. I dare not," he whispered. "You are still in terrible danger, Miss Llewellyn. In fact my blood runs cold when I think of what frightful danger you have been in throughout this trip. The only thing that has saved you is your ignorance—" he coughed apologetically. "If I were to tell you now the name of—er—this person, your face would betray your knowledge and you might never even reach your stateroom alive. You remember how the captain told you once that it was dangerous for you to know too much. He was right. It is, as I just said, your ignorance that has saved you, because the 'hunch' you mention is perfectly correct; you have the fatal clue to Robinson in your keeping. But there is a great deal to know. I myself feel nervous when I think of the amount of knowledge I have unearthed in the past few hours." He tapped the radiograms in his pocket.

"But aren't you ever going to make any disclosures?" I cried impetuously. "Are you going to keep us all in ignorance until we reach Georgetown?"

Daniels jumped up to his feet and gave me a disarming smile. "No," he said, "In fact I'm going to make you a promise, Miss Llewellyn—I promise you that you shall know at least two hours ahead of anyone else. How's that for a fair offer? But you've got to promise me something in return."

"I've got to the stage where I'd promise anything, Mr. Daniels."

"All right. Then you must do exactly as I say. I want you to stay up here exactly where you are until you hear the gong for lunch. During lunch you will receive an invitation for tea at 4:30. You will accept it. As soon as the meal is over—and without speaking a word to *anyone,* that is, anyone in private,—I want you to go straight down to your stateroom. Is that dear?"

"Sounds very mysterious."

"Not at all. I am just taking ordinary care for your safety. Later on you will see why. I don't want you to be alone with *anyone* until 4:30 today. After that, there will, so I hope, be no more danger. Do you promise?"

I nodded.

"All right. After lunch go and wait in your stateroom until I come. Lock your door and don't open it to anyone. I shall rap out 'God Save the King' on the panels with my knuckles. You know the tune? Tum—tum—tee—ta—tum—tum—. Whatever happens, be sure you don't open the door to anyone else. There'll be no guard in the corridor this afternoon. He'll be busy doing something else—something for me. As I was saying, I shall bring your journal and I will tell you the name of the—er—party concerned. I want you to spend the afternoon going through your record and checking my theories. I shall mark certain passages that seemed important to me. At half past four I'll come and fetch you—but, as you value your life do not open the door to *anyone*—anyone, mind—until I come. Remember 'God Save the King'—nothing else!"

The little man's tone was so intensely serious that I could do nothing but acquiesce. Besides, you can probably imagine, darling, that I am not anxious for a repetition of yesterday's little pantomime. I may be a bit thick but it's quite obvious, even to my somewhat limited intelligence, that Daniels believes Robinson to be *one of us.* And so I'll probably be better off by myself until we know exactly which one of us he is. And I'm afraid it's equally obvious that he is someone with whom I might, under normal circumstances, spend the afternoon.

All of which opens up vista upon vista of hideous suspicion—

Stateroom,
Sunday, November 22nd.
2:15. P. M.

Well, Davy, here I am locked in my stateroom, waiting for the sound of 'God Save the King' on the panels outside—waiting for my little man like patient Griselda.

It may interest you to know that I've been here only ten minutes and yet three people have knocked at my door already, or, to be accurate, someone or other has knocked on three separate occasions. I was a good obedient girl and didn't say a word. I sat perfectly still, just pretending I wasn't there, so of course I don't know who it was. Once the receding footsteps sounded like a man's—another time I thought I heard a woman's voice whisper my name—but I couldn't be sure. I was far too scared to speak or poke my head out. Daniels has filled me with such an unholy mistrust of all my little playmates that I find myself looking in the mirror and asking whether, even I, Mary Llewellyn, am entirely beyond suspicion.

And while I am waiting for my lord, I may as well tell you what happened at lunch time. There was an envelope at every place daintily disposed in the folds of the napkin. I opened mine with trembling fingers. I'll copy it out for you.

Commander Horatio Fortescue, R.N.R.
requests the pleasure of
Miss Mary Llewellyn's
company to tea at four-thirty
on
Sunday, November Twenty-second

Well, that was exactly as Daniels had prophesied. I was just about to slip the card nonchalantly into my bosom, when I noticed some small writing on the corner of the card. Printed in tiny capitals I read the extraordinary legend:

TO MEET MR. ROBINSON
Percy Daniels.

Immediately I hid the thing from sight as though it were something obscene and shameful. Then I glanced guiltily around. The others had opened their envelopes and were looking at the invitations with serene brows. Try as I would, however, I was unable to catch a glimpse of Adam's card.

Lunch was a tense, hurried sort of affair. We gobbled our food and all looked at each other with furtive distrust while we ate. Conversation was fitful and jerky. Even Adam seemed preoccupied. I was glad to escape to my stateroom.

And here I sit till 4:30. So far nothing has happened except the knocks on the door aforesaid. Patience, Mary—

Ah, there it is!

Tum—tum—tee—ta—tum—tum. Even the British National Anthem barely gives me courage to open the door.

God Save little Daniels!

• • • •

An Hour Later,
Stateroom.

Well, Davy, he's come and gone, and here I am sitting with my journal in front of me and a maëlstrom of conflicting emotions in my head.

Or, to put my state of mind in plain English—I am simply staggered. I just don't know what to say or do or think—I only know that my reason still refuses to accept the awful truth which has just come to me through Daniels.

At this point, darling, I want to stop and talk to you a moment. Tomorrow, God willing, I shall pack up this journal and send it off to you. There will be one more installment after this. That, I hope, will be written tonight and thus ring down the curtain on the fearful tragedies in which we have all been involved. But, as a matter of fact, the full story has been told already in these scribbled pages. Without realizing it, I have placed all the necessary threads in your hands. If you are as intelligent as I believe you to be, you will have guessed long ago the identity of the murderer of Mr. Lambert and Betty. Indeed, as Daniels has just pointed out to me, any person of super-intelligence reading this journal might have reached the right solution on page 21. (I've numbered the pages for your benefit.) For, on that page there is one word, one little word of four letters, which must have crept in out of my sub-conscious mind, but which, none the less, gives the key to the whole situation.

And now, my dear, if you haven't guessed already, go back at this point and read page 21 over four or five times. Then pit your brains against Daniels'.

Of course, Davy, I should have known all along, especially considering the way I pride myself on always spotting the criminal in a detective story. I may be fooling myself this time, but I honestly think that if I had been reading this in a book I should have guessed the solution. Somehow when you're living in the atmosphere of crime, it is very different from voluntarily steeping yourself in it for an hour or two by your own fireside. Your faculties seem to be alert enough, but in real life the issue is confused in a manner that the cleverest writer cannot imitate in a story. Your impressions of the actors involved, your instinctive belief in other people's good faith—not constant, heaven knows, but pretty fundamental after all—all such considerations keep you off that straightforward path from clue to clue which the detective fiction always seems to follow.

Then again, one can only believe in the things one sees and hears, and the things which we have seen and heard on board this ship have been no help in arriving at any reasonable solution. Several people have been nearly—so very nearly—correct with their theories. Everyone, however, seems to have missed several big, outstanding points, and a miss in this case has been far more misleading than a mile. But the murderer has taken good care to get us all thoroughly muddled. That was part of the job.

So much so that when Daniels crept into my stateroom an hour ago and whispered a name in my ear, I burst out laughing and told him that love—or something—must have gone to his head. In fact I laughed him out of the cabin and it was only after he had gone, when I gave the matter earnest, sober thought, that I realized there might be some truth in his ghastly accusation.

Immediately I snatched up my journal and read through the

passages he had marked (I shall rub them out before I send it off. You are quite clever enough to do without them.) Gradually I began to see the evidence piling up against the guilty party. Little by little I realized what an important rôle my journal will have played in this case; and by degrees it started to dawn on me why Robinson had been prepared to take such frightful risks in order to get the manuscript.

Davy, it is his death warrant!

And the word brings me to the question of my own personal danger. I came on this trip to rest up after my operation. I expected tranquil, care-free days. I expected safety. As a matter of fact I might as well have bivouacked in the most dangerous of New York's traffic intersections or pitched my tent among a tribe of Polynesian head-hunters. Unthinkingly I have walked on swords and played with dynamite. Death has been my companion every moment of this voyage. As Daniels said, it's only my blessed ignorance that has saved me. I tremble even now at the thought of leaving my stateroom and going all the way up to the captain's quarters at 4:30 this afternoon. Luckily I shall have an escort.

For there is still danger, Davy. Every time I hear a sound in the corridor outside I look at my door and reflect how, even though locked, it is a precious thin protection against a desperate criminal. I look in my mirror and see once again the face of Robinson as I saw it yesterday. I feel the loathsome pressure of his lips against mine, and I think now, even at this eleventh hour, if he could get hold of my journal and destroy it, he might be able to save his neck. And then I think of those knocks on the door that I heard earlier in the afternoon. Were they the innocent inquiry of some friend—or were they—were they *Robinson coming back?*

And now, perhaps, you see, Davy, why I dare not write the

name of the murderer until he is safely locked behind bolt and bar. Not even to you, my beloved, will I breathe the secret—at least not yet.

I don't want to tell you anyhow until the latest possible moment. Isn't that the correct technique for detective stories? You, as the reader, are supposed to exercise your ingenuity to the penultimate paragraph and then be amazed when you read the name in the last line. And the joke of it is that this journal—which started out as a series of love letters—might be dished up as quite a passable mystery story if one had the knack of arrangement. Not that I'd ever dare to put it out under my own name. I have my reputation to consider as a truthful journalist, and no one would ever believe that the perfectly fantastic happenings on board this ship had even a nodding acquaintance with the truth. And yet, though my climaxes are probably placed all wrong and the writing is perfectly appalling, all the ingredients are here. There have been a few false trails, but I have laid them in innocence and good faith. Yet, through it all, the path of truth has stretched out amazingly straight and steady like the shining furrow behind the stern of a liner. Circumstances have blinded me so that I've been unable to see it myself, but it's been there for all the time, Davy. I wonder if you have seen it—I wonder!

And now, having digressed to this extent, I suppose I should go back to Daniels and his final instructions. It's nearly half past four and he'll be here at any minute. I'm to bring my journal with me and be prepared for what will probably be the most exciting hour in my life.

Davy, there is to be a dénouement—an exposé—I can't think of any more French words to express it (they're bad copy anyhow), but still, it does sound as though it's all going to be very dramatic. Daniels says that it will start off like an ordinary tea or cocktail party and that nothing must be done to alarm Robinson or give him any idea that the game is up.

After that—well, it will have to wait. I hear heavy footsteps in the corridor outside. Daniels with two stewards! They have come to act as my bodyguard, and I shall proceed to the captain's quarters like a European potentate or the Queen of Sheba.

Room for Mary Llewellyn and her journal—!

Writing Room,
Sunday, November 22nd.
9:00 P.M.

At last, my darling, there is a period of tranquillity in which I can recollect the emotions of this afternoon. The shouting and the tumult have died. The ship seems strangely quiet. I am alone in this room.

The other passengers are all on deck trying to catch a glimpse of land or lights or some other outward and visible sign that the first stage of our journey is almost done. Ever since dinner the sea has been full of flotsam; strange, exotic sea-fowl have screamed at us as they swooped down on titbits belched forth from the ship's sides; the water is no longer a clear ultramarine; it is turbid and green—indubitable signs that land is near. We reach Georgetown at 6:30 tomorrow morning.

But the whole uncontaminated evening is before me, Davy, and I will not stint you on the last act of our little melodrama. You shall have it all to the minutest detail. My journalese shall have full rein. I leave you to judge whether or not the subject is worthy.

It seems like a month since I was sitting in my cabin writing to you last. In reality it was less than five hours ago when Daniels came down to take me to the captain's tea party. A great many people (including myself) must have lived through a whole lifetime since then.

Well, darling, picture me as you last saw me marching solemnly along with three men, my journal under my arm. At the captain's door it is handed over to the steward and Daniels and I enter alone, trying to look unconcerned. The stage is all set. There are teacups, a cocktail shaker, and highball glasses. The guests are seated and seem to be talking together quite merrily. Mrs. Lambert is being entertained on the sofa by Captain Fortescue. She looks pale and forlorn but is obviously making an effort. Silvera sits on her right—equally obviously making no effort whatsoever. In one corner Daphne is obscuring all the light from a porthole while Jennings plies her politely with tea and toast. Earnshaw is seated with his back to the purple curtains and is talking to Adam, who jumps up as I enter and knocks over the chair which he has vacated for my benefit. There are rather too many grim-faced stewards (including our old friends Trubshaw and Sam Bumstead) to pass round the cakes and sandwiches, but, apart from that, everything is calm and natural. There is no hint of the storm that is brewing in those peaceful teacups.

But surely someone is absent? Mentally I count noses as Daniels goes off to get what he calls a good stiff double Scotch. Of course—Mrs. Clapp! But she is coming: make no mistake about that.

There is rustle in the doorway. The rustling grows to a rumbling and the rumbling grows to a miniature whirlwind. The great actress is not to be done out of her entrance. It is dramatic. There is a pause while the press takes note. "Enter Marcia Manners in a trailing gown of black taffeta with which she wore her famous pearls." It is effective, but it is soon over. The party goes on, now a little livelier, a little more scintillating, thanks to the devastating arrival from the world of fashion.

And so, Davy, we eat, drink and flirt. As a matter of fact, Marcia has the monopoly of this latter activity. She gives all the men a break. She flirts with the captain; she does everything but kiss the purser; she darts amorous glances at Earnshaw; she stirs Silvera to the depths of his sombre soul; she even flings some playful badinage at Adam, which causes him to puff out his chest and look like a pouter pigeon. She is the life of the party on nothing stronger than tea. But the rest of us aren't so utterly lacking in social amenities either. Indeed, even our guardian angels, taking a bird's-eye-view of the situation, would never dream that we were gathered together for anything more sinister than cakes and chatter.

But even the cakes and chatter cannot go on for ever. There is a break and Mrs. Clapp rises from her seat—one small ringed hand stretched out in abortive valediction. It is ignored. The captain has also risen to his feet. There is no sound in the room but the tinkling of ice in the tumblers and the velvet pad-pad of the stewards as they clear away the tea things.

"Would you all be so kind as to remain seated?"

Captain Fortescue's voice sounds like a foghorn across the misty sea of our babble.

"Ladies and gentlemen, I am sorry to detain you, but I have a favor to ask. There is no need for me to tell you that there have been two terrible tragedies on board this ship. Directly or indirectly all of you have been involved. That is why I have invited you here today. It is my duty to tell you some more details about the sad deaths of Mr. Lambert and his niece. Mrs. Lambert will, I am sure, forgive me for bringing up this distressing subject at such a time. She is—as indeed we all are—anxious to get to the bottom of what has seemed like an insoluble mystery. Well, certain facts have now come to light which I think you should all hear. My friend and—er—colleague, Mr. Daniels, will present them to you. I am sorry to say that they bring accusations against a certain person in this room. That person will be given a chance for self-defense. The rest of you will be good enough to act as jury."

There was a long moment of silence. A dropped hairpin would have reverberated through the room like a pistol shot. Then Mrs. Clapp bent towards me and said in a stage whisper: "I've always wanted to be on a jury. When I think, my dear, of what Mrs. Fiske got away with—"

But Daniels had risen to his feet and all eyes were fixed on him. There was a nervous smile on his lips as he picked at a bunch of papers in his hands. I noticed that a steward had placed my journal on a small table at his side. Trubshaw and the other stewards were standing respectfully at attention in various corners of the room. At length the little man spoke, a trifle jerkily, reading from a paper which had obviously been prepared beforehand.

"I have been asked by the captain to put certain things before you. As some of you know, I am employed by this line in the capacity of detective or inquiry agent—and, although I was going to Rio on other business, throughout this voyage I have done little but try to solve the mystery of Mr. Lambert's death and the tragic disappearance of his niece. Let me confine myself for a moment to the case of Mr. Lambert. He was, as you know, poisoned during a game of bridge on the first night out from New York. Involved in his death there was a man who called himself Robinson. This man played bridge with myself, Mr. Burr, and Mr. Lambert, and then walked out of the smoking room and disappeared almost, as one might say, into thin air. Subsequently the ship was searched from bow to stern, but no trace was found of the missing fourth. At length there was only one conclusion to be reached. Mr. Robinson must have been—someone else in disguise.

"But he had done two very clever things with this disguise of his. In the first place he had assumed it on the first night—a time when everyone is a stranger to everyone else—the one evening when people hardly notice each other; and in the second place he had chosen a disguise which made him entirely inconspicuous. Although he sat opposite me as my partner during the better part of the evening—and although detection is supposed to be my business—I found I could remember nothing about him except the broadest outlines of his appearance. Nor could anyone else help me in this particular. Robinson was a clever actor and he knew how to avoid being noticed, but there *was* one thing about him that made him noticeable—one thing that he could not conceal. This was the badness of his bridge. He was an awfully rotten player—if he'll excuse my saying so. Far worse even than me and I'm pretty bad."

Here Daniels paused and smiled at his audience apologetically. Then he picked up my journal and shuffled the leaves, as he continued extemporaneously.

"Now, it so happens," he went on, "that Miss Llewellyn, who occasionally writes bridge problems for her paper, noted down two of the hands which Robinson played that night, and drew attention to the fact that he made certain mistakes which were of a rather extraordinary nature. I decided that if I could possibly get him to play them over again he might perhaps repeat his errors. By good fortune I was able to arrange for these particular hands to be repeated during the bridge tournament last night.

How I did it does not matter, but almost everyone who took part in the tournament played those same two hands. But one—only one person made the same mistake as Robinson made. That person is in this room now."

Everyone was staring at Daniels with the strained, uneasy expression with which people used to watch the ticker 'way back in 1929-30. It was Mrs. Clapp who broke the silence.

"Good heavens! Mr. Daniels. You surely aren't going to take that as conclusive evidence against anyone. My bridge game has always been appalling—I'm perfectly capable of making the most impossible mistakes; I revoke, I—"

Daniels smiled. "I'm no Culbertson myself, Mrs. Clapp, and you're quite right in saying there's nothing final about an error in bridge. But it's going to be very easy for everyone to clear himself. If you weren't acting as Robinson in the smoking room that night, presumably you were all somewhere else. If you have alibis for, say, between the hours of nine and ten last Friday week, well, obviously—"

A little buzz of conversation had sprung up. Daniels' voice was like a reedy pipe above the tumult.

"Come, it was the first night out. Surely you can remember what you were doing with yourselves?"

"If you demand the truth," snapped Mrs. Clapp, again acting as spokesman, 'I will tell you that I was doing what I always do every first night out—on principle. I was in my stateroom being violently seasick. Forgive the indelicacy, but you asked for it."

"And I was with her," said Daphne. "After I'd seen she was sleeping soundly, I came up and joined the bridge party, as you know."

No one else spoke for a moment. Daniels looked around encouragingly. "I know about you, Mr. Burr, and you, Mr. Wolcott, and Miss Llewellyn and Mrs. Lambert, we were all together in the smoking room. But what about you, Mr. Silvera?"

"Cabin—sick—ask steward," grunted the Brazilian and then turned his back as though he never expected to speak again.

"I was on deck with Miss Lambert," said Earnshaw. "Mrs. Lambert came out to fetch us somewhere around ten o'clock."

The widow nodded.

"And I was all over the ship," said Jennings. "Trubshaw must have seen me several times if you want to check on my movements."

"And you, Trubshaw?"

"I was taking care of me passengers, sir. There was some of 'em as needed me bad. I do remember going in once to Mr. Silvera, sir, but it wasn't till after ten o'clock."

You will say that none of this sounded very promising, Davy, but as a matter of fact, Daniels looked perfectly satisfied.

"Thank you, thank you," he said. "That is very satisfactory. Now, with your permission, I want to talk about the disappearance of Miss Lambert for a moment. No—I am not going to ask you for your movements last Sunday night. I have your statements, made at the time, that most of you were in your cabins. It was fairly late at night and there had been a nasty storm. The idea is that Miss Lambert was thrown overboard by Robinson at about 11:15. Miss Llewellyn was talking to Mr. Earnshaw in the smoking room at the time. These two—and Mrs. Lambert—heard the scream and were the first to run to the scene of action. Those three people—of us all—are the only ones that can be said to have alibis. Now, as I feel certain that the person who killed Mr. Lambert also killed his niece—"

"Oh, Mr. Daniels, please—please be brief," murmured Mrs.

Lambert, with her hand on her forehead. "I can't bear much more of this."

"Excuse me, Mrs. Lambert, but I'm coming to the point now. I believe that Miss Betty's death is the keynote—the crux, as you might say, of the whole problem. Who would want to kill such a nice, innocent young lady—and why? She had not been in the room during that first bridge game when—so we think—Mr. Lambert was poisoned. She could not have seen anything then that would have aroused her suspicions. And yet—and yet this man—this Robinson thought she should be destroyed—and destroyed her in a brutal, cold-blooded manner. He did a thing which— "

The voice of the captain cut across this monologue. "I think we'd better stick to the facts, Mr. Daniels."

"All right, sir. Such as they are—such as they are. But motives aren't facts and it was the motive that worried me in the case of poor Miss Betty. Then suddenly it came to me from an entirely outside source. It was given me by Miss Llewellyn here. She has, as you know, been keeping a journal of everything that's happened during this trip. Last night, she was kind enough to let me read it. Have I your permission now, Miss Llewellyn?"

I lowered my head in order to avoid the battery of eyes that were fixed on me. Mrs. Clapp was peering at me through a lorgnette as though Daniels had just denounced me as a scarlet woman. Silvera's keen glance was like a gimlet. Daniels continued:

"I am going to read an extract from Miss Llewellyn's diary, just to see if you catch the significance of the point I'm trying to make."

Here he read the passage on page 20 beginning, *"Mr. Daniels left the room with a grunt*" (this caused a laugh) and ending with, "*Mr. Daniels' rickey was positively poisonous.*"

The detective paused after reading and looked around him. The faces were blank and expressionless.

"Well, Daniels," said Adam Burr with a fatuous smile, "if you're trying to work out an elaborate case against yourself, that's very interesting and original, but—"

"Oh, doesn't anyone see it? cried Daniels impatiently. "That one word—one little word of four letters which explains the whole thing. I mean the word *back.*"

The faces were still vague. People were staring at one another with bewildered, half-pitying expressions. Mrs. Clapp went so far as to tap her forehead with an I-told-you-so look at Daphne.

"All right, let me read again what poor Miss Betty said that night when her uncle suggested that she should join the game. She replied and these were the very words according to Miss Llewellyn:

'I'm far too sleepy to play bridge; just one more turn on the deck with Jimmie, then I'm going back to my stateroom.'

"Now, ladies and gentlemen, does one say one's going *back* to a place unless one has just come from there? And if Miss Lambert said she was going back to her stateroom, that means she hadn't been spending the evening on deck with Mr. Earnshaw at all; and that means that his alibi falls entirely to the ground."

All eyes were now riveted on Earnshaw, who was sitting perfectly still with his legs stuck out in front of him.

"Daniels," he said, as an angry flush colored his cheek, "I don't know if you're accusing me of anything or not. I don't even care. The whole thing is so utterly absurd and preposterous. Miss Llewellyn is capable of inaccuracies like anyone else. Betty Lambert was on deck with me, but she did not choose to have it known. We were secretly engaged, if you must have the truth. And if you are making the ridiculous assumption that I am—or was—Robinson, let me remind you that I was the loser by Mr. Lambert's death in every way. I lost my position, the money he promised me—"

"Of course, of course, Mr. Earnshaw," said Daniels apologetically, "You must forgive me, but I wanted to show you—and everyone else—how easy it is to destroy an alibi. Miss Llewellyn's journal—"

"Well, even the omniscient Miss Llewellyn is bound to acknowledge my alibi in the case of Betty's murder," said Earnshaw indignantly. "I was talking to her when that devil threw her overboard. We had been talking together for the past hour—"

Daniels turned towards the speaker with a calm, level gaze. "Mr. Earnshaw," he said slowly, "I have already tried to show you that in this business we can attach no importance either to times or to alibis. If this statement holds good in Mr. Lambert's death it is doubly true in the case of his niece. I repeat—" here he paused and looked searchingly around the room "—I repeat that nobody had an alibi for the time when Miss Betty was killed, for the simple reason that no one—at least, no one except her murderer—knows . . . exactly . . . *when* . . . she was . . . killed. My own opinion is that it was sometime earlier in the evening—probably during the storm."

Mrs. Lambert was staring at Daniels in horror. "But, but," she mumbled, "I saw him—Robinson—they were talking together—and then that scream—and the shawl—"

"Yes, yes, Mrs. Lambert." The detective's tone was mollifying and polite. "I heard your story at the time. But did you actually *see* Miss Lambert thrown overboard? No. Did anyone see the crime, committed? No. You said that you saw two people talking together. There was a scream and a scarf floating out over the water. The scarf was seen by several people, including Miss Llewellyn—but did it necessarily prove that the owner of the scarf had—er—just been thrown overboard?"

Earnshaw had jumped to his feet. "Good God, man," he cried, "do you mean that there's a chance of Betty's still being *alive?*"

Daniels was shaking his head sadly. "No, Mr. Earnshaw. I'm afraid there's no chance at all—none whatsoever. Miss Lambert is dead. I am merely pointing out that the exact time of her death is unknown. Only Robinson can tell us that."

I think it was at this point that a steward came in and whispered in Daniels' ear. I noticed a gleam of satisfaction in his eyes as he replied, "All right. Let them wait outside." Then he continued:

"I say that only Robinson can supply the details. Well, in a very few minutes I think I shall be able to introduce you to Robinson—brown hair, spectacles, tanned face and everything."

There was another long moment of silence following this extraordinary announcement. Then Adam burst out with: "Daniels, I have been given to understand that Mr. Lambert had a son called Alfred who may or may not benefit by his father's will. Is there any truth in the assumption that he might be involved in all this—that he might actually be on this ship—that he himself might be Robinson?"

But Mrs. Clapp had now risen, stately and majestic. The look she gave Adam would have withered a rhinoceros. "Mr. Burr," she declaimed, "kindly remember that Alfred Lambert is my nephew. He is a fine, noble young man—a young man of the highest principles. He does not smoke; he does not drink; and he certainly does not commit—murder!"

Adam wilted and Daniels rushed to the rescue. "I was coming to that point, Mr. Burr. And I'm sure Mrs. Clapp will forgive me if I settled it once and for all. Alfred Lambert is not on board the *Moderna,* although the possibility that he might be had occurred to me—and to several other people. This morning I received a wireless message from the Chief of Police at Buenos Aires. He tells me that he interviewed young Lambert himself last night. He's running a cattle ranch out there and doing pretty well. The theory of his implication may have been likely, but I think we may now dismiss it altogether."

"I should hope so," snorted Aunt Marcia.

"Well, then, as far as I can see," rejoined Adam, meekly, "we cannot produce anyone who has any possible motive."

"Oh, there's a motive all right," replied Daniels grimly, "but before I come to that I want to make good to you my promise and introduce you to our old friend—Mr. Robinson."

He nodded to the steward who had entered last: "All right, Collins."

The man went out of the room and returned immediately with a small Gladstone bag. There was a whispered conversation during which I stole a glance around the room. The captain was sitting at his desk tapping a silver pencil against his writing pad. Jennings and Daphne were standing together, tall and aloof in the corner furthest from me. Mrs. Lambert and Silvera occupied the couch; the one looking tense and drawn, the other still bored and indifferent. Earnshaw was sitting with his back to the purple curtains, tilting his chair and whispering occasionally to Adam, who was his neighbor. Mrs. Clapp was magnificent in a solitary arm chair. Everyone was waiting. It was all ridiculously like a stage setting.

Daniels had taken certain articles from what appeared to be a false bottom of the Gladstone bag. He spread them out neatly on the table in front of him.

"Ladies and gentlemen," he said, smiling like a hired entertainer at a children's party, "allow me to present Mr. Robinson. Here we are, all complete. A brown wig—excellent workmanship. A pair of steel-rimmed spectacles—plain glass, I imagine. A box of Aubrey's Invisible Suntan. And here—here are two funny looking things."

He held up a pair of small objects that looked like part of a dentist's paraphernalia.

"I don't know what these are called in America, but in England they are commonly known as plumpers. They are, I believe, fixed to the upper row of teeth to swell out the cheeks and give a different shape to the face. Old ladies and actresses use them, I believe;—"

"Why, yes," cried Daphne from her corner, "I remember reading a feeble book by Elinor Glyn where the old duchess or someone dropped her plumpers in the soup tureen during lunch—"

"Daphne Demarest," cried her employer, "don't be vulgar. Duchesses don't serve soup out of tureens. As the granddaughter of an earl, you ought to know better than that."

"But, Marcia—"

"I think," broke in the captain, "you should explain where these articles were found, Mr. Daniels. Also, why there is a false moustache among these—er—effects. Robinson was cleanshaven—"

He bent forward and held up a small, dark object.

"Perhaps Mr. Earnshaw can explain," said Daniels mildly. "We took the liberty of searching his cabin while he was up here just now—"

Then, Davy, things began to happen so fast that I was utterly unable to follow them in detail. There was a flash from one corner of the room, followed by a howl of pain, and the next thing I knew was that two men had stepped out from behind the purple curtains and were standing one on each side of Earnshaw's chair. But it was not the same Earnshaw. The dapper little John Gilbert moustache had disappeared and Daphne—Daphne of all people—was standing in the middle of the room holding it aloft in her hand like the Statue of Liberty.

"Look, Percy," she cried, "it's come off and here it is. In books and plays the villain always puts on a black moustache to do his dirty work, but this one is quite original. He takes his off. A new idea, Percy, if ever you write your memoirs."

Earnshaw was fingering his denuded top-lip with a trembling hand.

"And this one," rejoined Daniels, as he took the other moustache from the captain's hand and replaced it on the table, "is what you might call a spare part. Very clever, Mr. Earnshaw. That explains why one hardly ever saw you in the daylight—why you kept yourself so much in your cabin—"

"You're crazy," screamed Earnshaw, as he moved his arms in an attempt to avoid contact with the two guards at his side. "And you needn't bother with all this fuss. I'm not armed."

"And I think you're crazy too," cried Mrs. Clapp, with a sympathetic glance at Earnshaw, who looked handsomer than ever without the moustache. "You'll need to do a great deal of explaining, Mr. Daniels. In the first place, speaking as one who is an expert in make-up—stage make-up, of course—I can tell you that it would have been virtually impossible for Mr. Earnshaw to disguise himself so that his own employer would not recognize him across a bridge table."

"That's another point where Miss Llewellyn's journal helped me, Mrs. Clapp," replied Daniels. "Mr. Lambert hadn't got his spectacles that night. He was very near-sighted. I have no doubt at all that Mr. Earnshaw could have told him where they were."

"But Betty's death!" continued the great actress hysterically. "You are surely not going to try and persuade us that any young man would be so completely devoid of humanity as to throw his own fiancée overboard!"

Daniels did not answer for the moment. Once again he was shuffling his bunch of radiograms. There was a sad expression on his face and I noticed that he shot a sentimental glance at Daphne, who was glaring at Earnshaw as though she were just about to murder him. "A very natural objection, Mrs. Clapp," he said mournfully. "But what proof have we that Miss Lambert *was* Mr. Earnshaw's fiancée? You must remember that he did not mention this interesting fact until after the girl was dead. We cannot prove his claim in any manner. Indeed, I have made inquiries which seem to point to the contrary. Here is a radiogram from the deceased young lady's father. He mentions a previous attachment which—"

"It's a damned lie," cried Earnshaw desperately, trying to jump to his feet. Restraining hands were immediately laid on his shoulder.

"Well, well," continued Daniels imperturbably, "I think I can show you that Mr. Earnshaw also had a previous attachment. An attachment which caused him to murder the man who had befriended him; an attachment which Miss Betty probably discovered on the night of her death. It was, if my guess is right, this fatal discovery which made it doubly necessary for Earnshaw to get rid of her before her last message reached Miss Llewellyn.

Is there any need for me to tell you what was the nature of this attachment?"

"There certainly is," cried Mrs. Clapp. "The man is talking in riddles. I for one may be exceptionally stupid, but so far nothing has been explained to my satisfaction."

"The whole thing is an outrage," said Mrs. Lambert, suddenly galvanized into life. "A perfect outrage—"

"A perfect piece of acting and a perfect piece of timing," replied Daniels. "Mr. Earnshaw was not alone in this, as you may have guessed. Someone else had to be at hand to see that he got into the game of bridge with Mr. Lambert. Someone had to help him with his alibi for the time that Betty was supposed to have been murdered. Well, here is his alibi—"

He took from the table a flat, round object and placed it in his mouth. A ghastly shriek echoed and re-echoed throughout the room. It was even more eerie and uncanny than the one which we had heard on the night when Betty was killed.

He removed the object from his mouth and held it up for inspection.

"This," he said, "looks to me like one of the devices used in the theatre to imitate screams off stage. Last Sunday night it was used to make people think they heard the death-cry of Miss Lambert. A scarf thrown overboard completed the illusion. The murder had been committed earlier in the evening—probably during the thunder-storm—but Mr. Earnshaw and his partner were so clever that we all believed that they both had perfect alibis. Later on they deflected suspicion still farther by a fake attack from Robinson; by a trumped-up stealing of Mr. Lambert's will; and by its equally dramatic return—to a fern-pot. Everything was thought out and timed to a nicety. It was perfect team-work and it took a pair of actors to carry it through. May I offer you my congratulations—Mrs. Lambert!"

The widow sat staring at her accuser as if thunder-struck. Then, slowly, I saw her hand moving towards the black velvet sack which lay at her side on the couch.

But Captain Fortescue had caught the movement too.

"Quick, Trubshaw—her hand bag." His voice cut across the room like a cracked whip.

The steward was just in time. A small revolver gleamed in the already opened hand bag.

There was a moment of ghastly silence as the weapon was laid on the table with the other exhibits. It was Mrs. Clapp who spoke. For the first time since I had known her, I noticed that her voice was neither well-pitched nor carefully modulated.

"Mabel Lambert," she screamed, "I always said you were a rotten actress. I apologize. You are a genius—you—"

But the sentence was not completed, for Mrs. Lambert had fainted—this time, I imagine, in grim earnest.

• • • •

There's no need for me to tell you any more, Davy. The case is open and shut. I've been through Daniel's radiograms, but I won't bore you with scabrous details wrested by the New York Police from all-too-willing chambermaids and other domestics in the Lambert home. The redoubtable Jimmie had been living there, you will remember, some time previous to the trip. They had planned the thing to perfection with Betty as a blind. They would have disembarked at Georgetown, returned to America, and, after a decent interval of mourning, presumably settled down to enjoy poor old Lambert's money. Certain things, of course, we shall never know. The details of poor little Betty's death will probably remain shrouded in mystery. We can only draw on our imaginations about what it was that she saw last Sunday night. Perhaps she went into her aunt's stateroom at an ill-advised moment; perhaps she over heard some conversation which gave her a clue as to their guilty relationship; perhaps—well, what does it matter? They're under lock and key now and I, for one, am utterly convinced that they deserve it.

But, as Daniels said, what timing—what perfect teamwork! The almost simultaneous visitation from Robinson to me and Mrs. Lambert was a masterpiece. He must have put on the disguise in Mrs. Lambert's room and, after that, everything was beautifully arranged so that Trubshaw would be absent in case I *did* manage to get my finger on the bell, and plenty of time was allowed for Earnshaw to go back to his cabin and change his clothes.

And when I think of that hideous brute standing on deck, straining his eyes over the ocean, in mock despair over the "fiancée" he had just murdered—and when I think of Mrs. Lambert lying pseudo-prostrate in her stateroom and gasping out "Robinson!"—then I can only go one better than Marcia Clapp and say with no uncertain voice that the stage has lost two accomplished actors. . . .

• • • •

Well, there's a big commotion going on outside, darling. The passengers are all twittering about with happy little squeaks. They've seen a lighthouse or something.

DISCUSSION QUESTIONS

- Were you able to solve the mystery before the final reveal? If so, how?
- Did any aspects of the plot date the story? If so, which?
- Would the story be different if it were set in the present day? If so, how?
- Did the social context of the time play a role in the narrative? If so, how?
- If you were Mary Llewellyn, would you have acted differently at any point in the story?
- Did you identify with any of the characters? If so, which?
- If you have read other "aquatic mysteries" from the era, how does this one compare?
- Did this book remind you of any present day authors? If so, which?

OTTO PENZLER PRESENTS
AMERICAN MYSTERY CLASSICS

All titles are available in hardcover and in trade paperback.

Order from your favorite bookstore or from
The Mysterious Bookshop, 58 Warren Street, New York, N.Y. 10007
(www.mysteriousbookshop.com).

Charlotte Armstrong, *The Chocolate Cobweb.* When Amanda Garth was born, a mix-up caused the hospital to briefly hand her over to the prestigious Garrison family instead of to her birth parents. The error was quickly fixed, Amanda was never told, and the secret was forgotten for twenty-three years … until her aunt revealed it in casual conversation. But what if the initial switch never actually occurred? **Introduction by A. J. Finn.**

Charlotte Armstrong, *The Unsuspected.* First published in 1946, this suspenseful novel opens with a young woman who has ostensibly hanged herself, leaving a suicide note. Her friend doesn't believe it and begins an investigation that puts her own life in jeopardy. It was filmed in 1947 by Warner Brothers, starring Claude Rains and Joan Caulfield. **Introduction by Otto Penzler.**

Anthony Boucher, *The Case of the Baker Street Irregulars.* When a studio announces a new hard-boiled Sherlock Holmes film, the Baker Street Irregulars begin a campaign to discredit it. Attempting to mollify them, the producers invite members to the set, where threats are received, each referring to one of the original Holmes tales, followed by murder. Fortunately, the amateur sleuths use Holmesian lessons to solve the crime. **Introduction by Otto Penzler.**

Anthony Boucher, *Rocket to the Morgue.* Hilary Foulkes has made so many enemies that it is difficult to speculate who was responsible for stabbing him nearly to death in a room with only one door through which no one was seen entering or leaving. This classic locked room mystery is populated by such thinly disguised science fiction legends as Robert Heinlein, L. Ron Hubbard, and John W. Campbell. **Introduction by F. Paul Wilson.**

Fredric Brown, *The Fabulous Clipjoint.* Brown's outstanding mystery won an Edgar as the best first novel of the year (1947). When Wallace Hunter is found dead in an alley after a long night of drinking, the police don't really care. But his teenage son Ed and his uncle Am, the carnival worker, are convinced that some things don't add up and the crime isn't what it seems to be. **Introduction by Lawrence Block.**

John Dickson Carr, *The Crooked Hinge.* Selected by a group of mystery experts as one of the 15 best impossible crime novels ever written, this is one of Gideon Fell's greatest challenges. Estranged from his family for 25 years, Sir John Farnleigh returns to England from America to claim his inheritance but another person turns up claiming that he can prove he is the real Sir John. Inevitably, one of them is murdered. **Introduction by Charles Todd.**

John Dickson Carr, *The Eight of Swords.* When Gideon Fell arrives at a crime scene, it appears to be straightforward enough. A man has been shot to death in an unlocked room and the likely perpetrator was a recent visitor. But Fell discovers inconsistencies and his investigations are complicated by an apparent poltergeist, some American gangsters, and two meddling amateur sleuths. **Introduction by Otto Penzler.**

John Dickson Carr, *The Mad Hatter Mystery.* A prankster has been stealing top hats all around London. Gideon Fell suspects that the same person may be responsible for the theft of a manuscript of a long-lost story by Edgar Allan Poe. The hats reappear in unexpected but conspicuous places but, when one is found on the head of a corpse by the Tower of London, it is evident that the thefts are more than pranks. **Introduction by Otto Penzler.**

John Dickson Carr, *The Plague Court Murders.* When murder occurs in a locked hut on Plague Court, an estate haunted by the ghost of a hangman's assistant who died a victim of the black death, Sir Henry Merrivale seeks a logical solution to a ghostly crime. A spiritual medium employed to rid the house of his spirit is found stabbed to death in a locked stone hut on the grounds, surrounded by an untouched circle of mud. **Introduction by Michael Dirda.**

John Dickson Carr, ***The Red Widow Murders.*** In a "haunted" mansion, the room known as the Red Widow's Chamber proves lethal to all who spend the night. Eight people investigate and the one who draws the ace of spades must sleep in it. The room is locked from the inside and watched all night by the others. When the door is unlocked, the victim has been poisoned. Enter Sir Henry Merrivale to solve the crime. **Introduction by Tom Mead.**

Frances Crane, ***The Turquoise Shop.*** In an arty little New Mexico town, Mona Brandon has arrived from the East and becomes the subject of gossip about her money, her influence, and the corpse in the nearby desert who may be her husband. Pat Holly, who runs the local gift shop, is as interested as anyone in the goings on—but even more in Pat Abbott, the detective investigating the possible murder. **Introduction by Anne Hillerman.**

Todd Downing, ***Vultures in the Sky.*** There is no end to the series of terrifying events that befall a luxury train bound for Mexico. First, a man dies when the train passes through a dark tunnel, then it comes to an abrupt stop in the middle of the desert. More deaths occur when night falls and the passengers panic when they realize they are trapped with a murderer on the loose. **Introduction by James Sallis.**

Mignon G. Eberhart, ***Murder by an Aristocrat.*** Nurse Keate is called to help a man who has been "accidentally" shot in the shoulder. When he is murdered while convalescing, it is clear that there was no accident. Although a killer is loose in the mansion, the family seems more concerned that news of the murder will leave their circle. *The New Yorker* wrote than "Eberhart can weave an almost flawless mystery." **Introduction by Nancy Pickard.**

Erle Stanley Gardner, ***The Case of the Baited Hook.*** Perry Mason gets a phone call in the middle of the night and his potential client says it's urgent, that he has two one-thousand-dollar bills that he will give him as a retainer, with an additional ten-thousand whenever he is called on to represent him. When Mason takes the case, it is not for the caller but for a beautiful woman whose identity is hidden behind a mask. **Introduction by Otto Penzler.**

Erle Stanley Gardner, ***The Case of the Borrowed Brunette.*** A mysterious man named Mr. Hines has advertised a job for a woman who has to fulfill very specific physical requirements. Eva Martell, pretty but struggling in her career as a model, takes the job but her aunt smells a rat and hires Perry Mason to investigate. Her fears are realized when Hines turns up in the apartment with a bullet hole in his head. **Introduction by Otto Penzler.**

Erle Stanley Gardner, ***The Case of the Careless Kitten.*** Helen Kendal receives a mysterious phone call from her vanished uncle Franklin, long presumed dead, who urges her to contact Perry Mason. Soon, she finds herself the main suspect in the murder of an unfamiliar man. Her kitten has just survived a poisoning attempt—as has her aunt Matilda. What is the connection between Franklin's return and the murder attempts? **Introduction by Otto Penzler.**

Erle Stanley Gardner, ***The Case of the Rolling Bones.*** One of Gardner's most successful Perry Mason novels opens with a clear case of blackmail, though the person being blackmailed claims he isn't. It is not long before the police are searching for someone wanted for killing the same man in two different states—thirty-three years apart. The confounding puzzle of what happened to the dead man's toes is a challenge. **Introduction by Otto Penzler.**

Erle Stanley Gardner, ***The Case of the Shoplifter's Shoe.*** Most cases for Perry Mason involve murder but here he is hired because a young woman fears her aunt is a kleptomaniac. Sarah may not have been precisely the best guardian for a collection of valuable diamonds and, sure enough, they go missing. When the jeweler is found shot dead, Sarah is spotted leaving the murder scene with a bundle of gems stuffed in her purse. **Introduction by Otto Penzler.**

Erle Stanley Gardner, ***The Bigger They Come.*** Gardner's first novel using the pseudonym A.A. Fair starts off a series featuring the large and loud Bertha Cool and her employee, the small and meek Donald Lam. Given the job of delivering divorce papers to an evident crook,

Lam can't find him—but neither can the police. The *Los Angeles Times* called this book: "Breathlessly dramatic … an original." **Introduction by Otto Penzler.**

Frances Noyes Hart, *The Bellamy Trial*. Inspired by the real-life Hall-Mills case, the most sensational trial of its day, this is the story of Stephen Bellamy and Susan Ives, accused of murdering Bellamy's wife Madeleine. Eight days of dynamic testimony, some true, some not, make headlines for an enthralled public. Rex Stout called this historic courtroom thriller one of the ten best mysteries of all time. **Introduction by Hank Phillippi Ryan.**

H.F. Heard, *A Taste for Honey*. The elderly Mr. Mycroft quietly keeps bees in Sussex, where he is approached by the reclusive and somewhat misanthropic Mr. Silchester, whose honey supplier was found dead, stung to death by her bees. Mycroft, who shares many traits with Sherlock Holmes, sets out to find the vicious killer. Rex Stout described it as "sinister … a tale well and truly told." **Introduction by Otto Penzler.**

Dolores Hitchens, *The Alarm of the Black Cat*. Detective fiction aficionado Rachel Murdock has a peculiar meeting with a little girl and a dead toad, sparking her curiosity about a love triangle that has sparked anger. When the girl's great grandmother is found dead, Rachel and her cat Samantha work with a friend in the Los Angeles Police Department to get to the bottom of things. **Introduction by David Handler.**

Dolores Hitchens, *The Cat Saw Murder*. Miss Rachel Murdock, the highly intelligent 70-year-old amateur sleuth, is not entirely heartbroken when her slovenly, unattractive, bridge-cheating niece is murdered. Miss Rachel is happy to help the socially maladroit and somewhat bumbling Detective Lieutenant Stephen Mayhew, retaining her composure when a second brutal murder occurs. **Introduction by Joyce Carol Oates.**

Dorothy B. Hughes, *Dread Journey*. A big-shot Hollywood producer has worked on his magnum opus for years, hiring and firing one beautiful starlet after another. But Kitten Agnew's contract won't allow her to be fired, so she fears she might be terminated more permanently. Together with the producer on a train journey from Hollywood to Chicago, Kitten becomes more terrified with each passing mile. **Introduction by Sarah Weinman.**

Dorothy B. Hughes, *Ride the Pink Horse*. When Sailor met Willis Douglass, he was just a poor kid who Douglass groomed to work as a confidential secretary. As the senator became increasingly corrupt, he knew he could count on Sailor to clean up his messes. No longer a senator, Douglass flees Chicago for Santa Fe, leaving behind a murder rap and Sailor as the prime suspect. Seeking vengeance, Sailor follows. **Introduction by Sara Paretsky.**

Dorothy B. Hughes, *The So Blue Marble*. Set in the glamorous world of New York high society, this novel became a suspense classic as twins from Europe try to steal a rare and beautiful gem owned by an aristocrat whose sister is an even more menacing presence. *The New Yorker* called it "Extraordinary … [Hughes'] brilliant descriptive powers make and unmake reality." **Introduction by Otto Penzler.**

W. Bolingbroke Johnson, *The Widening Stain*. After a cocktail party, the attractive Lucie Coindreau, a "black-eyed, black-haired Frenchwoman" visits the rare books wing of the library and apparently takes a headfirst fall from an upper gallery. Dismissed as a horrible accident, it seems dubious when Professor Hyett is strangled while reading a priceless 12th-century manuscript, which has gone missing. **Introduction by Nicholas A. Basbanes**

Baynard Kendrick, *Blind Man's Bluff*. Blinded in World War II, Duncan Maclain forms a successful private detective agency, aided by his two dogs. Here, he is called on to solve the case of a blind man who plummets from the top of an eight-story building, apparently with no one present except his dead-drunk son. **Introduction by Otto Penzler.**

Baynard Kendrick, *The Odor of Violets*. Duncan Maclain, a blind former intelligence officer, is asked to investigate the murder of an actor in his Greenwich Village apartment. This would cause a stir at any time but, when the actor possesses secret government plans that then go missing, it's enough to interest the local police as well as the American government and Maclain, who suspects a German spy plot. **Introduction by Otto Penzler.**

C. Daly King, *Obelists at Sea.* On a cruise ship traveling from New York to Paris, the lights of the smoking room briefly go out, a gunshot crashes through the night, and a man is dead. Two detectives are on board but so are four psychiatrists who believe their professional knowledge can solve the case by understanding the psyche of the killer—each with a different theory. **Introduction by Martin Edwards.**

Jonathan Latimer, *Headed for a Hearse.* Featuring Bill Crane, the booze-soaked Chicago private detective, this humorous hard-boiled novel was filmed as *The Westland Case* in 1937 starring Preston Foster. Robert Westland has been framed for the grisly murder of his wife in a room with doors and windows locked from the inside. As the day of his execution nears, he relies on Crane to find the real murderer. **Introduction by Max Allan Collins**

Lange Lewis, *The Birthday Murder.* Victoria is a successful novelist and screenwriter and her husband is a movie director so their marriage seems almost too good to be true. Then, on her birthday, her happy new life comes crashing down when her husband is murdered using a method of poisoning that was described in one of her books. She quickly becomes the leading suspect. **Introduction by Randal S. Brandt.**

Frances and Richard Lockridge, *Death on the Aisle.* In one of the most beloved books to feature Mr. and Mrs. North, the body of a wealthy backer of a play is found dead in a seat of the 45th Street Theater. Pam is thrilled to engage in her favorite pastime—playing amateur sleuth—much to the annoyance of Jerry, her publisher husband. The Norths inspired a stage play, a film, and long-running radio and TV series. **Introduction by Otto Penzler.**

John P. Marquand, *Your Turn, Mr. Moto.* The first novel about Mr. Moto, originally titled *No Hero*, is the story of a World War I hero pilot who finds himself jobless during the Depression. In Tokyo for a big opportunity that falls apart, he meets a Japanese agent and his Russian colleague and the pilot suddenly finds himself caught in a web of intrigue. Peter Lorre played Mr. Moto in a series of popular films. **Introduction by Lawrence Block.**

Stuart Palmer, *The Penguin Pool Murder.* The first adventure of schoolteacher and dedicated amateur sleuth Hildegarde Withers occurs at the New York Aquarium when she and her young students notice a corpse in one of the tanks. It was published in 1931 and filmed the next year, starring Edna May Oliver as the American Miss Marple—though much funnier than her English counterpart. **Introduction by Otto Penzler.**

Stuart Palmer, *The Puzzle of the Happy Hooligan.* New York City schoolteacher Hildegarde Withers cannot resist "assisting" homicide detective Oliver Piper. In this novel, she is on vacation in Hollywood and on the set of a movie about Lizzie Borden when the screenwriter is found dead. Six comic films about Withers appeared in the 1930s, most successfully starring Edna May Oliver. **Introduction by Otto Penzler.**

Otto Penzler, ed., *Golden Age Bibliomysteries.* Stories of murder, theft, and suspense occur with alarming regularity in the unlikely world of books and bibliophiles, including bookshops, libraries, and private rare book collections, written by such giants of the mystery genre as Ellery Queen, Cornell Woolrich, Lawrence G. Blochman, Vincent Starrett, and Anthony Boucher. **Introduction by Otto Penzler.**

Otto Penzler, ed., *Golden Age Detective Stories.* The history of American mystery fiction has its pantheon of authors who have influenced and entertained readers for nearly a century, reaching its peak during the Golden Age, and this collection pays homage to the work of the most acclaimed: Cornell Woolrich, Erle Stanley Gardner, Craig Rice, Ellery Queen, Dorothy B. Hughes, Mary Roberts Rinehart, and more. **Introduction by Otto Penzler.**

Otto Penzler, ed., *Golden Age Locked Room Mysteries.* The so-called impossible crime category reached its zenith during the 1920s, 1930s, and 1940s, and this volume includes the greatest of the great authors who mastered the form: John Dickson Carr, Ellery Queen, C. Daly King, Clayton Rawson, and Erle Stanley Gardner. Like great magicians, these literary conjurors will baffle and delight readers. **Introduction by Otto Penzler.**

Ellery Queen, *The Adventures of Ellery Queen.* These stories are the earliest short works to feature Queen as a detective and are among the best of the author's fair-play mysteries. So many of the elements that comprise the gestalt of Queen may be found in these tales: alternate solutions, the dying clue, a bizarre crime, and the author's ability to find fresh variations of works by other authors. **Introduction by Otto Penzler.**

Ellery Queen, ***The American Gun Mystery.*** A rodeo comes to New York City at the Colosseum. The headliner is Buck Horne, the once popular film cowboy who opens the show leading a charge of forty whooping cowboys until they pull out their guns and fire into the air. Buck falls to the ground, shot dead. The police instantly lock the doors to search everyone but the offending weapon has completely vanished. **Introduction by Otto Penzler.**

Ellery Queen, ***The Chinese Orange Mystery.*** The offices of publisher Donald Kirk have seen strange events but nothing like this. A strange man is found dead with two long spears alongside his back. And, though no one was seen entering or leaving the room, everything has been turned backwards or upside down: pictures face the wall, the victim's clothes are worn backwards, the rug upside down. Why in the world? **Introduction by Otto Penzler.**

Ellery Queen, ***The Dutch Shoe Mystery.*** Millionaire philanthropist Abagail Doorn falls into a coma and she is rushed to the hospital she funds for an emergency operation by one of the leading surgeons on the East Coast. When she is wheeled into the operating theater, the sheet covering her body is pulled back to reveal her garroted corpse—the first of a series of murders **Introduction by Otto Penzler.**

Ellery Queen, ***The Egyptian Cross Mystery.*** A small-town schoolteacher is found dead, headed, and tied to a T-shaped cross on December 25th, inspiring such sensational headlines as "Crucifixion on Christmas Day." Amateur sleuth Ellery Queen is so intrigued he travels to Virginia but fails to solve the crime. Then a similar murder takes place on New York's Long Island—and then another. **Introduction by Otto Penzler.**

Ellery Queen, ***The Siamese Twin Mystery.*** When Ellery and his father encounter a raging forest fire on a mountain, their only hope is to drive up to an isolated hillside manor owned by a secretive surgeon and his strange guests. While playing solitaire in the middle of the night, the doctor is shot. The only clue is a torn playing card. Suspects include a society beauty, a valet, and conjoined twins. **Introduction by Otto Penzler.**

Ellery Queen, ***The Spanish Cape Mystery.*** Amateur detective Ellery Queen arrives in the resort town of Spanish Cape soon after a young woman and her uncle are abducted by a gun-toting, one-eyed giant. The next day, the woman's somewhat dicey boyfriend is found murdered—totally naked under a black fedora and opera cloak. **Introduction by Otto Penzler.**

Patrick Quentin, ***A Puzzle for Fools.*** Broadway producer Peter Duluth takes to the bottle when his wife dies but enters a sanitarium to dry out. Malevolent events plague the hospital, including when Peter hears his own voice intone, "There will be murder." And there is. He investigates, aided by a young woman who is also a patient. This is the first of nine mysteries featuring Peter and Iris Duluth. **Introduction by Otto Penzler.**

Clayton Rawson, ***Death from a Top Hat.*** When the New York City Police Department is baffled by an apparently impossible crime, they call on The Great Merlini, a retired stage magician who now runs a Times Square magic shop. In his first case, two occultists have been murdered in a room locked from the inside, their bodies positioned to form a pentagram. **Introduction by Otto Penzler.**

Craig Rice, ***Eight Faces at Three.*** Gin-soaked John J. Malone, defender of the guilty, is notorious for getting his culpable clients off. It's the innocent ones who are problems. Like Holly Inglehart, accused of piercing the black heart of her well-heeled aunt Alexandria with a lovely Florentine paper cutter. No one who knew the old battle-ax liked her, but Holly's prints were found on the murder weapon. **Introduction by Lisa Lutz.**

Craig Rice, ***Home Sweet Homicide.*** Known as the Dorothy Parker of mystery fiction for her memorable wit, Craig Rice was the first detective writer to appear on the cover of *Time* magazine. This comic mystery features two kids who are trying to find a husband for their widowed mother while she's engaged in sleuthing. Filmed with the same title in 1946 with Peggy Ann Garner and Randolph Scott. **Introduction by Otto Penzler.**

Mary Roberts Rinehart, *The Album*. Crescent Place is a quiet enclave of wealthy people in which nothing ever happens—until a bedridden old woman is attacked by an intruder with an ax. *The New York Times* stated: "All Mary Roberts Rinehart mystery stories are good, but this one is better." **Introduction by Otto Penzler.**

Mary Roberts Rinehart, *The Haunted Lady*. The arsenic in her sugar bowl was wealthy widow Eliza Fairbanks' first clue that somebody wanted her dead. Nightly visits of bats, birds, and rats, obviously aimed at scaring the dowager to death, was the second. Eliza calls the police, who send nurse Hilda Adams, the amateur sleuth they refer to as "Miss Pinkerton," to work undercover to discover the culprit. **Introduction by Otto Penzler.**

Mary Roberts Rinehart, *Miss Pinkerton*. Hilda Adams is a nurse, not a detective, but she is observant and smart and so it is common for Inspector Patton to call on her for help. Her success results in his calling her "Miss Pinkerton." *The New Republic* wrote: "From thousands of hearts and homes the cry will go up: Thank God for Mary Roberts Rinehart." **Introduction by Carolyn Hart.**

Mary Roberts Rinehart, *The Red Lamp*. Professor William Porter refuses to believe that the seaside manor he's just inherited is haunted but he has to convince his wife to move in. However, he soon sees evidence of the occult phenomena of which the townspeople speak. Whether it is a spirit or a human being, Porter accepts that there is a connection to the rash of murders that have terrorized the countryside. **Introduction by Otto Penzler.**

Mary Roberts Rinehart, *The Wall*. For two decades, Mary Roberts Rinehart was the second-best-selling author in America (only Sinclair Lewis outsold her) and was beloved for her tales of suspense. In a magnificent mansion, the ex-wife of one of the owners turns up making demands and is found dead the next day. And there are more dark secrets lying behind the walls of the estate. **Introduction by Otto Penzler.**

Joel Townsley Rogers, *The Red Right Hand*. This extraordinary whodunnit that is as puzzling as it is terrifying was identified by crime fiction scholar Jack Adrian as "one of the dozen or so finest mystery novels of the 20th century." A deranged killer sends a doctor on a quest for the truth—deep into the recesses of his own mind—when he and his bride-to-be elope but pick up a terrifying sharp-toothed hitch-hiker. **Introduction by Joe R. Lansdale.**

Roger Scarlett, *Cat's Paw*. The family of the wealthy old bachelor Martin Greenough cares far more about his money than they do about him. For his birthday, he invites all his potential heirs to his mansion to tell them what they hope to hear. Before he can disburse funds, however, he is murdered, and the Boston Police Department's big problem is that there are too many suspects. **Introduction by Curtis Evans**

Vincent Starrett, *Dead Man Inside*. 1930s Chicago is a tough town but some crimes are more bizarre than others. Customers arrive at a haberdasher to find a corpse in the window and a sign on the door: *Dead Man Inside! I am Dead. The store will not open today*. This is just one of a series of odd murders that terrorizes the city. Reluctant detective Walter Ghost leaps into action to learn what is behind the plague. **Introduction by Otto Penzler.**

Vincent Starrett, *The Great Hotel Murder*. Theater critic and amateur sleuth Riley Blackwood investigates a murder in a Chicago hotel where the dead man had changed rooms with a stranger who had registered under a fake name. *The New York Times* described it as "an ingenious plot with enough complications to keep the reader guessing." **Introduction by Lyndsay Faye.**

Vincent Starrett, *Murder on 'B' Deck*. Walter Ghost, a psychologist, scientist, explorer, and former intelligence officer, is on a cruise ship and his friend novelist Dunsten Mollock, a Nigel Bruce-like Watson whose role is to offer occasional comic relief, accommodates when he fails to leave the ship before it takes off. Although they make mistakes along the way, the amateur sleuths solve the shipboard murders. **Introduction by Ray Betzner.**

Phoebe Atwood Taylor, *The Cape Cod Mystery*. Vacationers have flocked to Cape Cod to avoid the heat wave that hit the Northeast and find their holiday unpleasant when the area is flooded with police trying to find the murderer of a muckraking journalist who took a cottage for the season. Finding a solution falls to Asey Mayo, "the Cape Cod Sherlock," known for his worldly wisdom, folksy humor, and common sense. **Introduction by Otto Penzler.**

S. S. Van Dine, ***The Benson Murder Case.*** The first of 12 novels to feature Philo Vance, the most popular and influential detective character of the early part of the 20th century. When wealthy stockbroker Alvin Benson is found shot to death in a locked room in his mansion, the police are baffled until the erudite flaneur and art collector arrives on the scene. Paramount filmed it in 1930 with William Powell as Vance. **Introduction by Ragnar Jónasson.**

Cornell Woolrich, ***The Bride Wore Black.*** The first suspense novel by one of the greatest of all noir authors opens with a bride and her new husband walking out of the church. A car speeds by, shots ring out, and he falls dead at her feet. Determined to avenge his death, she tracks down everyone in the car, concluding with a shocking surprise. It was filmed by Francois Truffaut in 1968, starring Jeanne Moreau. **Introduction by Eddie Muller.**

Cornell Woolrich, ***Deadline at Dawn.*** Quinn is overcome with guilt about having robbed a stranger's home. He meets Bricky, a dime-a-dance girl, and they fall for each other. When they return to the crime scene, they discover a dead body. Knowing Quinn will be accused of the crime, they race to find the true killer before he's arrested. A 1946 film starring Susan Hayward was loosely based on the plot. **Introduction by David Gordon.**

Cornell Woolrich, ***Waltz into Darkness.*** A New Orleans businessman successfully courts a woman through the mail but he is shocked to find when she arrives that she is not the plain brunette whose picture he'd received but a radiant blond beauty. She soon absconds with his fortune. Wracked with disappointment and loneliness, he vows to track her down. When he finds her, the real nightmare begins. **Introduction by Wallace Stroby.**